MAGE'S END GAME

TILLY WALLACE

ONE

THE BITING wind tried to find a way through Seraphina's woollen cloak as she arched her back to relieve tired muscles. She had never thought that being branded an outlaw would result in her fantasising about baths. Just because they were riding from one safe place to another in search of answers, didn't mean she had abandoned all thought of cleanliness. A sigh frosted on the air as she remembered the copper tub in the Fae palace.

She cast a sideways glance at Hugh, and her mind tumbled into much *warmer* memories of baths.

With each step her horse took, Sera's determination grew stronger, somewhat fuelled by her desire for the comforts of her little home. Lord Rowan's plan to seize control of the throne would fail. After she defeated him, she would carve a place for herself in the world. Until then...oh, how she wanted a bath.

Her breaths left puffs of fog in the frigid air, but

there was no time to stop. Elliot Brynn, her insolent yet charming and infinitely useful footman, led the way towards the Crow's Nest, a secluded estate belonging to his cousins.

"Nearly there," Elliot called over his shoulder, his voice carrying on the gusting wind.

The path they followed through the trees grew darker as the old oaks clustered closer together. Even stripped bare of their leaves, their skeletal branches formed arms that enclosed them. Up ahead, a pair of wrought-iron gates appeared, the metal overgrown with ivy. A crow perched on one pillar and called out at their approach before taking flight.

"You'd better tell Fiona to make sure the coffee is hot!" Elliot yelled after the bird.

Their horses perked up, as though sensing they would soon be tucked up in a stable with a warm feed in their bellies. As the group rounded a corner, the trees pulled back to reveal a two-storey house built of pale-grey stone.

Ancient trees surrounded the Crow's Nest, their gnarled branches reaching up to the heavens like grasping hands. The old manor house stood proudly in the winter landscape, as if daring the frigid air to even attempt to penetrate its walls. The slate roof glistened with a dusting of snow, while tall chimneys puffed smoke into the grey sky.

As they approached the house, laughter rang through the air. Children bundled in thick coats dashed across the frozen ground, their cheeks rosy with joy.

The three remarkable women who called the Crow's Nest home had rescued them all. The Crows were descendants of Morag, a long-ago mage—the only other female mage permitted to live. Her daughters were born with the ability to transform into crows, and when they combined their magic, they were the equal of any mage.

Erin emerged from the manor house, bundled up in a dark-purple woollen shawl, a wide smile on her face as she hurried to Sera's side.

"Lady Winyard! Come inside. There is more snow on the horizon." Erin gestured for two of the older boys to approach. "The lads will take your horses to the stables. Warin is out there to help them."

After they dismounted, each boy took hold of two horses and led them around the side of the house.

Erin turned to her cousin. "The coffee is hotter than you can handle, Elliot."

The lanky footman chuckled as he embraced his shorter cousin.

Kitty and Hugh stood on either side of Sera, and she laced her gloved fingers with Hugh's.

"Let's observe the niceties inside. I'm freezing my buttocks out here." Kitty pushed them all towards the front door.

Inside, they walked past the dim parlour and followed Erin into the kitchen—the heart of the home. The fire burned bright, and enchanted lights cast a golden glow over the long oak table. Two long benches were positioned on either side, and Fiona carried a pot from the stove. Anna stirred another pot that wafted a meaty aroma that made Sera's stomach rumble.

"Lady Winyard," she murmured. Then she glanced at her cousin. "Elliot. Don't bother sitting—earn your keep and fetch cups and plates for our guests."

A frown flashed across Elliot's face, then the footman heaved a dramatic sigh and walked to a cupboard.

Sera peeled off her outer layers and tossed them over a ladder-backed chair. Then she sat on the worn bench that had supported dozens of bottoms over its long life.

The kitchen was a warm embrace after the biting cold outside. The roaring fire at one end cast flickering shadows across the whitewashed plaster. Sera wondered at the countless stories and secrets hidden within the timeworn walls.

She drew in a deep breath and savoured the aromas of stew, coffee, and freshly baked bread. "May we stay for a few days while we figure out what to do next?" she asked Erin as Fiona poured coffee and passed around the steaming mugs.

"Of course you can. You and your friends are always welcome here," Fiona said. "Anna and I will feed the children upstairs, so you can have some privacy."

The two older Crows arranged a pot and stack of bowls on a tray, and they piled another with bread and a pitcher of lemonade.

Warin, the head of the Londinium gargoyle clan,

stomped snow off his boots at the kitchen door. He nodded to them in greeting, then took a seat opposite Hugh.

Conversation flowed as freely as the rich gravy that accompanied their stew. Sera listened intently, her mind racing with how best to bring down the old mage who thought her but a pawn in his scheme.

"Lord Rowan has men scouring the countryside for you." Worry etched itself across Erin's forehead. "Perhaps you should consider a new life in the Americas?"

"No. I will not falter now. Not when we have come so far, and no matter the danger swirling around us." Sera straightened her spine. She would not be driven from the country of her birth like a pheasant flushed from the undergrowth.

"Whatever you decide, we will be beside you," Hugh said in between taking bites of stew spread over a thick chunk of bread.

Sera's heart swelled with appreciation for the unwavering support of her companions. She could not have come this far without them. Determination to repay their kindness filled every fibre of her being.

"I'm sticking with you because you owe me a personal performance by Selene the dancer." Elliot waved at her with his fork.

Beside Sera, Kitty snorted. "As if we could forget with your constant reminders."

Elliott had sacrificed his handbill of the exotic beauty so that Sera and Kitty would have a means to communicate between the Fae realm and the human one.

The laughter of children echoed through the manor house, a stark contrast to the worries building in the kitchen. As night fell and the fire burned low, Sera and her friends huddled together, planning their next move. The future was uncertain, but one thing was clear: they would face it head-on, united in their quest for freedom and justice.

Sera finished her meal and pushed the bowl away. Hugh poured more coffee into her mug, and she flashed him a smile of thanks. Wrapping her hands around the uneven pottery, she studied Warin.

The centuries-old gargoyle had an imposing build, even in his human form. His shoulders were almost the width of two men. His hands dwarfed the plate before him. When he glanced up, a keen but weary intelligence lit his pale-grey gaze.

"What news from London?" she asked.

He swallowed his mouthful. "Troubling news. No one has seen the king or queen for many weeks now. King George's health continues to deteriorate, and Queen Charlotte remains absent from public view. Rumours swirl like the winter winds, but none can say for certain what has befallen her." Warin's stony gaze met Sera's.

"The official word is that they are merely sequestered for the winter," Kitty murmured at her side. "But the court has never been cut off from them for such a long time."

"I need to find a way into Buckingham House to speak with the queen." Sera sipped the strong coffee, and her face screwed up. While it would keep her awake, she didn't think she would ever develop a taste for the drink.

"It will be too risky to use your magic. The mages at court will detect you," Kitty said.

On other occasions, Sera had cast a glamour to change her features. But any mage positioned near the queen for her *protection* would sense the faint tingle of magic being used in their presence.

"There are other, non-magical ways to make you look different. No one will be looking for a man, for starters," Elliot said with a grin and a wink.

"Oh, you are brilliant, Elliot." Her footman's suggestion sparked an idea in Sera's mind.

Kitty regarded her friend with a keen eye. "We could draw stubble on your face with coal, or a rakish moustache."

"A larger coat and some, um...padding to hide your...shape, will help." Hugh drew curves and lines in the air with his hands, and a faint blush crept up his neck as he indicated the issue with Sera's bosom and hips.

Sera and the others plotted late into the night, huddled in the warmth and protection of the thick stone walls. Shadows stirred outside the Crow's Nest as if sensing an approaching storm.

SERA SLEPT SOUNDLY, safe in the Crow's Nest and Hugh's heated embrace. The next morning, she stretched and yawned as the first light of dawn crept through the frost-laced windows. Pale shafts of light caressed the furniture in the room.

The Crow's Nest came alive around them, a sanctuary amidst the desolation of winter. The ancient manor house seemed to exude a sense of ageless wisdom, its ivy-covered walls whispering secrets from centuries long past. Outside, a patchwork of snow-dusted fields stretched out around the estate, crisscrossed by winding paths that disappeared into the shadows of the surrounding woodlands. It was a place that seemed untouched by time, a bastion of solace amidst the chaos and uncertainty that threatened to engulf the world beyond its borders.

Laughter echoed from the rafters as the children who called the Crow's Nest home chased each other along the halls, racing to the kitchen for breakfast.

"Shall we give the children a head start?" she murmured to Hugh.

A pained look crossed his face as the need to satisfy two quite different appetites conflicted. Then he grinned when he settled on a compromise. "Perhaps just a *quick* head start?"

When they left their room a short time later, the cheery atmosphere of the kitchen enveloped them like a friend's embrace. With a much lighter heart, Sera took a seat at the table for breakfast. Restorative sleep and good company did much to buoy her mood. Outside the window, snow flurries swirled. Sera sipped at her steaming mug of spiced tea, feeling the comforting heat spread through her bones.

The three sisters served bowls of porridge drizzled with honey and cream, while Hugh and Warin tucked into sausages, bacon, and mushrooms piled on thick chunks of toast. Even Elliot watched the two eat with wide eyes.

"Not sure I want any gargoyle in my blood if you eat that much. It would ruin my much-admired figure." He swept a hand down his lean length.

"You're just jealous of us magical folk, and you always have been." Erin poked her cousin as she moved down the table.

"I wasn't jealous. You lot cheated at games." He stabbed his spoon into his porridge.

Kitty nudged him. "If it makes you feel any better, I am also without any magical traits. Although I surpass them all with my wit and intelligence. I'm not sure what the Fates gave you as compensation."

Laughter broke out around the table.

A red-headed boy raced into the room, waving a letter. "A rider brought this for you, Miss Napier." He skidded to a stop before her and handed it over.

"Who is writing to you here?" Sera asked with a niggle of anxiety.

"Father. Some months ago, our carriage brought you here, remember? I asked Father to send any news here." She turned the letter over and slit the wax seal. Unfolding the sheet of paper, she scanned the lines and sucked in a breath.

"This is an interesting development. It seems Lord Rowan has declared you a dangerous traitor, Sera. There's a bounty on your head, and people are warned not to approach you, but to report any sightings to the local authorities."

"How can he do that?" Elliot said.

Kitty lowered her teacup. "Because he has control of England now."

The news hung heavy in the air, casting a shadow over the gathered group. Sera's heart skipped a beat as fear and anger warred within her. Her grip tightened around the mug, her knuckles turning white. The others in the room exchanged worried glances, the tension palpable.

"Lord Rowan's shadow grows longer over this country. We must tread carefully," Hugh said, resting a hand on her knee under the table.

"It becomes even more crucial that we find a way to speak with the queen. The fate of England, and my future, depend upon it." Determination flared hotter inside Sera, even as her time ran out. "Today, we plan. Tomorrow, we act."

Wind howled outside, buffeting the old stone walls

of the house. As though even the weather sought out Sera and wished to expose her.

"It's a long ride to London, and that wily old mage will have agents everywhere," Elliot said.

Kitty sipped her tea and regarded Sera over the rim of her mug. "Abigail has eyes and ears in every parlour because of her standing in society."

Sera grinned. The strengths of her enemies were also their weaknesses. "Luckily, we won't be patronising anyone in society, so there will be little to tell."

Elliot barked in laughter. "Please tell me we'll be visiting the more entertaining pubs?"

Sera tapped the side of her nose. Moving around London without using magic would be possible if she dressed like a working-class boy and stuck to the shadowy places avoided by society.

As they spoke, ideas unfurled like tendrils of ivy, each presenting new possibilities and challenges. Kitty poked holes in everyone's suggestions until they had the outline of a plan.

"Above all else, we must be careful who we trust." Kitty glanced at Sera, remembering the betrayal of the woman they'd once considered a friend.

"Never again will I be fooled." Sera took Kitty's hand and squeezed.

The door burst open, and children raced through the room, their cheeks flushed pink as they shrugged on warm layers to go play outside. Voices dimmed to muffled bursts as the solid door to the kitchen garden closed behind them.

Sera stared at the door, thinking of the new life gifted to the children under the care of the sisters. "That is what I fight for—a world where laughter and hope can thrive, unburdened by fear and oppression."

"It is what my kind has strived for over the centuries. It is a battle that often demands sacrifice." Warin's features softened with a hint of melancholy.

"Nothing worthwhile was ever easily won." Hugh's gaze fell on Sera.

The group shared a solemn nod of understanding. Their chosen path was treacherous and littered with unseen pitfalls and hidden enemies. But together, they would forge a way forwards.

"Are we truly ready for what awaits us in London?" Kitty asked, her brow wrinkling. Her gaze darted between Sera's confident expression and the more worried faces gathered around the kitchen table.

"We don't have the luxury of waiting. We must face Lord Rowan. There are only a few moves left in this game," Sera replied. In her mind, she could visualise a decimated chessboard. A lone pawn bravely marched towards the other side of the board. But there were still pieces to rally behind her—the rooks, a wise bishop, and her faithful knight.

Sera's gaze wandered to the frosted window panes, the world beyond obscured by the swirling snow. The road ahead was a fraught one, but there was no turning back. With a deep breath, she refocused her attention on her companions, resolve hardening within her.

"Personally, I want to see the look on Abigail's face

when you defeat her grandfather and she realises all her scheming was for nothing." Kitty winked at Sera.

"I want to see the king free of whatever spell has poisoned his mind," Hugh said.

Elliot grinned. "I want—"

"Your exotic dancer. We know!" Kitty and Sera shouted in unison, then burst into laughter.

Even in the darkest hour, there remained a glimmer of hope. A flame keeping the encroaching shadows at bay, fuelled by the tight bond between Sera and her friends.

"Where will you go, though? Lord Rowan will expect us all to return to my family's home." Worries clearly continued to nibble at Kitty.

Sera tapped a fingernail against her mug. "You will return to your home and continue as usual. That will infuriate him—and we have ways to communicate that he cannot intercept. As for me, I am going to call on Ethel."

"Isn't that the ancient crone who lives in a hovel surrounded by graves?" Some of the colour drained from Elliot's olive complexion.

"The very one. She's going to love you, Elliot." Sera chuckled into her tea.

There was a place right under Lord Rowan's nose that he couldn't infiltrate. Nor would the residents give her up to the soldiers for any price, regardless of their poverty.

The settlement beside Bunhill Fields cemetery gave its loyalty to the night witch who protected them.

Two

THE STORM BLEW through overnight and left a clear sky with only a few lingering clouds. The golden haze of dawn touched the horizon as Sera and her friends prepared to leave the sanctuary of the Crow's Nest. Sera breathed deeply of the cool, crisp air, taking a moment to appreciate everything the journey had brought her so far. Most important were the friends who had become family.

"I will meet you in London," said a gruff voice from nearby.

Sera turned to face Warin, the gargoyle who had taken up the role of guardian of the women and children of the Crow's Nest. His stone skin glinted in the dim light of early morning, his large wings spreading out behind him like a cloak.

"How will we find you?" Last time, Sera had climbed to the belfry of a deserted church in a meeting arranged by her aunt, the gargoyle Natalie Delacour.

"I roost close to the church and will look out for you." He shifted completely to his stone form and took to the sky, disappearing into the clouds above.

Hugh gazed after his distant relative, a look of wonder on his face. "I will never tire of seeing such wondrous things. What a world we live in."

"Why did we have to be up at sparrow's fart to see it?" Elliot grumbled as he checked the contents of his saddlebag. "Couldn't we have had a sleep-in, had a large breakfast, and then headed out at a civilised time...like noon?"

"The days are short. I want to be in London before dark." Sera hugged Hugh before she moved to her horse. The surgeon's warm presence radiated a sense of security and grounded her in moments of uncertainty.

They had left the three sisters in the warm kitchen, preparing breakfast for the children who had also roused early. Erin could always meet them in London, to be ready should Sera need to call on the assistance of the Crows.

"You should leave Mr Brynn in my household, Sera. We will soon have him accustomed to early starts," Kitty said as she took the reins of her horse.

Elliot shuddered and shook his head at Sera while mouthing *No*.

Sera hid a chuckle as she climbed onto the saddle. Soon, they were all mounted and trotting down the curving drive.

Conversation was subdued among them as they travelled less populated roads. As the sun progressed across the sky, they wound their way through the countryside, avoiding larger towns wherever possible. It was a longer route, but one that would keep them safe from unwanted attention.

After a long day, they finally spied the lingering haze from the coal fires that blanketed London. Sera guided her horse to a spreading elm and dismounted. Here, she would have to say goodbye to Kitty. But only for a little while.

She wrapped her friend in a tight embrace. "We have our paper and the mage silver rings to communicate. I will keep you abreast of whatever we discover."

"Good. I have appointed myself campaign general, and I need intelligence to do that successfully." When Kitty broke their hug, her eyes glistened with unshed tears. "I shall set to work with Father to counter this ridiculous edict proclaiming you a traitor."

Sera swallowed, a lump of gratitude stuck in her throat. "Thank you."

Not one for lingering farewells, Kitty waved Elliot over to give her a leg up, then put heels to her horse and cantered off towards London.

Sera tugged her hood over her head to cast her features in shadow. Her skin prickled with awareness as they continued on their way. Lord Rowan sought to turn the people against her by offering a reward for any sightings. Anybody who shared the road with them might recognise her and seek to line their pockets with coin.

The winter sun dallied above the horizon as they

reached the small settlement nestled beside Bunhill Fields. The ancient gravestones cast eerie shadows as they approached the dwellings sheltered by rolling hills. A sense of foreboding raced down Sera's spine, but she pushed it aside. Fear would not control her decisions.

They tied their horses to a tree, and the mounts munched on the short grass.

Sera cast a critical eye over the little village, one that existed beneath the notice of most Londoners. But not her. Over the course of many visits, Sera had done what she could to improve their lives. Their tiny cottages were now warmer and drier, thanks to her enchantments that had repaired holes and added invisible layers of insulation. Gravelled pathways crunched beneath their boots, preventing the mud that would otherwise have been an issue during the wet winter months. Despite the challenges she faced, Sera couldn't help but feel a swell of pride at the positive impact she'd had on these people's lives.

A group of children ran up to her, all with wide grins. One had a gap where two front teeth were missing, the adult teeth just peeking through the gumline. "What have you got for us, Nyx?" she lisped through the space.

On previous visits, she had given the children magical lanterns that emitted a soft glow when tapped and that were safer than the exposed flames of candles. She'd also distributed her incredibly bouncy balls for their amusement. Today, she would create a different toy. Rubbing her hands together, she murmured a spell. Sera visualised the final effect in her mind as she whispered it into being between her palms. When she threw her hands apart, half a dozen dragonflies darted forth and hovered over the children.

"They will land on your hand, and you can launch them into the air." She demonstrated by placing an outstretched hand under one and then casting it high to buzz around the group. "They also glow at night."

Excited chatter broke out, and soon the luminous insects were making patterns in the evening sky. Leaving them to play, Sera and her two companions walked among the cottages, following the gravel path. Many residents called greetings to her, and all seemed genuinely pleased at her return. Sera's boots crunched on the gravel as she made her way up the winding path towards Ethel's cottage. The scent of lavender-infused tea wafted through the air, mingling with the faint aroma of wood smoke and the earthy musk of damp soil. The sun dipped lower, casting its watery light across the settlement below.

At the top of the hill sat the cottage with the crooked chimney and mismatched windows. As was her habit, Ethel sat on the porch in her rocking chair. Wispy white hair framed her weathered face like a halo of moonlight. A shawl was wrapped around her shoulders to guard against the chill of the day. Her gnarled hands gripped a wooden pipe, from which tendrils of fragrant smoke curled upwards, dissolving into the twilight.

"Knew you'd be back. And you've brought old Ethel a treat." Her rheumy gaze roamed over Hugh's bulk and Elliot's lean frame. She chuckled as her attention settled on Elliot, and she withdrew the pipe to lick her lips.

"I'm not paid enough for this job," Elliot muttered as he kicked a loose stone.

Sera stood on the bottom step. "Behave, Ethel. This is Mr Hugh Miles and Elliot Brynn. Both gentlemen are my friends."

"A woman can dream, and I know who'll be running through them tonight." Ethel laughed, a wheezy sound that made Sera worry as to the condition of her lungs.

"I'd be running all right," Elliot muttered.

Sera ignored him. If he wanted his private performance by the exotic dancer, he would have to earn it. "Mr Miles is a surgeon. Is there anyone in the village who might need his assistance?"

Ethel tilted her head at Hugh and then gestured to a cottage off to the right. "Mrs Cooper's youngest has a terrible cough. She can't afford a doctor."

"I shall see what I can do." Hugh touched Sera's hand and then set off for the indicated home.

"How have you been?" Sera sat at the old woman's feet. Elliot wandered off after Hugh, clearly preferring sick children to amorous old crones.

"The spirits are noisy. Keeps me awake at night." As she spoke, she poured tea into two chipped mugs from a pot snuggled in a knitted cosy. Then she handed one to Sera.

Sera held the mug in two hands and inhaled. The liquid was aromatic with lavender and just a hint of bitterness to sharpen her senses. "Is Lord Thornton no longer supplying you with tea?"

"That's a brew for letting the mind unwind. You need something to keep you alert." She gave a knowing wink and exhaled a plume of smoke.

The spirits who communed with Ethel passed on all sorts of interesting titbits, such as when Sera would visit and where hidden valuables could be found.

Sera sipped the tart blend, and her brain did indeed perk up in the same way it did with Hugh's campfire coffee. There was a question she needed to ask and didn't want to risk offending. "Am I safe here?"

"If any of this lot dared turn in our Nyx for a stack of coin, they would answer to me in this life and the next." A hard tone entered Ethel's voice.

Sera had hoped that caring for the people cast off and ignored by London would earn her their loyalty. It reassured her to hear it. "Good. I need somewhere safe to lay my head tonight, if you would offer shelter to Nyx and her friends."

"You're one of us, and Bunhill folk stand shoulder to shoulder." She set down the pipe to drink her cooling tea.

The sun dipped and cast long shadows across the small settlement. With the loss of light, the temperature dropped rapidly. Sera cast a warming spell around them as the old aftermage enjoyed sitting on her porch, whatever the weather.

"Lord Rowan seizes control of England, and I doubt he will better your lives." Never once had he mentioned improving the lot of the lowest class of citizen. He wanted the political power to accompany his magical one for his own benefit.

"None of them gives a fig about us. Centuries come and go, but such men never change. Our men are arrow fodder in their battles. Our women to be badly used." Ethel drained her mug with one long slurp.

"All it takes is one troublesome woman to make a stand," Sera murmured into her mug. The odds were stacked against her. Lord Rowan would rally the Mage Council behind him, and he controlled the king's army. But she had friends.

Ethel cackled with laughter. "You will show him. You are the spark that will start a forest fire."

Sera focused on the path before her and didn't waver. She would oppose Lord Rowan not only for herself and her friends but for those faceless souls so often trodden into the mud of their society. The ordinary people depended on her, and she would not let them down.

Age might cloud the old aftermage's eyes, but she had a mind sharp with wisdom that bored into Sera's soul as she spoke. "You're safe here, but out there"—she gestured with her pipe beyond the trees to the barely visible rooftops—"are those who will turn on their own kind for a ha'penny, let alone what the old man is offering for you."

"Don't worry. Nyx will not leave this community but another will." A lad would take Sera's place as she altered her appearance to avoid Lord Rowan's spies.

"There's power in numbers but also danger." Ethel tapped the pipe against the post to empty the ash.

"But multitudes cannot be held back. We are water. A swollen river about to rupture its banks," Sera murmured as ideas and hope swirled inside her.

"The shadows will protect you." Ethel picked up the cane beside her chair and stood. "Go, eat. There'll be room on the floor to lay your head when you return."

Sera strode down the hill, her footsteps soft on the gravel path. A trickle of magic laced around the cottages had, over time, asked the stones and gravel to push through the earth and form paths.

At the base of the hill, the cottages clustered around a common area. Laughter and chatter washed over Sera as she joined the residents. In the centre, a bonfire kept the cold at bay. A variety of items were arrayed around the edge for people to sit on—a chair here, a keg on its side there, an upturned box big enough to seat three children.

Sera sat on a rotund log, dragged in to serve as a bench seat. Hugh and Elliot joined her.

"How is the child?" Sera asked as she leaned into Hugh's side.

"It's a nasty bout of bronchitis. I've given the mother a few ways to ease the boy's lungs tonight. In the morning, I'll fetch a potion from the apothecary." Hugh stretched out his legs and warmed his boots before the fire.

Potatoes were rolled in the embers at the base of the fire, and children watched them, ready to flick them out with a long pole when they were ready. The evening air was alive with the scent of roasting vegetables and sizzling meat, mingling with the earthy aroma of smoke. The crackling fire cast a warm, flickering glow on the faces of the villagers who had gathered to share a meal with Sera and her companions.

A shy young woman approached with a steaming bowl of root vegetables. She held it out to Sera and ducked away when she took it. Two older women passed bowls to Hugh and Elliot. While the village had little, they shared it with no hint of grumble or complaint. As Sera ate, warmth seeped into her chilled bones.

Beside the village lay a field where they grew their crops. Before she left, Sera would murmur to the soil and ensure it continued to provide the basics for the families who relied upon it.

Around the roaring flames, Elliot's laughter rang out as he swapped stories with the young men of the village. A few admiring women circled him, like moths to a flame. His eyes sparkling with mischief, his grin infectious, he drew even the weariest villagers into his tales of daring escapades in the Fae realm. None of it was true, since he had returned to London after Sera and Hugh had crossed Shadowvane, but

Sera wouldn't let the truth ruin his entertaining yarns.

After he had finished his supper, Hugh excused himself to move among the assembled people. He quietly tended to their ailments and injuries with gentle hands. His tall, broad frame exuded reassurance. The faint trace of long-ago gargoyle in his blood lent him an air of solidity that others found comforting. Sera watched him with admiration, and her love for the gentle surgeon deepened.

Two of the children with the glowing dragonflies sat beside Sera, and they played a game, tossing it from one hand to another. They giggled and stole glances at her.

"I wish I were a mage. Then we could have thousands of toys," one girl said.

Sera caught her gaze. "If you had lots of toys, you would grow bored with them and none would excite you. Magic isn't about having everything. It's about having exactly what you need."

"I need new boots. These are too small, and my toes hurt," the other girl lisped between the gaps in her teeth.

"That I can help with." Sera wriggled her fingers and laid one palm on each boot. A big toe poked up under the leather on each. The girl had outgrown them, but her mother probably couldn't afford a new pair. When Sera lifted away her hands, the girl wore dark-red leather boots with enough space for growing feet.

"Thank you, Nyx." The girl jumped up and down

a few times, then leaned forwards and kissed Sera's cheek.

"Your influence here is palpable. These people love you for what you've done," Hugh said as he took a break from his rounds to eat an apple roasted in the fire and drizzled with honey.

"And yet it's not enough." She could mend roofs and broken windows, give them magical lanterns and toys. But they needed education and better opportunities. They needed to be seen and heard.

"You can't change the entire world at once, remember?" He stroked the arch of her neck with one hand.

"Do one small thing," she murmured. Words he had spoken to her in a tenement in what seemed like a lifetime ago.

"Your efforts will build, and others like me and Kitty will augment it with actions of our own." He lowered his hand to take hers. "Where exactly are we sleeping tonight if we cannot risk venturing into London?"

Sera suspected they had an uncomfortable night ahead of them, and she couldn't risk using too much magic that other mages might sense. "On the floor of Ethel's cottage. I suspect Elliot will prefer to sleep here."

As night settled over the village, the shadows reached towards the ancient gravestones of Bunhill Fields cemetery, where centuries of stories and secrets had been laid to rest.

"May they guide our way," Sera whispered as night

claimed the tombstones and the world beyond the circle of light disappeared.

As the fire burned low, more stars became visible above them. Tomorrow, she would begin her covert mission to defeat Lord Rowan. She only hoped she could sneak into Buckingham House without stumbling into a magical trap.

Promise me, she whispered to the night, *that I shall return victorious and bring hope to these people who have given us so much.*

As the flames flickered their last dance, a single spark rose into the air, answering her plea with a silent promise of its own.

THREE

SERA WOKE to the sound of rain pattering on the slate roof of Ethel's one-room cottage. She allowed herself a moment of satisfaction at having ensured all the homes were watertight and holes were plugged to keep out drafts. The previous night, the old woman had dragged out a thin mattress from under her bed for Hugh and Sera and laid it before her little hearth. She offered to share her narrow pallet with Hugh, but the surgeon declined. Elliot had slept outside by the bonfire, muttering that he didn't trust the old woman not to try to warm her bones against his.

Every muscle in Sera's body ached. The mattress gave them a scant inch of comfort before the hard floor, but she couldn't afford to use her magic to make them more comfortable. The sort of spell she would have to cast to persist all night while she slumbered would have alerted Lord Rowan to her presence. As she stretched her limbs, she considered that the ground might have been the better choice. Inhaling deeply, she found the air thick with the scent of earth, herbs, and something faintly metallic—an aroma created by the dead that frequently visited the dwelling.

When she attempted to sit up, Hugh's powerful arms wrapped around her, his warmth a slight comfort amidst the larger discomforts.

"Morning," Hugh murmured, his voice rough from sleep as he sat up beside her, his tousled hair casting shadows over his chiselled features that bore the dark lines of stubble.

"Good morning." A smile crossed Sera's lips, gratitude washing over her for his steadfast presence. As she rose to her feet, her thoughts were already racing ahead, consumed by the need to speak with Queen Charlotte.

Ethel snored on from her corner. The old woman was indistinguishable from the pile of blankets.

Hugh poked the embers of the fire and threw more coal on to warm the interior of the cottage before Ethel woke.

"I'll make some coffee," he said.

Sera padded to the window in her stockings and watched the village wake. Some children burst from their homes and raced along the paths, heading on some errand for their mothers before breakfast.

A familiar lanky form strode up the hill with a bundle in his arms. Sera opened the door and slipped out into the frigid air. "You're awake early," she called out to Elliot.

"The fire went out, I got cold, and the ground was hard. Tonight, I demand a bed and a pub meal or I'm going on strike." He paused at the bottom step.

"If we can find somewhere safe, you have a deal. I shall also report to Kitty that she has been a positive influence on you." Sera didn't mind early starts. She loved to watch the colours nature painted across the sky and hear the bustle of birds flying off to find their breakfast.

Elliot, on the other hand, might have been prodded from sleep early by circumstances, but the scowl on his face made it obvious what he thought about the situation.

"What do you have there?" Sera pointed to the bundle in his arms.

"One of the lads volunteered some of his old clothes for you. You can't pretend to be a boy in your fancy boots and trousers." He stepped up on the porch and held out the bundle.

Now Sera scowled. She liked her boots; they were stylish and comfortable. But Elliot had a point. "Hugh is making coffee, but Ethel is still asleep." She gestured for him to follow her inside the cottage.

Hugh had drawn water from the barrel in the corner and had a battered pot sitting on the cast-iron plate over the fire. They spoke in murmurs so they didn't wake the old woman. Sera pulled her piece of ensorcelled paper from her saddlebag and dashed off a quick note to Kitty.

Heading into London. Can you meet me in Hyde Park?

The reply came a few moments later. Sera imagined Kitty sitting at the table, eating toast while she surveyed her morning correspondence and discussed events with her father.

Yes. Use your ring when you are near.

"What is the plan for today?" Hugh asked as he handed around the mugs of strong coffee.

"We drink this to wake us up. I disguise myself as a lad, and we ride to Hyde Park. I need a footman's uniform from Buckingham House, and we need a safe place to sleep tonight," Sera said.

Elliot sipped from his mug, and his eyes screwed shut for a moment as the brew hit his senses. "I can rustle up a uniform. Might take me a few hours."

"And I can find a safe house," Hugh said.

Eager to be on the move, Sera drank her foul coffee as quickly as she could without scalding her throat. Elliot went to saddle up their horses while Sera stripped off her finer clothes to don the borrowed ones.

Ethel stirred in the corner and sat up with a start. Her gaze was almost milky white. "Oh, it's you lot. I thought the blasted spirits had finally decided to keep house for me."

Hugh took her a cup of coffee, and she winked at him in thanks.

After disrobing, Sera first bound her breasts with a length of cloth. Then she dressed in the borrowed clothes. She bit her lip as she adjusted the unfamiliar clothing. The coarse fabric of the shirt chafed against her skin, and the trousers were ill-fitting. With each layer, the weight of the disguise settled upon her. Or it might have been the fleas in the fabric. Her skin began to itch. She would thank the lad who owned them by buying him a brand new set.

"You still look like our Nyx," Ethel helpfully called from her bed.

"There is a cap." Hugh handed it to her, and Sera coiled all her long hair up underneath.

"Some final touches." He wiped his hands over the hearth and then dabbed coal dust onto her face, creating the illusion of stubble. When he finished, he stepped back and gave a satisfied nod. "You could fool even the sharpest-eyed observer, if I say so myself."

"Let us put that to the test and see if I can fool Kitty." Sera couldn't imagine a more eagle-eyed observer than her friend.

"You look like a ruffian who is going to shank someone in a dark alley," Ethel said.

Sera swept a bow to the old aftermage. "Thank you, Ethel. You say the loveliest things."

Grabbing her saddlebag, Sera stuffed her usual clothing inside and did up the buckles so that a boot didn't escape. Taking Hugh's hand, she stepped out into the cold air.

Elliot waited at the grove of trees, reins in his hands, their horses snatching a few last mouthfuls of grass before they headed off. It was a brief ride of less than five miles from the cemetery to the edge of Hyde Park, where they left their horses at a mews that Kitty had once recommended for its discretion.

Sera rubbed the mage silver ring on her finger and thought of the other woman, to alert her to their being not far away. As they walked the packed dirt paths, around them throngs of people went about their everyday business. Sera's heart raced as they walked, her senses hyper-aware of every glance and gesture in her direction. But no one looked twice, nor did recognition light any curious eyes.

"You need to swagger. You're a man about town now," Elliot muttered from her side.

"Right." She adjusted her posture and focused on each step. It wasn't that hard to pretend to be a man. She simply acted as though she owned the world and everyone in it was hers to command.

A street vendor shouted of his wares for sale nearby, and the smell of roasting chestnuts filled the air. Hugh broke away to purchase them a bag each, and they munched on the warm nuts as they walked.

As they entered Hyde Park, Sera breathed in the crisp scent of dew-covered grass and the earthy aroma of damp soil. Birds flitted through the branches over-head, their songs filling the air. The sun filtered through the trees, casting dappled shadows on the ground beneath them.

They sat on a bench overlooking the pond to finish their breakfast.

"I'd love a bit of bacon," Elliot grumbled.

"If today goes well, we shall have supper in a pub tonight." Sera glanced at her footman. She struggled to remember how he had survived life in a Mayfair home, wearing livery and doing whatever his employer told him to do.

As she finished her roasted chestnuts, the ring on her finger tingled. "Kitty," she murmured as she traced a fingertip along the metal.

Searching the people in the park, she couldn't spot her friend. Odd. Reaching under her coat, Sera tugged out the piece of paper she had tucked into the top of her cloth binding. A hurried sentence scrawled its way along the page.

Being followed. Go on without me.

"Blast. Kitty is being followed." She showed the note to Hugh before tucking it back into its safe spot.

"Elliot, you go find the footman's livery. We'll meet at noon in the East End. Somewhere." Sera wracked her brain, trying to think of a safe spot to meet.

"The Apothecary's Poison. It's a pub tucked off the main road. I know the owner," Hugh offered.

Elliot nodded. "I know the place." He screwed up the paper that now held only a few flakes from the chestnuts and dropped it into his pocket. Then he set off with a long, determined stride.

As Sera and Hugh walked in another direction, she had to shove her hands into her pockets to stop herself from taking Hugh's hand. They walked across the grass and watched children out for an early walk with their nannies.

"If Elliot can't find the queen's livery, I will figure out another way to gain access to her this afternoon." Sera didn't want to waste time. Lord Rowan must know she had escaped the Repository of Forgotten Things, hence his decree labelling her a traitor. But did he know she had restored her magic?

As she turned to watch a group of children playing under a tree, Sera stumbled and fell, her foot caught on something invisible. She gasped as a white-hot wire pulled tight around her ankle. She swore under her breath as her fingers scrabbled against the worn leather of her borrowed boot and grasped nothing but the familiar brush of magic.

"What is it?" Hugh knelt to help her to her feet.

"It's a snare." Sera leaned back on the grass as though she had chosen that exact spot to lie in the sun.

"But I can't see anything." Following her example, Hugh sat on the damp grass beside her.

"It's an invisible trap, triggered by anyone with a trace of mage in their blood." As she watched a little girl of about ten years old make a leaf dance between her outstretched palms, a vague idea formed in her head.

"Can't you just use your magic to release it?" Hugh stared at her trouser leg, where the fabric seemed to bunch for no apparent reason.

"I could. But then Lord Rowan will know that someone powerful enough to disarm his trap had been caught in it." Sera caught the eye of the girl who could make leaves dance. Sweeping her hand over the grass, Sera made the fallen leaves stand to attention and march in straight rows.

"You need another rabbit to take your place," Hugh murmured.

"Yes. One who might have inadvertently triggered the spell while playing with her friends." Sera smiled at the girl and hoped her altered appearance didn't make her too scary.

The little girl approached and stopped a few paces from Sera. She frowned and pointed to the foliage soldiers. "You can do magic, too. I thought I was the only one."

"There are a few like us in London. With my magic, I have discovered something very special in this park, and only people like you and I can sense it." Sera crooked her finger and lowered her tone to ensure the girl would come closer.

The frown deepened, and the girl took another step towards Sera. "What?"

"A magical thread. When you tug on it, someone very important feels it on the other end. They will be along shortly. When they get here, they will do something magical just for you. Would you like to see that?"

The frown disappeared, along with any natural reservations the child harboured. "Oh, yes."

"All you have to do is put your hand on the thread and wait for the nice man to come." Sera coaxed the spell to widen enough to allow her to slip her boot out. Then she draped the invisible strand over the girl's outstretched hand.

"It tickles." She giggled and turned her wrist this way and that, as though she wore an expensive piece of jewellery.

"Remember, when the man gets here, you are to ask him to do something for you." Sera placed a hand on the girl's silky hair and whispered a spell. While she couldn't remove the memory of having seen Sera, she could blur the edges. The child would only remember seeing two men before she stumbled into the snare.

Sera walked away as fast as she could without attracting attention.

"Do you think Lord Rowan will come?" Hugh lengthened his stride to keep up with her.

"I doubt it. But I wouldn't be surprised if Lord Ormsby or Lord Tomlin are monitoring the traps." *Please let it be Lord Ormsby.* Sera liked the idea of the grumpy mage being asked by the little girl to produce a unicorn or a troupe of dancing fairies.

Hugh caught her arm and slowed her down to guide her back onto the path. "If there's one snare in the grass, there are likely to be more."

"While it's a greater risk, we need to stick to more populated areas. I doubt they have scattered traps around the London streets. They'd capture every after-mage in the city." They exited the other side of the park and kept walking into the heart of London.

As they navigated the treacherous city, Sera tried to push aside the nagging doubts that threatened to over-whelm her. How could she possibly stand against Lord Rowan's power and resources? His influence seemed to touch every corner of London, and with each trap they evaded, Sera questioned her own abilities a little more.

"You're very quiet," Hugh observed after several minutes of silence.

"I'm just tired and imagining a hot bath." She nudged him with her elbow.

Hugh turned red and coughed. "I don't think the pub has anything as large as the Fae realm offered. They probably only have a tin bath that would fit a small child."

"A girl can dream." Sera kept mental notes of what she liked for the house she would one day build at Westbourne Green on her little parcel of land. It would now have to include a tiled bathroom with an enor-mous copper tub. She made a promise to herself. Once she had defeated Lord Rowan, she would ask her father and Nat if they would begin the stonework for her home.

They rounded a corner as fog rolled in and muffled the sounds of the bustling city. They appeared to walk through a drizzly cloud, completely cut off from the world. Sera took a deep breath, inhaling the air that hung heavy with the scent of moss and decay. Then her skin tingled as though she had brushed against nettles.

"It's another trap." Grabbing Hugh's arm, she hurried him down an alleyway, where the tendrils of fog didn't reach.

Sera leaned her head against the damp brick as the fog slithered on down the street. Frustration made her teeth ache, and she screwed up her eyes. Doubt bombarded her. At this rate, she would make a mistake and put her friends in danger.

"Hey." Hugh's voice was gentle, his touch warm as he placed a hand on the side of her neck. "We can do this."

Uncertainty pressed her down. *Thinking* she could succeed and truly *believing* it were two different things. The truth was the icy fingers of self-doubt tightened around her like a vice.

"I can't avoid every trap for long." She drew a shuddering breath and reminded herself that she refused to cry or let Lord Rowan win.

"We tackle what is in front of us." Hugh turned her towards him and leaned his forehead against hers. Their breath mingled. She drew in his love, strength, and belief in her. "We get to the pub. You can contact Kitty while we wait for Elliot."

"How do we get there if the main roads have the guard fog, and they have laid lures in the back alleys?" They could fly if Warin were handy, and they could persuade him to transport them. But soaring over

London in the grips of a gargoyle would also give away her position.

Hugh took her hand and winked. "I grew up in these alleys. I can get us there by a route where I doubt any of your colleagues would dare venture to lay anything to catch you."

"You're right. I can't imagine Lord Tomlin dirtying the soles of his boots in the lower-class neighbourhoods." While Sera feigned a more cheerful mood, her thoughts churned like the muddy waters of the Thames.

The chill in the air was tinged with the scent of coal smoke and horse manure and stung Sera's cheeks and nose, but she pressed on. She clung to Hugh's promise that they would be safe when they reached the Apothecary's Poison...assuming they weren't murdered in a darkened alley. Eyes watched them, feet shuffled in the shadows, and sometimes, a baby cried from an overhanging tenement.

After what seemed like a journey through the bowels of hell, Hugh led the way through a narrow passageway that opened up into a modest intersection. Three roads joined in a Y, and in the triangular space bordered by two roads sat the pub. The sign swinging on a pole jutting out from the whitewashed wall bore a carved and painted potion bottle with a skull and crossbones on it.

"Are you sure we're safe here?" It looked like the sort of place where pirates gathered when ashore.

Hugh chuckled. "You'll see." He held the door open for Sera.

As his bulk crossed the threshold, the man at the bar stopped wiping a tankard and looked up. "About bloody time you turned up. My knee is killing me."

Sera wasn't that surprised Hugh was recognised. Most people knew the surgeon.

Hugh approached the bar with Sera in tow. "Sera, this is Imp. The closest thing I have in this world to a brother. He's also a terrible hypochondriac."

"Yeah. That's playing up an' all," Imp grumbled.

Four

"Brother?" Sera looked from Hugh to the pub owner. Apart from their muscled physiques and both looking like they could easily throw kegs of beer, any similarity ended there. Imp had a dark swarthiness to him that spoke of origins in more tropical climes.

"Brothers by choice, not blood. We grew up on the streets together. Imp taught me to throw a punch, and he's the one who encouraged me to become a doctor." Hugh leaned on the bar.

"We needed someone to patch us up, and Hugh here was the runt among us." Imp placed a clean tankard in front of Sera and filled it from a nearby pitcher.

She snorted to think of Hugh being the smallest in their group. She sipped the ale, which was surprisingly good, given its location. Perhaps the Apothecary's Poison kept many secrets behind its half-timbered Tudor exterior.

"You must be in a pickle if you're coming here." Imp poured a drink for Hugh.

"We need somewhere safe for a few nights, and a meal." Hugh surveyed the few customers hunched over their tankards.

"No one here will rat out Nyx, or they'll answer to me," Imp murmured, his gaze lingering on Sera.

"How did you know?" Sera blew out a sigh. So much for her disguise. If Imp recognised her, how many people on the street would, too?

Imp chuckled. "Oh, you pass for a lad, all right, milady. But Hugh told me a few months ago that you and he are—"

"Imp knows I love you," Hugh interrupted before his adopted brother said something entirely more colourful, given his hand gestures.

The big man shrugged. "Is love what you're calling it? Anyway, I've seen the posters offering a reward for you. And I know how hard the runt will fight to protect his family."

"I appreciate your discretion. Elliot Brynn will join us here, too, if we could have two rooms for tonight." Sera had better not forget her footman, or she'd never hear the end of his complaining.

"Oh, that one, too? I'll find somewhere for 'im." Mischief glinted in Imp's eyes. "Take a seat. I'll send Evie over with a meal." He waved them away with his cloth.

The dark wooden beams overhead were stained with years of smoke and grime, but the walls were clean. The rickety tables scattered across the uneven floor were populated by an assortment of rough-looking patrons, their whispered conversations barely audible over the crackling fire in the hearth. Hugh led Sera to a corner close to the fire where shadows lingered.

By the time they sat, a middle-aged woman approached. She grinned at Hugh but cast a curious look at Sera. She set down two plates laden with slices of roasted beef and rosemary potatoes.

Sera murmured her thanks. Once the barmaid had retreated, Sera pulled out the ensorcelled sheet of paper. Kitty had penned a new message.

"Kitty couldn't shake those who followed her and went to a bookshop instead before returning home," she told Hugh. "Blast. Abigail knows how close I am to Kitty and must have told her grandfather to keep a close watch on her, hoping she would lead them to me." Sera stabbed a piece of tender meat and chewed while she thought. "She needs to slip out in disguise. But I don't like the idea of her walking the streets alone."

"Send Elliot. He can fetch her and bring her safely here." Hugh stabbed beef and then potato before popping the fork-load into his mouth.

"Good idea." Pulling a stub of pencil from a pocket, Sera wrote a reply to her friend, urging her to find a disguise and wait for Elliot.

They had finished their meal, and Sera was savouring a cup of tea when the door was pushed open to admit Elliot. He nodded to Imp and then made a beeline for their corner. He carried a cloth-wrapped bundle, which he set down on the table with a flourish.

"I have found the key you need." He peeled back one corner of the protective outer wrapping to reveal the pristine livery of a royal footman. Sera's eyes widened as she took in the soft navy wool with the silver piping.

"I am impressed, Elliot. How did you secure it?" she asked, her voice hushed.

"Let's just say I have friends in high places...and low ones, too." He winked at the barmaid, who returned with a plate and a tankard for the cheeky footman. "Thank you, Evie. You are an angel who has saved me from starvation."

She giggled and blushed. "Get away with you, you rogue."

"You certainly have friends in many places," Sera said as she watched the interaction between the two.

"I'm a lovable fellow," Elliot mumbled around a mouthful of food.

While he ate, Sera instructed him to fetch Kitty first thing in the morning and guide her out through the kitchens of the Napier house and safely to the pub. Then she took the bundle upstairs to the little room she would share with Hugh.

"It's no Fae palace," Hugh murmured. The bed was barely big enough for two and was pushed up against the wall. A table with two chairs sat under the square window overlooking the street. A narrow sideboard held a mirror, ewer, and basin.

"I don't need anything fancy. I just need you." Sera dropped the bundle on the bed and wrapped her arms around the man she loved.

After a gentle kiss, she shrugged out of her dirty clothes and wiped her face and limbs with the cold water. After a brisk rub, she changed into the footman's livery. Hugh restored the stubble on her face with a bit of coal. She looked smart and, hopefully, beneath the notice of any courtiers roaming the queen's residence.

"Your hair." Hugh held out a powdered wig that the queen's male staff wore. It took some effort to cram all her hair up under it, but they managed.

Finally, she donned a thick, hooded cloak to obscure her new disguise.

As an early twilight settled over the city, Sera, Hugh, and Elliot made their way towards Westminster, sticking to the shadows as they navigated the narrow alleyways. As they neared Buckingham House, Sera's heart pounded. She couldn't use magic and would have to rely on her wits to navigate the traps the Mage Council had no doubt set to guard the queen.

The grand house loomed before them, its elaborate façade illuminated by mage lights set on the lawn. Following Elliot, they went around the side to the smaller doors used by merchants and servants.

"You can do this," Hugh whispered before he placed a swift kiss on her lips.

Sera slipped away from her companions and approached the servants' entrance. Her timing was perfect. The kitchens were bustling as the staff prepared the queen's supper. The aroma of roasting meats and fresh-baked bread filled her nostrils as she navigated the chaos, careful not to draw attention to herself. She observed the other servants as they hustled about their tasks and mimicked their actions. Picking up a silver tray with a small bowl of marzipan treats on it, she fell into line behind three other footmen in the same livery, who marched towards a door on the other side of the enormous kitchen.

With each step, Sera's confidence grew. Now that she was inside, all she had to do was find the queen. Fortunately, she had previously been invited to afternoon tea with her and had some idea of where she would find her private apartments.

She slipped out of line and down a corridor, her footfalls muffled by the plush carpets. The air was heavy with the scent of beeswax, old wood, and the lingering stale perfume of courtiers. Turning a corner, Sera spotted a group of patrolling guards approaching from the opposite direction. She kept her gaze on the tiny orange balanced on top of the pyramid of marzipan fruit and kept her steps slow and steady.

One guard glanced at the contents of the tray as he drew near. "Lucky buggers, getting to eat those whenever they want," he muttered as they continued on their way.

Sera let out a sigh. No one expected the dangerous woman mage to be dressed as a footman and carrying sweet treats. Her mood lightened as she neared the queen's apartments. *Almost there.*

As she rounded another corner and neared her destination, her heart plummeted to her toes. Before her was the one person she absolutely did not want to encounter—Lady Abigail Crawley.

Anger surged through Sera, and her magic pooled in her fingertips, demanding she lash out at the treacherous woman. To mar her perfect face with a pig's snout. Or better yet, immolate her on the spot.

But she couldn't. *Revenge is a dish best served cold.*

Sera dropped her gaze to the rug and let her shoulders sag. She held the tray with the porcelain bowl as though it were an offering to the gods. As Abigail neared, Sera stepped to the side as a servant would and bowed.

Her heart pounded so loudly that she wondered how Abigail did not hear it. But the woman who had once been her friend didn't even cast a glance at a footman. A servant was beneath the notice of a woman engaged to the son of a duke.

Sera stood still long after Abigail had disappeared around the corner, waiting for her heart to calm. She had faced an obstacle more dangerous than any mage.

A few more feet, and she stood before the double doors of the queen's apartments. She tugged on the brass handle, but the door didn't budge.

Locked. Setting down the tray, Sera knelt on the carpet.

Using any magic risked alerting Lord Rowan to her presence. She only hoped the tiny amount required to unlock the door was as far beneath the old mage's notice as a footman had been to his grand-daughter.

Using a tendril of magic as thin as the most delicate spider-spun silk, Sera encircled the lock and tickled it. The metal yielded to her gentle touch, and a whisper-soft click sounded.

Picking up the tray once more, she opened the door and entered the queen's private parlour. The monarch sat at a round table before the window, the shutters now closed to keep out the cold of night. She was playing cards with two of her ladies. Plush sofas uphol-stered in white-and-blue chintz were placed facing each other before the massive fire. Lapdogs dozed on the rug, warming their tummies before the flames.

An open door gave a glimpse of the queen's private bedchamber beyond.

"Oh, marzipan!" one lady exclaimed on spying the tray Sera carried.

Sera set the bowl in the middle of the table and tucked the tray under her arm.

The queen discarded one card and picked up another. "Why are you still here? Have you come to tell me that I am to be let out of my cage at last?"

There was a sentiment Sera could understand. "Forgive the intrusion, Your Majesty, but I require a private word."

Queen Charlotte looked up and narrowed her gaze. She tilted her head as she studied Sera's features. Then she pointed to her ladies. "You two, get out. Since the door is unlocked, take the dogs so they can do their business elsewhere."

The ladies dropped their cards and hurried to do the queen's bidding. Each picked up two of the little dogs and slipped out the partially open door.

"You took your time in getting here, Lady Winyard. What exactly is happening in our country?" The queen abandoned her cards and laid her hands flat on the table.

There were many similarities between Kitty and the queen. Both women possessed a sharp intellect and were direct in their manner. Which meant Sera could cut straight to the point. "Lord Rowan imprisoned me and seized control of England. I believe that he has placed some enchantment over King George to muddle the king's mind and make it easier to assume power. First as regent, and then to style himself as emperor."

The queen sucked in a breath. "He has caused this harm to my George?"

"Yes. I only need to get near the king to confirm my suspicion and to determine the nature of the spell, so I can break it." How to make her way through St James's Palace, where the king was sequestered, was a problem for tomorrow.

The queen rose and walked to the fire. Sera followed. The monarch was kept in a much nicer cage than the one Sera had escaped at the Repository of Forgotten Things. Still, a prison was a prison.

"Rowan is an old man. Why do such a thing when

he has only a few years left at most?" The queen's gaze demanded answers from Sera.

"He intended to use a magical child, called a Nereus, born of two mages, to turn back the hands of time and make himself young once more." The plot tasted repugnant on Sera's tongue.

The queen's eyes widened in surprise. "If this creature can do such a thing, why have we not heard of it before?"

Sera recalled the sad fate of the little boy. "Because a Nereus is as dangerous as it is powerful. The last Nereus caused fractures that tore through the Fae realm and nearly destroyed this country. It took the entire council and the Roman army to defeat him. That is why those druids decided to ensure there could never be another, by ending the life of any girl mage born."

The queen clenched her hands around the marble mantel. "Your child would do this?"

A snort welled up in Sera's throat. "Only if I bore the child of a fellow mage. That is why Lord Rowan had me imprisoned. He thought mistreatment would make me comply with...the proceedings."

Queen Charlotte barked a laugh and turned to stare at the flames. "You escaped. No wonder he is fuming. Smoke swirls around him, his temper is so high. He said I had to be detained here for *my* protection. I knew that was damned odd. My mage would never harm me."

"Of course not, Ma'am. I swore to protect and serve you, the king, and this country. Lord Rowan thought imprisoning both of us would allow his scheme to proceed." The old mage had not only underestimated Sera but also the queen.

The queen huffed and sat on the sofa, then gestured for Sera to sit. "What do you need from me?"

Sera sat, only to find the sofa not as comfortable as it appeared, having only a small amount of padding over the wooden structure. "I need to identify how Lord Rowan is affecting the king's mind. Has he ever cast any spells over the king, given him a potion to drink, or placed any magical talismans on his person?"

"Our lives are full of incantations and vile potions. Things to stop a blade, a shot, or to protect us from poisoners." The queen rapped her knuckles on the arm of the sofa as she thought.

"This would be something different. Something kept from the other mages and courtiers. Something administered privately."

Enough seconds passed to make Sera fear she had been wrong. Then the queen huffed.

"Some years ago," she said with slow, measured words, "in a private audience, Lord Rowan gave George an amulet. He said it was very old and imbued with ancient wisdom. He told George not to take it off and it would ward off evil."

Sera's suspicions grew stronger. "Do you recall any change in the king's behaviour after receiving this gift?"

"Yes," the queen said softly, her eyes half-closed as she lost herself in memory. "He threw the most uncommon tantrum after Lord Rowan left—when I tried to lift the thing from around his neck to have a closer look. I had never seen George in such a rage before. Since that day, his mind has been...clouded."

"Your Majesty, I believe that amulet may be the cause of the chaos within the king's mind." At least now she knew what to focus on. But if the king never took it off, how to inspect the thing?

"You will get close to my George, ascertain the truth of it, and then you will make Lord Rowan pay for what he has done to the king." The queen rose, her voice silk-wrapped in steel.

Sera leapt to her feet. "I promise, Ma'am. I also hope the edicts incarcerating me in the Repository and declaring me a traitor will be rescinded?"

The queen waved a hand as though that were a simple matter. "Once the king and I are *both* free, it will be done, and you shall have our thanks."

That would have to do. The price on her head made life more difficult, but she couldn't hide at the Apothecary's Poison until the order was reversed. Not with Lord Rowan's grip growing tighter every day.

"One more thing, Lady Winyard," the queen called as Sera approached the door.

She paused. "Yes, Your Majesty?"

"Don't get caught. I am rather fond of having a woman mage at my command." Queen Charlotte grinned and then returned to the card table.

With a final bow, Sera left the queen's private chambers. With the silver tray tucked under her arm, she navigated the quiet corridors back to the kitchens.

Each time another person appeared in front of her, her heart skipped a beat in case it was Abigail returning to the queen.

As she trod the expensive carpets, she marvelled at what she had done in her short life. The only woman mage, escaping the unescapable Repository, travelling to the Fae realm, freeing a dragon, and now turned resourceful spy, infiltrating the very heart of the English monarchy.

Closer now, she wound her way to the kitchens. The hushed whispers of servants scurrying about their tasks grew louder. As she turned a corner, Sera found herself face-to-face with a young maid carrying a tray laden with cups of steaming tea. For a moment, they merely stared at one another, caught in a tense standoff.

Then Sera stepped out of the woman's way. "Pardon me," she intoned in what she hoped would pass for a masculine voice.

As she passed through the kitchens, Sera deposited the tray on a table. Once outside, she collected her cloak from where she had hidden it between two crates of potatoes.

Only when she left the glow of the lights from Buckingham House and slipped into the embrace of the dark did Sera relax. Two shadows detached themselves from a tree and fell into step beside her.

"I saw Abigail," Sera murmured in a small voice.

FIVE

Hugh took her hand and pulled her to a halt. "Did she recognise you?" Worry was carved into the lines of his face.

Sera closed her eyes and let the scene play in her head once more. Had any spark of recognition flared in the other woman's face? Could she have missed it if there had been any hint? "I don't think so. There was no pause in her movement, nor did she glance back at me."

"That one wouldn't have looked at a footman," Elliot said. "When she came to visit you, her eyes just bounced right over me, even when I was right in front of her pulling a face."

A smile warmed Sera's insides. "You used to pull faces at Lady Abigail Crawley?"

"I would have spat in her tea, too, but I didn't want you to drink it." He landed a mock punch on her shoulder.

A chuckle bubbled through her and dissolved the worry. "Let's get back to the pub. We need to figure out how to get close to the king."

The group hurried back through the dark streets of London. This time, they worried less about magical snares and more about cutthroats and thugs thinking them easy targets. Fortunately, Hugh's size and Elliot's wiles kept them out of trouble.

At the little junction, which made Sera think of a clearing among towering trees, Hugh held open the door to the Apothecary's Poison. In her mind, the warm pub became a dimly lit bastion of mystery and intrigue, its name whispered only among those who knew where and how to find it. The pub's worn wooden floorboards creaked beneath the tread of its patrons, while the air hung heavy with the scent of tobacco and damp wool.

"I'll change out of these." Sera touched the edge of the livery visible beneath the fastening of her cloak.

"Good. I need to put them back before the owner realises I nicked them," Elliot said.

"I'll order something to warm us up." Hugh headed for the bar.

Upstairs, Sera stripped off the uniform but couldn't bring herself to put the itchy old clothes back on. Instead, she retrieved her trousers, boots, and black shirt from her saddlebags.

"That's better," she murmured as she laced up the knee-high boots. She left her long-skirted coat in the room as it was too uniquely...*her*. Instead, she grabbed the old jacket. At least with her shirt underneath, it didn't scratch as much. Sera refolded the livery and wrapped it once more in its protective layer. All the while, she wondered who Elliot had stolen it from. Most servants lived in or near the palace. Perhaps he had swiped it from a laundry. But that didn't explain the wig. With those thoughts dancing through her mind, she made her way back downstairs to their corner.

Overhead, a haphazard collection of lanterns hung from iron hooks and swayed gently, casting eerie shadows that seemed to dance in time with the lilting notes of a fiddle. The flickering glow lit the weathered faces of the pub's regular patrons. Sera placed the bundle of clothing on the seat next to Elliot and slid in next to Hugh.

He reached for her hand under the table, giving it a reassuring squeeze as if to say they would conquer whatever challenges lay ahead. "Imp is bringing you a pot of hot chocolate and some bread-and-butter pudding."

"I knew there was a reason I loved you." That was exactly what she needed—a steaming mug of chocolate goodness.

"I'm having supper and ale since you are paying." Elliot winked.

"You had supper not so long ago." Sera smiled at Evie as she laid mugs and plates on their table.

"The way things are with you, I'm getting in as many meals as possible. I can't live on roasted chestnuts, you know." Elliot took up his cutlery and attacked a slice of savoury pie.

Around them, people drank, laughed, and whispered secrets into each other's ears, their faces half-hidden in the dim light. Yet even amidst this cacophony of mirth, tension coiled within her. Obstacles littered her path. Every time she thought they had events under control, something else cropped up that she needed to figure out. Like escaping from an inescapable prison. Or freeing an ancient guardian of the Fae. Now she had to find a way to get close to the king when one of the senior mages would be constantly at his side.

"We need to get into St James's Palace. Elliot, you're the most devious one. What ideas have you got?" Sera's voice was barely above a whisper as she leaned in closer to her friends.

"Do you really think Lord Rowan would stoop so low as to cast a spell over the king himself?" Hugh asked as he reached for the battered pot containing hot chocolate.

Sera steeled her spine as she recalled her encounters with the man she'd once thought of as her mentor. "Yes. Or do you consider altering the king's mind worse than commanding Lord Tomlin to assault me?"

"I supposed I hoped there was some limit to his depravity." Hugh poured them both a mug of the steaming chocolate drink.

"The queen said that some years ago, Lord Rowan gave the king an amulet. One he never takes off." She sipped her chocolate and detected a hint of heat from a pinch of chilli. "Oh, this is good. Where does Imp get chilli?" One problem was momentarily set aside as she considered a mystery closer to where she sat.

Hugh swallowed his mouthful before answering. "He was wasted as a fighter. Just as I had a higher purpose with my hands in healing others, Imp's calling is in the kitchen. As to where he gets his spices, I wouldn't dare ask for his sources."

"I shall have to procure some for Rosie once we can return to our normal lives." *Normal lives.* What would that look like? Sera dreamed of a life that held chilli, cinnamon, and vanilla. Some spices were worth their weight in gold, so she'd better figure out a way to afford such luxuries for her cook.

"Life with you will never be ordinary." Hugh's warm gaze rested on Sera.

"And at least she's the only one wearing livery and not me," Elliot joked around mouthfuls of sliced beans.

"From what I have heard, the king grows increasingly delusional. His physicians say he is sequestered and refuses to admit anyone into his presence he doesn't know or trust." Hugh leaned against the wall and stretched one arm along the back of the bench. From that position, he could see both Sera and the others in the pub, to spot any trouble headed towards their corner.

"I need to examine the amulet to figure out what sort of spell Lord Rowan is using. But how do I do that if the king won't let anyone near? Disguising myself would be pointless as I won't be admitted. But if I walk in there openly, I'll be seized by whichever mage is watching over him." Sera was facing a circular problem with no way to break into it.

"He trusts me," Hugh whispered, almost as though he was thinking out loud.

"I'm not sure how to use you in this instance. I need to inspect the amulet. The king won't remove it, and you can't discern any magic it contains." She wanted to throw her arms up in frustration.

"What you need is a way for the king to trust you, long enough to let you do whatever witchy stuff you have to do." Elliot spoke the words, but his gaze followed the barmaid who threaded her way between tables.

Sera considered that for a moment. "Sometimes, Elliot, you scare me with how smart you are."

Hugh frowned. "That will work?"

Elliot placed one hand to his heart, as though Hugh's doubt had wounded him.

"The king trusts you. As his physician, you can administer potions to ease his complaints. What we need is a spell that will clear his mind long enough to allow me close to him." Sera teased out the idea, testing the way it sounded.

"Something that will pass the taster's lips without notice," Hugh said.

Blast. She'd forgotten that everything the king consumed was first tasted by an aftermage, who sampled everything to check for either poison or a spell against the king. She sipped her hot chocolate and let the rich flavour swirl in her mouth as she thought of possible solutions.

She swallowed. "We need a potion that works on the king but registers as harmless to the taster." The first hurdle was easily jumped. Whatever they brewed would do no harm to the king or to the unfortunate person who put themselves in the way of death with every bite and sip. The more troublesome question was how to add something that wouldn't appear untoward when the taster sensed the spell the liquid contained.

"Lucidity," she breathed, and her brain said *yes*. That was the right path. "What if I brewed a potion for a clear mind? It would help the king, even if only temporarily, and the taster wouldn't notice anything amiss."

Hugh made a noise in the back of his throat as he considered her idea. "We have tried such potions on the king with little success. While I believe in you, it has a high chance of failure."

Her excitement grew, certain she had grasped hold of the right solution. "But all the other physicians and mages brewing their concoctions haven't considered the basic problem—the influence of the amulet. They have been trying to address a purely physical origin for his symptoms. If I incorporated a shielding component, it could protect his mind at the same time as clearing his thoughts."

Hugh's expression remained neutral, but his hand tightened on his mug. Then he blew out a sigh.

"Hypothesise, then test. It sounds as though it should work, but we won't know until he swallows it."

"I could be as close to hand as possible, ready for you to give the word. But it means you take the greater risk." Sera laid her hand on his forearm. "Assuming I can concoct such a potion, you have to gain admittance to the king and get him to drink it. Abigail will have told her grandfather that if he finds you, he will find me. They might try to seize you."

"Some things are worth the risk." Hugh stroked his thumb along her cheek.

"Let's assume you can boil up whatever will do the trick. Where will you do it? Or find all the ingredients you need?" Elliot waved his fork as he spoke.

"Or the spell to adapt to our needs?" Sera leaned her head against the wood of their nook, and a shaft of despair carved a path through her. "It's not as though I can do a spot of research in the library at the mage tower."

The accumulation of centuries of knowledge...all out of her reach. If she had had more time, she could have asked Queen Deryn if she could talk to the Fae mages and study in their libraries.

"What if there was another library?" Hugh leaned forwards and rested his arms on the table.

"I'm sure there are many in London. But I need arcane law, not a travel guide of Europe or a naughty novel." Under other circumstances, Sera could have used trial and error to produce the desired effect. But that could take weeks or even years.

A gleam entered Hugh's eyes. "When we were at the Crow's Nest, I asked Warin about his time in London and how it had changed over the centuries. He mentioned a library kept by his clan, where their scribes once recorded the stories of Londinium. He said that it had fallen into disuse as there are so few of them now."

"So it's not even full of travel stories, but boring everyday ones about poor sods like us? Although if they recorded tales of the brothels, I'd be interested." Elliot pushed his plate away and turned his attention to his ale.

Hugh glanced at the footman and shook his head. "They didn't just keep memoirs. They also collected dangerous books that needed the protection of gargoyles."

Sera's breath left her in a quick gasp. What sort of books needed gargoyles to keep them safe? "It's worth a chance if we can find this place. Warin said he would meet us in London and keep watch over the church. Let's hope that if we return there, we will find him."

She ate her pudding while a tight knot grew in her stomach. How could there be such a hidden store of magical knowledge and the Mage Council not know of its existence? It could simply be a tale, and she tried not to get her hopes up. A yawn nearly cracked her jaw. The stress of the last few days since they had left the comfort of the Fae realm had taken a toll. "We seek him out tomorrow after Elliot has fetched Kitty. She'd never forgive me if she missed a visit to a library."

They made their plans, and Sera passed them on to Kitty with the enchanted paper. Then she climbed the stairs, undressed, and fell into bed.

THE NEXT MORNING, Sera awoke with renewed determination. The Fates might toy with her by tossing obstacles in her way, but they strengthened her and made her more intent upon stopping Lord Rowan. As Sera and Hugh sat at the corner table and ate breakfast, a grumbling Elliot set off for Mayfair.

An hour later, he returned. Kitty wore a simple gown under a dark-blue cloak, and her thick hair was tied in a knot at her nape, such as a laundress or maid might do.

"Blasted rude of Abigail to have me watched," Kitty said as she dropped to the bench beside Sera. "More tea." She instructed Elliot when he tried to sit across from the women, next to Hugh.

Sera hugged her friend. "I saw her at Buckingham House, but she didn't recognise me."

"She always had her nose too high in the air to see what was right under it. Now, what is this about a secret library?" Her eyes were luminous with curiosity.

"Have your tea and we shall find Warin to learn more." Sera tapped the rim of her cup and hoped there was such a place. Otherwise, she didn't know what to do.

The inn was quiet at such an early hour, and apart from one man dozing in a corner, they had the place to themselves.

"While we are gone, I need you to find either a livery or a maid's uniform for St James's, please," Sera told Elliot as he brought to the table a plate laden with sausages, toast, eggs, and a kipper.

"Yes, ma'am," he said before tucking in.

Leaving him in peace, they set off to find the old gargoyle. Sera took Kitty's arm, and Hugh guided them through the back streets and alleys to the old church. Its once-grand façade was now scarred by neglect and the relentless passage of time. The belfry loomed overhead, a shadowy sentinel against the tempestuous sky.

"Do we have to climb all the way up there?" Kitty asked, glancing at the tall, spindly belfry.

"If he is agreeable, Warin can fly you back down to the ground." Hugh grinned, excited at the prospect of flying or gliding, again.

"I prefer my feet on the ground," Kitty murmured.

One by one, they squeezed in through the partially blocked doorway. The smell of mouldering wood hung in the air as the leaks in the roof spread rot in decaying pews. Only the magic-infused stained-glass window remained intact.

Kitty stood in the nave and stared up at the panes lit by the morning light. "How beautiful."

Before they could pick their way to the narrow stairwell that wound up into the belfry, a shape moved in the gloom beneath the beams of a collapsed transept roof on one side. In his gargoyle form, Warin approached.

"Rain is making the stairs slippery, and it is less windy down here," he said.

"I need your help, Warin. Hugh said you told him of an old gargoyle library. Does it by chance contain any spell books?" Sera didn't have time to engage in chitchat, nor were gargoyles fond of it.

His slate-grey gaze lingered on her for a long moment. "Yes. But only my kind are allowed there."

Sera curled her hands in frustration. It must be like the mage library. Not only did you have to be a mage to enter, you had to grow a stupid blade of grass first. Or an oak tree, in her case. Why was nothing she had to do easy?

"Oh, for goodness' sake." Kitty placed her hands on her hips, squarely facing the creature that had seen Roman centurions walk the streets. "We're not going to loot it. We are trying to protect the king and this country. Which is exactly what you are supposed to be doing. Sera needs to find a particular spell. Are you going to help us or be all...*dense* about it?"

A rumbling growl came from deep within the gargoyle's chest, but Kitty never flinched. Instead, she pointed a finger at his head and shook it. "We haven't got all day. Either show us this library, or we need to figure out another way."

The rumble turned into a rolling chuckle. "I will show you. It is at Bone Hill. Meet me there."

The three of them shared a look. Kitty's was more thoughtful. "That's the Saxon name for Bunhill Fields. Who better than the dead to keep a secret through the centuries?"

By the time they squeezed back out the door, Warin was gone. Hugh hailed a hackney, and they piled in for the short trip. The weather behaved, and the sky remained clear, even though the air contained a bitter edge.

"Spring is not far away. A time of new beginnings." Through the window, Sera watched the streets peter out into fields. Hope pushed through her like a daffodil poking through the cold soil.

At the old cemetery, it didn't take long for them to find Warin. He waited on the path by the sexton's hut and led them into the older area with its mature trees, whose skeletal branches clawed at the sky like pleading hands.

The gargoyle stopped at a mausoleum that was being reclaimed by the earth, its worn façade covered in moss and lichen. The lettering was long gone, but a stone gargoyle perched on each corner. One had lost a wing at some time, but the caress of wind and water had sanded the wound over. The tomb had no door or any obvious way inside.

"It's in there?" Kitty glanced at Sera, doubt colouring her words.

"The library was first. We built this to conceal the

entrance." Warin placed his hands flat on the stone. A *crack* sounded as a line raced around the solid surface and created a door. With a push, it creaked open. A blast of musty air came from the black void that reminded Sera of the inky well that had trapped Ebonfyre.

But she had to step into this one.

SIX

"AFTER YOU, WARIN." Sera swept her arm towards the gaping entrance.

The ancient gargoyle chuckled, ducked his head, and the dark swallowed him. With a glance at Kitty and Hugh, Sera followed. Kitty came next, her gown hitched up to avoid snagging on loose rocks and roots that might encroach upon their path. Hugh took the rear.

Inside the squat tomb, Sera cast a globe of soft amber light and instructed it to hover in front of them. The flickering light revealed a narrow, winding tunnel that angled down into the earth. As they descended, the air grew colder and damp, with a cloying stench of decay. The macabre whispers of the dead echoed around them, sending shivers down Sera's spine. Kitty reached for her hand, and the two women drew strength from each other.

Warin led them through a labyrinth of tunnels, the

walls lined with the bones of those who had succumbed to the plague and wars a thousand years ago. Sera tried not to linger on the macabre sight, focusing instead on the promise of hidden knowledge that lay ahead.

The air grew colder, and Sera shivered, her mage-flame doing little to dispel the chill that crept through her bones.

"Watch your step," she said, letting the glowing orb linger to illuminate where the ground beneath them became treacherous with fallen rock and debris.

"Good Lord, look at this," Hugh whispered, his voice hushed with reverence as they rounded a bend in the tunnel.

Sera's heart raced at the sight laid out before them. They had come upon a narrow passage, flanked on all sides by skeletal remains embedded within the very earth. Shapes in white to dark cream created a gruesome sort of masonry. She shuddered, imagining the lives of those who had been entombed here, their bones now a part of the foundation of the world above.

"Do you think they are Saxon?" Kitty asked, a fingertip hovering above a skull that displayed its profile, the jaw open in a half scream.

"Older," Warin replied. "Humans have buried their dead here for millennia. This is a sacred site."

"I wonder what these remains could tell us about the sort of lives they lived. Did they die of old age, sickness, or injury?" Hugh peered closer, his hand tracing a fracture in a long bone.

"Perhaps Warin will let you return another day to

study those who protect his library." Sera gestured for the gargoyle to carry on. Her friends could either stay in the dark or follow the bobbing light.

The deeper they went, the more Sera became aware of an odd phenomenon. The air was no longer chilly; indeed, she found it a tolerable temperature. "Does anyone else notice that it's getting warmer down here?"

"Yes. Do you think all the earth above us has something to do with it? Rather like piling on woollen blankets?" Kitty asked from close behind Sera.

"I don't know." Sera tucked the knowledge away to ponder later. Perhaps she and Hugh could return; he could examine bones, and she could fathom why the air grew warmer when she expected it to be frigid. If the air in the tunnels was temperate in the middle of winter, could there be a way to harness that to make the homes of those above warmer?

"We are here." Warin stopped at the end of the tunnel.

Before them stood a round piece of granite some nine feet in diameter, its surface covered in runes unlike any Sera had ever seen before. The ancient symbols seemed to pulse with a power that both drew her in and set her on edge.

"This isn't Fae." She peered closer. These runes didn't have the familiar shape of the Fae language. She studied the markings. The faintest touch of an eerie magic emanated from the symbols, different from anything she had encountered before.

Warin leaned back against the curve of the tunnel and crossed massive arms over his broad chest, the faintest trace of a smile on his square face. "Why don't you try opening it?"

If he was giving her the chance, it meant he didn't think she could. There was undoubtedly some trick to triggering the lock, rather like the one in the mage tower where you had to ask the metal ouroboros to move out of the way.

With a deep breath, she started with a simple air spell. Gathering her focus, she whispered the incantation, waving her fingers in a fluid motion before the granite. The stone remained unyielding.

"Try something else that doesn't work," Kitty helpfully suggested.

Curling her hands while she thought, this time, Sera invoked the power of fire, calling forth the essence of heat and combustion. A soft glow emanated from her hands, casting flickering shadows over the walls. As she thrust her palms towards the granite, sparks flew, but the stone merely absorbed the heat without so much as a crack.

Hugh rapped a knuckle on the warm stone. "It's gargoyle construction. Could the solution be the earth that contains the library?"

"Good idea," Sera replied, already visualising the spell. She reached out, fingers splayed, and chanted the words that would call forth the power of the earth—the very force that shaped mountains and carved valleys.

Had the door shifted?

No, any effect was gone, and the granite proved impervious to her efforts.

"You have had your little game. How does it open?" Her hands itched for a sheet of paper and a piece of charcoal to take a rubbing of the unusual markings in order to learn of their origins.

"Only a gargoyle can access the library. Our elders made this two thousand years ago." Warin laid one dinner-plate-sized hand flat on the stone.

"Gargoyles are impervious to magic. Are you saying you have your own sort of magical ability?" Sera's mind lit up with ideas. She had assumed gargoyles were powerless save for their ability to shift their shapes, but perhaps their rock-solid bodies contained a different sort of ability, gifted to them by Mother Earth.

"We are part of the earth, only our forms are different," he said in a deep, gravelly tone.

Which wasn't an answer at all.

With both hands flat on the carved surface, Warin's fingers seemed to meld with the stone as he whispered a guttural incantation in an ancient language. One by one, the runes glowed a deep amber, pulsating like the heartbeat of the earth itself.

Before their eyes, the granite shifted and groaned, transforming into a door that creaked open to reveal a room beyond.

Warin let them go first. Sera took a cautious step over the threshold—perhaps the first human to do so—Kitty and Hugh crowding behind her. The room was oval and windowless. Its walls curved like the belly of a great serpent. Sera crafted more light orbs and set them at regular intervals around the walls. The flickering light revealed shelves soaring two storeys above their heads, laden with books and scrolls so numerous that they seemed to defy the laws of space. A magical, ancient, and mystical air filled the chamber.

Kitty tilted her head to stare at the curved ceiling high above them. "How deep underground are we? I cannot recall any structure poking out of Bunhill Fields...other than the hill itself."

"We are deep enough for our knowledge to remain concealed from prying eyes," Warin answered, casting his gaze over the vast collection.

"One could almost suspect you built this library first and then created the hill and surrounding cemetery, piling up the bones of the dead to hide it." Kitty turned her sharp gaze to the gargoyle.

Warin remained silent, his features unreadable.

"How did you conceal it from the mages? They must have questioned you." Sera wandered to the closest shelf and murmured titles under her breath.

Warin shrugged. "We told them it was a catacomb to house the dead. They lost interest."

Sera swallowed a snort. She could imagine the mages recoiling in horror, scurrying back to the mage tower, and the existence of the catacombs under the cemetery becoming lost to time.

The room held the musty odour of aged parchment mingling with the tang of leather bindings and the faint scent of something else—the smell of magic itself. Soft whispers echoed around them as if the very spirits of the long dead holding the library in their embrace guarded their secrets jealously.

"Look at these," Kitty murmured. She ran her fingers reverently over a row of ancient tomes, their spines embossed with letters from languages Sera had never encountered before.

"Many of these texts are written in tongues now lost to time," Warin said, following the line of Kitty's gaze.

Kitty pulled a face at Sera and muttered out the side of her mouth, "That will not help our search."

Apart from the rows of books, there were also diamond-shaped compartments crammed with scrolls.

"How are the books organised?" Sera asked, surveying the labyrinthine stacks with a mixture of awe and trepidation. "Is there any method to this madness?"

"Yes," Warin replied, a sly grin playing on his stony features. "Each section is dedicated to a particular branch of knowledge, from arcane lore to the natural sciences. The books are arranged by subject matter and then further divided according to the age and origin of their authors."

That must be the gargoyle's idea of a joke. Who used an organisation method that required the seeker to have an in-depth knowledge of both the writers and their works over the last two thousand years?

"We are here. Let's make a start." Determination flared inside Sera. Somewhere in the pages of one of these books, there had to be a spell that would work to help King George.

The group split up, each of them tackling a different point on the compass. Sera's fingers traced the spines of ancient tomes, their surfaces cold and smooth, like the scales of some long-forgotten serpent. The air in the library was heavy with the mustiness of time and a tinge of sadness that it had sat for so long with no one to visit it.

Silence fell as they each became lost in the task. The only noises were the shuffle of pages, a soft tread, and a few muttered words. At length, Kitty approached Sera with a thick volume.

"This one has a spell for cleansing the spirit." Kitty's hands held it open at the page.

Sera scanned the intricate symbols and arcane diagrams. "No," she said with a sigh, shaking her head. "This is for purging demonic possession. We need something more refined, something that will restore memories and protect against dark magic."

Kitty returned to her side of the room. More time elapsed, and this time, Hugh presented a book for her inspection. "What about this one?" he asked hopefully. "It mentions a spell to shield the mind from enchantment."

"Oh, that sounds promising." Sera's brow furrowed as she read the faint text. "Unfortunately, this would make the king immune to all magic, including our own attempts to help him. We need something more... targeted."

Warin, who had perched on a high shelf, unfurled his wings and leapt into the air. He soared gracefully above them, his stone hands reaching out to pluck volumes from the uppermost reaches of the library.

"These may be of help. They contain protective magic." He swooped back towards the group and placed the stack of books at Sera's feet.

"Thank you, Warin," she murmured and reached for the top volume.

As Sera delved deeper into the labyrinth of knowledge, the ancient texts surrounding her blurred together, forming an indecipherable mass of words and symbols. Her hands flew between pages and scrolls, her fingers dancing as if possessed by the spirit of some long-dead mage.

She paused as a chill ran down her spine and a chorus of moans and whispers filled the library. The sound was like the sigh of a thousand restless souls, their voices echoing through the chamber in a haunting lament.

"Does everyone else hear that?" Hugh asked, his voice low and uneasy.

Kitty's eyes were wide. "It seems we are not alone in this place."

Sera swallowed. The weight of the dead pressed upon her from all sides, their ghostly whispers urging her to hurry. "Stay focused. Don't let restless spirits distract us from our task," she said, even as the hairs on the back of her neck bristled.

They continued searching, spiralling higher in the

shelves, while Sera focused on the books Warin fetched from near the ceiling. Her pulse quickened as her fingers traced the ancient parchment, the inked symbols seeming to dance and spin before her eyes. It was as if the very air within the library hummed with an unseen energy. The moans and whispers of the dead continued to swirl around them, but Sera ignored them. If they wanted to chat, they should go find old Ethel.

"Here!" she cried, her voice cutting through the spectral cacophony like a blade. "I have found two spells that I can combine to create the potion we need."

"Show us." Kitty placed the book she held back on the shelf and rushed to where Sera sat on the floor.

Hugh walked more slowly, careful not to step on the scattered volumes.

Sera picked up one open book and pointed to a page. "This spell restores lost memories and brings clarity of thought. And this one"—Sera pointed to the book open on her lap—"is a protection spell to ward off evil magic."

"And combining them will work?" Kitty asked cautiously.

"It has to," Sera whispered. "All I need to do now is copy out the spells."

Warin swooped down from his perch, clutching a stack of parchment, an inkpot, and an odd quill fashioned from a small bone. He placed them before Sera with a nod, his stone hands rough yet surprisingly gentle in their movements.

"Thank you, Warin," Sera murmured, taking up

the pen and dipping it into the small pot of ink. She copied out the spells carefully, while Kitty and Hugh gathered up the discarded books for Warin to return to the shelves.

Then both her friends began pulling books at random, devouring every scrap of mystic lore in the time left to them.

As Sera completed the final stroke of her penmanship, her breath shuddered in her chest, relief washing over her. She cast a simple spell to ensure her version was an exact duplicate and every punctuation mark was identical. Any tiny mistake might cause the spell to fail or deliver an unexpected result.

She waved the pages through the air to let the ink dry before folding them up and tucking them safely under her stays and against her skin.

"Time to leave." Kitty heaved a sigh and stared at the shelves as though she were being parted from a lover.

"The dead grow restless. We have lingered too long," Warin intoned. His voice was a low rumble that seemed to echo through the stone walls.

As one, the group turned away from the towering shelves, and Sera snuffed out the hanging orbs. Their eyes adjusted to the dim light from the one remaining globe that hovered before them. A pang of loss passed through Sera as they left behind the trove of knowledge, knowing there were so many secrets to uncover. Yet another marvellous thing to revisit once she had dealt with Lord Rowan and freed the king and queen.

Once they were all back in the tunnel, Warin swung the granite door shut and placed his stone hands on the cold rock. He closed his eyes and murmured in a language that sent shivers down Sera's spine. The runes glowed a soft amber as the stone responded to his gentle commands. Rock shifted and groaned as it knitted itself back together, sealing off the hidden library from the world above.

"Goodbye. We shall return another day." Sera touched the smooth stone one last time.

"*All* of us," Kitty added.

In silence, they retraced their steps along the winding tunnel, their faces illuminated by the flickering glow of Sera's magical light. The bones that lined the walls seemed to press in on them, eager to touch those who had been inside death's library.

"Can you feel it?" Kitty whispered, her voice barely audible above the shuffle of their feet over rough dirt. "Thousands of lives, trapped in the soil and rock."

"The gargoyles could not have enlisted better guardians. The dead may be at rest, but they never sleep," Hugh said.

As they emerged from the tunnel into the mausoleum, Sera blinked against the sudden brightness that filled the room. The contrast between the tepid, shadowy depths and the cold, sunlit world above was stark, a reminder of how far they had journeyed—both physically and metaphorically.

"Thank you." She placed a hand on Warin's

forearm as they stepped out into the frosty grass. "We wouldn't have found what we needed without you."

"I was too long wrapped in my grief and forgot my duty. We protect, and I thank you for reminding me of that." He took her hand in his larger one. He had lost the woman he loved and the family they might have had, but Sera had found another for him at the Crow's Nest.

"Say hello to Meredith and Hannah for me, please." They had missed the mother and daughter during their recent stay. The pair had travelled to town to buy supplies for the classroom, as Meredith taught the children.

A grin spread over Warin's face, and he nodded. Stone encased his human form as he shifted into his gargoyle one. Spreading his monstrous wings, he leapt into the air, and the grey of stone blended with the overcast sky.

"Now what?" Kitty asked, trying to find the gargoyle among the stormy clouds.

"The Apothecary's Poison. I need to make a list of ingredients for the potion." Her stomach rumbled, and the friends laughed. "How long were we down there?"

Hugh consulted his pocket watch. "Most of the day. It will be dark soon."

Kitty pushed Sera towards the entrance to the cemetery. "Let's get moving then. I will do many things for you, Sera, but I'm not staying here after dark."

SEVEN

LIKE A DETERMINED MOTHER HEN, Kitty chivvied them along the paths and back to the entrance of the cemetery. Hugh strode along the road to find them a ride back to the East End. While not a carriage, he found a merchant driving a wagon in that direction. They sat in the rear among crates and kegs for the journey.

Kitty passed the man a coin for his trouble when he stopped some distance from the pub. Then Hugh led the way through the maze of alleyways to the quiet intersection. As they stepped through the door of the Apothecary's Poison, the now familiar aroma of ale, spiced meats, and unwashed bodies tickled Sera's nostrils.

Elliot occupied their corner, a deep frown on his face as he kept glancing at the door, his shoulders tight. When he spied them, he let out a sigh and his lanky frame relaxed.

Sera grinned at him as they approached the table. "Admit it, you were worried."

"Only because I didn't want to be left with the bill. You lot have been gone all day. What happened?" He slid over to make room for Hugh as Kitty and Sera took the bench on the other side.

The low din of chatter provided a comforting backdrop as Sera leaned against the worn timber that formed the back of the bench seat. "Warin showed us the most amazing place, but it took some time to find what I needed."

Elliot's eyebrows shot up with curiosity. "Oh, yeah? Where is this amazing place?"

"Somewhere held in the clutches of death. How do you feel about skeletons, Mr Brynn?" Kitty inquired.

Elliot stared and paled a shade or two. "Guess I don't have to know."

Imp came over with two tankards for Sera and Hugh and a goblet of wine for Kitty. "Food will be out shortly," he said, then bustled away to serve his other customers.

Kitty picked up the goblet and toasted her companions. "I'm quite enjoying being in the thick of it. I never thought I'd find myself in a place like this, but I must admit, it has its charms."

"Charms?" Sera echoed, her nose crinkling in amusement. "You have a peculiar taste in charms."

Kitty gestured to the bar, where Imp poured ale into pitchers. "We have found a place that affords privacy, not to mention companionship and good food. There are places frequented by the aristocracy where you would struggle to find just one of those three."

"Excellent point, Kitty. This is one of the few places where it is safe for Sera to show her face." Hugh raised his tankard.

Elliot huffed. "I'm starting to think I should be worried about keeping such company as you lot. A footman has a reputation to uphold, you know."

"If you want a more refined environment, my father can talk to his brother, the earl. I'm sure the Napier family can find a place for you in the ancestral pile," Kitty offered.

Elliot paled once more. Sera wondered if it was the idea of having to wear livery or of being on his best behaviour day and night that horrified him.

"I might stick it out with Sera for a bit longer. See how this whole magic battle goes." He shrugged and wrapped both hands around his mug.

Hugh reached across the table and touched Sera's hand. "If you make a list of what you require, I can gather the ingredients from the apothecaries."

"Thank you. It might be best to spread the list over a few of them, so no one can figure out what I am doing." She pulled the sheets of paper free of her stays.

Evie the barmaid approached with a tray laden with plates of delicious-smelling food.

"Could we trouble Imp for paper and pencil, please?" Hugh asked before she turned to leave.

"Of course—anything for you." She winked and

returned a few moments later with the requested materials.

Flattening the sheets on the table and avoiding any flicks of gravy from supper, Sera made a list of ingredients. Some of them would be easily obtained, like rosemary and thyme. Others would be harder to locate.

Kitty leaned over, scanning the list with interest. "Dragon's breath and moonstone dust? Who keeps such things, and where on earth did they get them?"

"Some of these ingredients are exceedingly rare and difficult to come by," Hugh muttered, his brow furrowing as he studied the list.

"Yet again, I am reliant upon you, Hugh. Do you think you can find them all?" Sera tightened her grip on her knife and fork.

Hugh grabbed the spare sheet of paper and the pencil. "I'll split this list in two. Elliot can purchase the more readily available herbs and tonics. I'll have to talk quietly with my associates to find the more unusual items."

"I am sure that between your connections, Elliot's resourcefulness, and my coin, we shall be successful," Kitty said.

Sera drew a breath and leaned against her friend. "Thank you for paying for everything. We would be lost without you."

Kitty kissed the top of Sera's head and then nudged her upright with a pointed elbow. "Oh, don't you worry about that. I am keeping every invoice and intend to submit a claim for reimbursement to the king once this business is settled."

Sera laughed. The situation was dire and there were still Lord Rowan's magical traps to avoid, but the support of her friends meant the world to her. The Mage Council could strip every material thing from her, and she would still be a wealthy woman if she counted their friendship.

"To King George and a clear mind." She held her mug aloft.

They toasted their cause, then fell to the serious task of eating supper.

THE NEXT MORNING, Sera made her way downstairs to the kitchen. Hugh and Elliot had set off to visit the apothecaries. Kitty had refused to go home, determined to be at Sera's side each step of the way. She also sensibly pointed out that the more often she went back and forth from the pub to her Mayfair home, the greater the chances of someone following her. Instead, she sent a note to her father and took a room beside Sera's.

The kitchen was busy, despite the early hour, as Imp and his wife Evie prepared the dishes they would serve. Kitty was already up and sipping a hot chocolate, sitting on a stool out of the couple's way.

"Good morning, milady. I have gathered a variety of bowls and glasses for your use. What else do you require?" Imp gestured to the collection of crockery piled up before Kitty.

"Sera, please. There is no need to *milady* me." She cast a quick eye over the assortment. It would serve her well. "A mortar and pestle, too, if you have them."

Evie reached under a cupboard and produced a stone mortar with a notch for the pestle to rest in. Sera added it to the collection. "I'll also need to cast a magic flame, so something fireproof for it to sit on and a way to suspend a pot over it."

After sorting through a myriad of pots and pans, they found a set meant to keep coffee warm. A hand-sized, shallow cast-iron bowl would hold the flame, and the stand would hold a pot above it.

"Perfect," Sera murmured as she created a work-space close to the back door and window in case there were noxious odours wafting off her work. As she surveyed her corner of the kitchen, a tendril of doubt clawed its way into her mind. What if they couldn't find the necessary components? What if the shield failed?

She brushed the worries away with one hand, as though they were lazy summer flies buzzing around her head.

"Let us hope Hugh and Elliot are successful," Kitty murmured into her drink, as though she'd plucked the thoughts from Sera's mind.

Elliot returned first. He pulled the strap of the

satchel over his head and deposited the bag before Sera. "I got everything on your list. Got some right odd looks. But I told them I'm not a doctor, just the bloke fetching what he's told to get."

Sera unpacked the stoppered bottles and paper-wrapped parcels. "Brilliant, Elliot, thank you. I can start with these."

"Why don't you take a seat out there, and Evie will bring you coffee." Kitty pushed Elliot towards the door.

"A scone or two wouldn't go amiss," he called as he went through to the main part of the bar.

Sera and Kitty worked side by side, her friend following every instruction as they unpacked the herbs and liquids and lined them up. They weighted the sheet of paper bearing the first part of the spell with a heavy tankard, so it didn't blow away should a gust burst through the back door when it opened.

Sera was grinding rosemary in the mortar when Hugh finally strode in, his expression triumphant. "Success!" he declared, proffering a small cloth pouch and a delicate glass vial. "Dragon's breath and moonstone dust, as requested. It cost most of your coin, though, Kitty, and I had to pull in a few favours besides. The apothecary asked some very pointed questions, but I merely told him Lord Viner was working on a possible way to clear the king's mind."

"You stuck close to the truth, good man. And do not worry about the coin. There is more where that came from." Kitty took the little vial and held it to the light. It sparkled and glinted as though it contained ground-up diamonds. "Do you think it really is from the moon?"

Sera leaned over her friend's shoulder. "I doubt it. I think the name was given because it looks like something scooped up from its surface."

"Shouldn't it be cheese if it comes from the moon?" Imp was chopping vegetables and looked up with a frown on his broad face.

Kitty swallowed a snort. "Since you now have a more qualified assistant in Hugh, Sera, I shall keep an eye on Mr Brynn and give him some other tasks to keep him occupied today."

Hugh took down an apron from a hook by the door and tied it around his waist. Then he rolled up his shirt sleeves. He took over weighing and measuring ingredients for the potion, while Sera did the processes that required a swirl of magic.

They worked slowly and methodically, not wanting to make any mistakes. A faint tremor shook Sera's hands as she measured out the correct weight of the iridescent moonstone dust. Then she gently tapped it into a narrow-necked glass container. Next, she added one drop at a time of the liquid called dragon's breath. The two sizzled as they combined and changed into a luminous-purple cloud.

Hugh hovered at her side, a mixture of admiration and concern etched into his strong features. "Are you certain about this step? We've not had any success so far, and our supplies are dwindling."

"I know this isn't what I wrote out, but the other

mix failed, and this way seems...right," Sera murmured, her brow furrowed in concentration. She couldn't let doubt creep in now. Two more drops and she quickly added a stopper to the flask before the swirling cloud escaped.

In the mortar waited the other component of the spell. Taking up a pitcher holding the liquids they had combined, Sera poured a little into the mortar. The concoction bubbled and frothed. Her heart raced with anticipation, but as moments passed, the potion settled into a dull, murky colour, devoid of any magical glow.

"Blast!" Sera slammed her fist on the table, frustration boiling over. They'd been at this for hours, trying myriad combinations of quantities and order for the first part of the spell. Every time, it turned listless.

Hugh laid a hand on her shoulder. "The clarity part is working. Look." With a gentle touch, he picked up the flask where the storm cloud was shaking off the purple and slowly changing to the blue of a clear ocean.

She grudgingly admitted that it was pretty. "The storm has passed in the flask, much like the way it will clear troubled thoughts. But it's useless without the shielding potion to augment it."

"Then we try again and keep trying until it works. You can do this." Hugh folded her into his embrace.

Sera rested her cheek on his shoulder and let his love seep through her. She could do this. Potions had always been her favourite thing to work on. Perhaps, like the clarity spell, she had to follow instinct rather than every word of the old spell.

As they continued to labour in Imp's kitchen, the atmosphere grew heavy with the weight of failure. Time and time again, they mixed, heated, and experimented, only to be met with disappointment. Some attempts resulted in small explosions that left them coughing amidst clouds of acrid smoke, and they quickly flung the door and windows open. Other brews simply had no effect at all.

Exhaustion settled into Sera's bones, but she refused to yield. When she considered giving up, she remembered the anguish and love on the queen's face as she implored Sera to heal her George. She worked to save not their king, but the man who was much loved by the woman she respected.

Inspiration struck her like a bolt of lightning, and she could scarcely believe they hadn't considered it sooner. "It's the *order* of the ingredients. Tincture of bloodworm should be first. It dwells under the soil and should be the base layer, not thrown in at a later stage as though it were an air creature."

Hugh raised an eyebrow, considering the idea. "Let's try. There is not much left, but we can send Elliot for more."

Drawing a sigh and arching her back to relieve stiff muscles, Sera started again. Grinding herbs, measuring tinctures, and chopping pieces that resembled dried tendons. As the last ray of sunlight slipped below the horizon, Sera held her breath and combined the ingredients one final time.

Please let this work, she entreated Gaia.

As they waited, Sera wearily surveyed the cluttered workbench, strewn with the detritus of their many failed attempts—charred remains of parchment, blackened glass vials, and the mortar stained with the remnants of crushed herbs. Her fingers ached with the effort of grinding the herbs into a fine powder, but she dared not stop. Her determination burned as fiercely as the lanterns illuminating their efforts.

When no sparks emitted from the mortar, nor puffs of sulphurous vapour, she leaned forwards to peer within. The mix had combined into a solid lump. But it emitted a soft glow that reminded her of flames frozen in amber.

"It worked. The shielding spell worked!" She glanced at Hugh with excitement in her eyes.

"I knew you could do it, Sera. Now you have only to combine them." He moved the coffee pot warmer closer.

Sera placed the piece of amber-like substance in a small bowl and set it over the warmer. A whisper lit the stub of candle that she had imbued with more spells. The flame flickered through shades of blue, from a deep navy to that of a pale spring sky.

When the edges of the lump in the bowl rounded as it melted like a slab of butter, she uncorked the flask and used her magic to capture the blue cloud and wrap it around the solid substance. The delicate cloud settled over its companion like a blanket draped over a person. Then the mixture began to bubble and froth, emitting a sweet aroma that filled the air.

"Come on," Sera whispered under her breath, watching the potion with bated breath.

Slowly, the bubbling subsided, and the two different spells combined into a liquid that glowed a bright blue.

"You did it!" Hugh grinned at her.

"*We* did it." She kissed him most soundly. They had surmounted another obstacle and were one step closer to the goal.

Kitty and Elliot were drawn from the bar by Hugh's excited shout.

"Oh, brilliant!" Kitty exclaimed as Sera poured the luminous potion into a small glass vial.

"Shouldn't you test it?" Elliot eyed the concoction suspiciously.

"There's a small amount of residue in the bowl." Hugh swiped a finger around the surface, then popped a glowing blue digit into his mouth.

"I wouldn't have done that. I'd have made *her* test it," the footman muttered.

Sera glared at her employee. "Still, Elliot? You know I didn't poison Lord Branvale."

He shrugged and gestured to the dirty bowls and containers scattered along the bench. "I was referring to your cooking in general."

"Can you feel anything, Hugh?" Kitty asked, bringing the conversation back to the matter at hand.

"It's...warm and comforting. Like a nip of brandy on a chilly day that has been heated and mixed with honey." He turned his hands over, one tip still a pale blue.

"Can you feel any effects, though? Sera, cast a spell at him and see if it works." Kitty pointed from one of her friends to the other.

Sera didn't want to hurt Hugh, but they needed to know if the shield worked. Given he'd only ingested a fingertip's worth, she pushed a tiny spell of crackling lightning at him. It rippled over his bare forearm, and a look of disappointment fell over his face.

Her stomach dropped. "It didn't work." Her voice wavered a little.

"Yes, it did. I never felt a thing. And you know how much I enjoy your electrical displays," he murmured in a tone that made heat flush through her body. "And my mind is as clear and focused as if I'd had a solid night's sleep and drunk an entire pot of coffee."

Kitty threw her arms around Sera. "You did it. I always knew you could. Now Hugh has only to ensure the king drinks it."

Sera had been so focused on creating the potion, she had forgotten about administering it. "How on earth am I going to sneak into St James's Palace when Lord Rowan is hovering beside the king?"

Eight

Hugh

THE MORNING SUN cast a golden glow through the windows of the pub, adding a touch of warmth to the otherwise dim room. Hugh stood before a smudged mirror, carefully adjusting his fine court clothes. The crisp white shirt and richly embroidered waistcoat seemed out of place in the shabby pub, yet they were an essential part of their plan. He glanced at Sera, who had transformed herself into a maid with the help of a plain black dress and a white apron.

"You will need to stoop. You are tall for a woman," he murmured as he tugged on his cuffs so that a thin strip of white was revealed below his sleeve.

"And you are broad. Wherever did you find court clothes to fit?" She walked to his side and brushed a mote of dust from the shoulder.

"A patient of similar build died some months ago

and had no need of them." Hugh had no shame about being passed a dead man's clothes. While he could have earned a comfortable living tending to the headaches and hangovers of the wealthy, he preferred to look after the common man—who rarely had the means to pay him.

"Your patron had a discerning eye. The cut is impeccable and stylish without being garish like some of the courtiers favour." Leaning up, she kissed him, then rested her arms over his shoulders. "This will work, and we will be another step closer to defeating Lord Rowan."

Hugh placed his hands on her waist. "I don't like placing you in danger. There will be a mage at the king's side. What will you do if it is Lord Rowan?"

Lines briefly marred her sun-kissed forehead. He marvelled that even after her months of captivity, she retained a golden hue to her skin. "I don't know. Let us simply hope it is not him. Lord Pendlebury would not stand in our way, but I believe he is still in Scotland."

Hand in hand, they left the pub. Sera stayed alert to any traps set by the Mage Council as they journeyed towards St James's Palace, their footsteps echoing on the cobblestone streets. The palace loomed large before them, its majestic façade emanating an oppressive air, as though the very bricks were infected by the king's chaotic mind.

As they reached the palace gates, Hugh and Sera parted ways with a lingering glance. While Hugh would walk straight through the front doors, Sera would sneak around the back, using her disguise and wits to evade the guards.

Upon entering the palace, Hugh found his mentor, Lord Viner, waiting for him in the grand foyer. The older man bore the dignified countenance of a seasoned royal physician, his silver hair neatly combed into a queue and his eyes sharp as a hawk's.

"Ah, Hugh." Lord Viner greeted him, clasping his former pupil's hand. "I must admit, it surprised me to receive your note asking to join me here. You have not been seen for some time. There is talk you are consorting with that rogue mage."

"While I consider Lady Winyard a friend, I have not seen her for some time." *At least fifteen minutes.* "I have been absent from court as I have been engrossed in my studies. I believe I have brewed a potion that would offer the king some clarity of thought. I seek your permission to administer it to him."

"Indeed?" Lord Viner raised an eyebrow, intrigued by the proposition. "Well, we could certainly use all the help we can get. His Majesty's suffering is great, and no potion, poultice, spell, or any amount of bleeding has offered any relief."

As Hugh spoke to the man who had taken him under his wing and ensured he received the best medical education, his thoughts drifted towards Sera. If there were a god, Hugh silently prayed that she had slipped past the guards and made her way closer to the king. Their plan hinged on both of them being able to carry out their tasks. As much as he trusted in Sera's abilities, nowhere would there be more guards and traps than around the king.

"Come, then." Lord Viner motioned for Hugh to follow. "Let us see if your elixir can bring some relief to our troubled monarch."

The palace's opulence made a stark contrast to the modest pub where Hugh had dressed that morning. As they walked through the grand corridors, their footsteps rang out against the marble floors and echoed off the gilded walls. Tapestries depicting ancient battles and mythical creatures adorned the walls, while crystal chandeliers cast shimmering light over the ornate furnishings.

"His Majesty's condition has worsened over the last few months. Lord Rowan thought it best that he be sequestered in the countryside with fresher air. He has only recently returned to St James's, but continues to be kept isolated," Lord Viner explained as they approached the king's private quarters. "King George has become increasingly erratic, plagued by fits of rage and despair. It is a sight best kept from the court and the people."

Armed guards in bright-red livery stood on either side of the double doors leading to the king's chambers. They bowed their heads to Lord Viner, recognising the renowned physician. A bored courtier stood near them, an open book in his arms.

Lord Viner addressed the courtier. "This is Mr Miles, my associate. He is assisting me today as I attend His Majesty."

The man with the powdered wig and heart-shaped beauty mark scribbled in his book then gestured for the guards to open the door. Within was a scene of chaos. The once-regal room lay in disarray, with shattered porcelain and torn draperies strewn about. In the centre of the destruction, King George paced back and forth like a caged animal, his face contorted in anguish. His eyes darted around the room as if searching for an unseen enemy.

"Your Majesty," Lord Viner bowed deeply, his voice soft and measured. "I have brought my former pupil, Hugh Miles, who believes he might offer some assistance."

King George's wild gaze fixed upon Hugh, his eyes narrowing with suspicion. Hugh felt the weight of the king's suspicious scrutiny, but he held his ground, meeting the monarch's stare with a kindly regard.

"Your pupil, you say? He looks like a man who breaks bones, not sets them." The king resumed pacing, beating at his chest in time with each step.

Lord Viner continued to speak in a calm tone. "Mr Miles is an extraordinary surgeon, Your Majesty. He has been sequestered for some months, working on a remedy for you."

"They will not catch me. No, they will not," the king muttered, seeming to have forgotten their presence already.

Four men clustered by a sideboard covered in an array of foods to tempt the royal palate. Half-eaten pieces of cheese and abandoned slices of cake were scattered on stacked plates. Hugh recognised the men by sight. Two were old doctors who thought they could cure the king by continuously opening up a vein—a process which Hugh believed only weakened the monarch and made it harder for his body and mind to fight whatever assaulted him.

A third man was the royal taster. He had the job of sampling a portion of everything that passed the king's lips. With an aftermage gift for detecting magic and poisons, he would sense any threat to the king in the food and drink he ingested.

The fourth man made Hugh's blood run hot. Lord Tomlin. The man Lord Rowan had commanded to... *lay his hands* on Sera in hopes of producing a Nereus. Hugh's own hands curled into fists, and he longed for a scalpel. One swipe and he would end the other man's involvement in such a plot. But he couldn't do that and also discover what plagued the king. Damn it.

The mage turned a critical gaze on Hugh, and he huffed in recognition. Had he already alerted his brethren that Sera might not be far behind? He needed to remove the mage from the plan running through his head.

"Good day, Lord Tomlin. I hear the Mage Council is doing all they can to find a cure for the king." Hugh attempted to mask his unease with a smile.

"We all labour to serve the greater cause," the mage answered.

Hugh bit the inside of his cheek. The only cause

Lord Tomlin served was whichever one benefited him the most.

"Aren't you a *friend* of Lady Winyard, the traitor?" Lord Tomlin narrowed his gaze, and his lips moved in unspoken words.

Hugh's skin prickled. If Lord Tomlin thought to use a compulsion spell against him, he clearly didn't know about the trace of gargoyle blood that lent him some immunity to magic. His love for Sera encased his thoughts in layers of steel that no spell would ever penetrate. "I aided her in a few of the council's investigations, yes. Ones in which she had a particular need for my medical knowledge."

The mage huffed and, with a bored expression on his face, dropped to a padded chair by the sideboard. "Tea," he commanded and turned to watch the king pace.

Hugh's mind had raced, wondering what to do about Lord Tomlin. He would raise the alarm the instant Sera walked into the room unless he did something. Since Hugh was always prepared for a variety of ailments and injuries he might encounter with his patients, his little field kit contained more vials than the luminous one for the king.

Hugh picked up the teapot and laid out fresh cups, then poured fragrant tea into them. As Lord Viner engaged the others in conversation, Hugh took advantage of everyone's attention being elsewhere. He took a small brown vial from his kit and quickly poured a few drops into the mage's teacup, then slid it along the side table so it sat by his elbow.

Putting the vial back, he slipped out the blue one and tapped the taster on the shoulder. The man had been listening to Lord Viner but turned and cast a tired look at Hugh. He held up the little vial. "I will be administering this to the king. It will clear the mind, rather like a good night's sleep."

"I could certainly do with a sip of that," the taster said.

Hugh moved the king's teacup closer, with its delicate band of gold around the rim. He counted out nine drops, as instructed by Sera, while from the corner of his eye, he watched as Lord Tomlin took a sip of his tea. Hugh had dosed his brew with the powerful sedative he used during amputations. It should work quickly and give the appearance that the mage had nodded off in his chair.

Hugh stirred the tea. A blue haze simmered over the surface and released a fresh spring scent. He handed it to the taster. The man brought it close to his nose and sniffed. Then he took a cautious sip, followed by another. He rolled the liquid around in his mouth as he used his gift to detect anything that would harm the king.

Then they waited in case the taster keeled over dead from poison. They were long minutes in which Hugh could count his heartbeats by the thrum of blood in his ears. When he glanced at Lord Tomlin, the mage's eyelids had begun to droop. With each laboured blink, the sedative took a stronger hold. His limbs grew heavier until finally, his head dipped forwards, chin resting on his chest.

At last, the taster made a satisfied noise in the back of his throat. "My mind does feel a little clearer. You could command a high price for such a brew if you were inclined to provide it to the courtiers." He held the cup in both his hands, and Hugh worried he might not relinquish it.

"It was a long and arduous process. I was driven by my desire to aid our king." Hugh took the teacup, thankfully without a tussle for possession of it, and approached King George.

The monarch had slumped in a gilded chair, his body sprawled, his eyes bloodshot and unfocused, hands trembling as he grasped the armrests.

Hugh passed the cup and saucer to Lord Viner. "The taster approves," he murmured.

The older physician approached the king with slow movements. "You must drink this, Your Majesty. It will ease your mind," Lord Viner urged in a gentle tone.

The king sat up and scrambled back further on his chair. He eyed the cup suspiciously.

"It is a calming brew, Your Majesty," the taster said from behind Lord Viner. "I can vouch for its effect."

King George took the cup with shaky hands and brought it closer to his face. He sniffed much like his taster had. Then he grunted and took a deep drink. As he swallowed, the room seemed to hold its collective breath.

Sera's elixir would flow through every part of the king's body, unseen but potent in its effects.

"Your Majesty, the effects of the potion may take up to thirty minutes to fully manifest," explained Hugh, taking care to maintain a respectful tone. "You might experience slight warmth and tingling sensations as it works through your system."

The king didn't reply but thrust the empty teacup at his physician. Then he slumped back in his chair, one hand shielding his face.

As the minutes ticked by, an uneasy silence settled over the room, punctuated by the occasional snore from the sleeping Lord Tomlin. Lord Viner fidgeted with the buttons of his waistcoat, while Hugh's gaze remained fixed on the steady rise and fall of the king's chest.

Worry for Sera consumed Hugh's thoughts. Had she evaded detection? Was she even now hovering at the door, trying to convince the guards to let her in? He forced himself to focus on the task at hand, but concern for her safety gnawed at him.

Twenty-five minutes had passed when King George suddenly turned his head towards them. "I—I do believe it's working," he said, his voice stronger than before. "My mind feels lighter, like a fog has lifted. And my body...it's as if a great weight has been removed. Is this truly the power of the tea?"

"I laboured for some time over the potion it contained, Your Majesty. The elixir is designed to bring clarity to the mind," Hugh explained.

"This is most remarkable, Mr Miles. I do feel... clearer." As the king spoke, his voice grew more certain.

"It gladdens me to hear that, Sire. The potion should continue to improve your condition over the next few minutes," Hugh said, relief evident in his voice.

The physicians clustered around the king, eager to examine the miraculous change.

"We should bleed him and see if his humours are in balance," one muttered, while the other claimed leeches would be superior.

Hugh rolled his eyes and sucked in his lips to stop himself from shaking the duo and inviting them to step into the eighteenth century, where a doctor used reason and not antiquated methods.

King George answered their questions in a calm and reasoned tone. The agitated, jerky movements of his body were gone.

"Remarkable," whispered Lord Viner, his gaze filled with awe when he turned to Hugh. "Truly remarkable."

"Long may it continue," Hugh replied as he rubbed the ring on his pinkie finger.

Shaped like a bone, Sera had crafted it from mage silver—the rare material that allowed a mage, and those she loved, to stay in touch. He stroked the warm metal and thought of her.

The king was lucid. Lord Tomlin was snoring. But where was Sera?

NINE

Seraphina

SERA WALKED with a determined stride through the kitchens, snatching up a tray as she passed. Nobody stopped a servant who was carrying something and looked like they were following instructions. Hesitation was a weakness. A sign that she didn't know what she was supposed to do.

Guards and courtiers patrolled the corridors, but she kept her cap pulled over her forehead and her eyes downcast. Remembering Hugh's warning about her height, she rounded her shoulders and slouched. The curved posture also made her look older, along with a little flour in her hair to make the visible strands appear grey.

Further into the palace, she walked rapidly along halls and up staircases as she worked her way towards the king's private apartments. Her senses were on alert to avoid the magical traps laid throughout the palace. Her servant's guise helped, as she pressed herself to the wainscoting to avoid the courtiers and skirted around the patches meant to ensnare those with magic in their blood.

She suppressed a snicker when a foppish courtier stepped in one. A trace of aftermage in his blood triggered the trap, and it took hold of his stocking-clad leg and refused to let him go. His companions tried in vain to free his foot from the invisible snare.

"Don't just stand there, girl—fetch the mage and tell him to let me go before my stocking is ruined!" he shrieked at Sera.

She bobbed a curtsy and took off at a faster pace. Let them think she sought rescue for the man. She did race towards a rescue, just not for the person they thought.

As she turned a corner, she saw a group of ladies with icy-blue powdered wigs and matching gowns walking towards her. She held her breath as she scanned their faces, but thankfully none was Abigail. Sera clutched the tray to her chest like a shield and pressed herself to the wall to give them room to pass.

"Do you think the rumours are true?" one whispered to her taller companion.

"Oh, indeed. Look how strenuously the lady is denying it. Some say that her grandfather is using magic to quash the rumours," she replied.

"That shows the truth of them," a third pronounced.

The fourth member of the group tittered. "*I heard the truth is even more scandalous. That she gave herself to a man *not* her intended.*"

Gasps of shock ran through the group, then as they turned into the next corridor, they dissolved into fits of laughter.

Sera allowed herself a moment of smug satisfaction. No need to guess who they were gossiping about. There was only one woman with a mage grandfather who would try to stamp out the wildfire of scandal.

Abigail. Sera's little birds had done their work and augmented the story created by Kitty of a pregnancy.

Continuing on her way, at last Sera reached the carved double doors and the guards at the entrance to the king's private rooms. She ruined her posture a little more and clutched the tray, affecting a tremble in her hands as she addressed the courtier in charge.

"If it pleases you, milord," she lisped. "They have sent me to clear the dishes." She kept her eyes focused on the toes of the guard's boots while she addressed the courtier, who tried to stare at his reflection in a crystal vase holding magical roses.

"Make it quick, girl." He waved a hand, his attention on his own face, and he barely glanced at her.

Sera bobbed a curtsy while internally she raged. The fact that she could walk through two royal homes and gain access to the monarchs simply by pretending to be a servant showed how utterly oblivious the aristocracy was to common folk.

If she had swanned in through the main doors

below and announced herself as Lady Winyard, she would have been tackled to the ground before she took three steps.

The guard opened one door, and Sera slipped inside with a whispered, "Thank you."

The first person she saw was an anxious-looking Hugh. Relief and pride flashed over his features before he waved her further into the room.

King George glanced up, but his attention returned to the physicians around him. As Sera approached the side table, the king's once-feverish eyes seemed clearer, and the wild energy that had radiated from him was now dampened.

About to place the tray on the table, her heart skipped a beat when she spotted Lord Tomlin. The mage's head was thrown back, resting against the wall, and a soft snoring came from his open mouth. She shot Hugh a questioning glance.

Hugh whispered close to her ear, "I gave him a sedative. He won't be a problem for a while."

She dared a quick touch, grazing his hand in thanks for his resourcefulness. As she set about gathering the dirty dishes on her tray, she stole glances at the slumbering mage. Her gaze moved to the king, seeking a hint of the mysterious amulet that hung around his neck, hidden beneath his clothing.

With Lord Tomlin incapacitated, her mission now hinged on gaining the king's trust and examining the amulet before the elixir wore off. She also had to hope the physicians present didn't summon the guards to seize her. A sense of urgency mounted as time slipped through her fingers like sand.

Steeling herself, she made a decision. Sera approached the king and ducked around the bickering physicians without making a sound.

"Your Majesty," she murmured as she reached for the teacup set on the ground by the king's chair. "It is I, your royal mage Lady Winyard. I must speak with you on a most urgent matter."

Sera was crouched at the side of the chair upholstered in gold brocade, and King George leaned forwards to peer at her.

"Why, so it is. I always enjoyed your entertainments. But Lord Rowan tells me you have turned upon us." His voice hardened on the last few words.

"That is not so, Sire. It was I who laboured alongside Mr Miles to brew the potion that has brought peace to your thoughts. I fear there is dark magic poisoning your mind." She curled her fingers around the edge of the saucer.

The king sucked in a breath. "My oldest and most loyal mage has detected no such magic about my royal person. Indeed, Lord Rowan himself gave me this amulet of protection." King George tugged on the silver chain and pulled forth the round pendant.

"Sometimes it is those who stand closest to the throne who pose the greatest risk. I believe the amulet is the source of your malady. Do I have your permission to inspect it?" Sera pitched her voice low. So far, no one apart from Hugh had taken note of their conversation.

The royal physicians were measuring out drops of Hugh's potion into their own teacups as they loudly discussed its effects.

The king rubbed his thumb over the smooth stone. "I will think on what you have said. But you may look at the amulet. I never take it off, and indeed, if I try, the chain shrinks so it will not fit over my head and a thousand demons torment my mind."

Sera tucked that effect away to add to what else she could learn about the piece. She shuffled forwards on her knees. It appeared to be a simple polished stone, but a pretty one, with a dark-green vein running through the grey surface. It reminded her of the rocks that rested at the bottom of a river. When she used a tendril of magic to examine it, the surface seemed to absorb light, making it difficult for her eyes to focus on its details. Then she reached out a hand. The moment her fingers brushed against it, a cold darkness flooded her mind, and she bit back a cry.

Sera sat back on her heels and used her other senses to examine the amulet. She noticed an absence of any magical resonance. This was nothing constructed by Lord Rowan, but something ancient he had ferreted out to use against the king. It could be Fae magic. When she returned to the pub, she would use her ensorcelled paper to ask Elowyn if she knew of such a thing. Instead of emanating energy, the amulet seemed to draw it in, its own darkness devouring magic and light. She knew, without a doubt, that this object held dark powers beyond her understanding. That meant it could be Unseelie or from another realm entirely.

"I believe this amulet *causes* your affliction, Your Majesty," she whispered, careful not to alert anyone else in the room. "I fear the longer you wear it, the stronger its effects will become."

The king's eyes widened, and his lips formed a thin line as he took in the information. He stared at the amulet, his expression a mixture of fear and determination. "I cannot remove it, but I shall demand that Lord Rowan do so."

Sera doubted that the old mage would comply with such a request.

"I will do all I can to reverse its dark curse," Sera murmured. Then she rose with the teacup in her hands.

Lord Tomlin stirred as Sera returned to her tray. The sedative was wearing off, and she needed to be gone before he woke. She piled teacups and plates on her tray until it was full.

A shout from behind made her whirl around. Had Lord Tomlin awakened? The noise came from the king, and his physicians rushed to his side. The elixir's effects had faded. King George's eyes grew wild and unfocused, his pupils dilating as they darted around the room. His breath came in shallow gasps, and his hands trembled as he clutched at his head.

"Your Majesty must remain calm," one physician urged, his voice tight with concern.

"More tea with the potion," another called out.

They clustered around him like a murder of crows, their dark coats flapping as they attempted to administer more tinctures and procedures in a vain effort to prolong the moment of lucidity.

The king's fingers dug into his scalp. His voice grew desperate, the words spilling from his lips like water from a broken vase. "No, no, please...not again," he muttered, breath hitching with every syllable.

But Sera knew their efforts would be in vain. The elixir's effects were fading all too quickly. Whatever magic emanated from the amulet, it had pushed back the clarity spell and cloaked the king with its foul stench once more.

"The shadows! They return. Get away from me!" King George roared, shoving aside the physicians who tried to restrain him. His body convulsed in violent spasms as the last vestiges of sanity poured from him like wine from a bottle. "Cold. Cold. Why is the water so cold?"

Sera's heart twisted with sorrow as she watched the king's mind slip away once more. Guilt speared through her at leaving him in such a state. But she needed to discover what sort of magic the amulet contained so she could destroy it.

"Who are you?" King George shouted, panic creeping into his voice as his gaze swept over the faces of his physicians. "Help! Help!" The king's voice cracked, and he raised his arms as though trying to dislodge a swarm of invisible insects.

"Please, Sire, we will find a way," a physician said in a desperate tone. "Where are my bloodletting tools?"

Sera turned her back on the heart-wrenching scene and approached the doors. The king's distress was a noose tightening around her heart.

"Charlotte...Charlotte, where are you?" The king's voice grew weak and desperate. "I need you, my love."

Hugh held the door open, the lines of his face tight as he glanced back at the king struggling against his physicians. "Go. Lord Tomlin is waking," he whispered.

Sera carried her laden tray from the room, stooping as she ventured past the guards. The corridor seemed a thousand miles long as she walked away, the king's tortured cries following her. As she rounded the corner at last, a heavier tread followed her. Her heart leapt into her throat. Was it a guard, or worse, Lord Tomlin?

"Sera," a familiar voice murmured.

She swallowed a sob of relief. Hugh.

"Lord Tomlin has awakened, and I thought it better to leave than answer awkward questions." He fell into step beside her.

"I will go back out through the kitchens." She kept to the wall side of the corridor, her eyes downcast. Thankfully, the screams from the king had diminished.

"I'll be waiting by the wall outside." Hugh touched her hand, then strode away as a group of courtiers walked towards them.

Sera navigated the palace corridors, the tray of dirty dishes clutched tightly in her hands. While she walked, she picked apart what she had learned about the amulet with its malevolent aura. What stone could hold such power, and why had no other mage detected the dark void it contained?

The kitchens were busy as always, staff bustling in one direction and another.

"Oi, you!" A shrill voice cut through Sera's thoughts. One cook gestured at her with a spoon. "Put the tray down and get to scrubbing pots. We're running out."

"Sorry, ma'am," Sera replied meekly, pitching her voice higher to hide her true identity. "I was told to fetch the used dishes."

Casting around, she spotted the pile of dirty pots and pans stacked up on a bench. A maid poured hot water into a deep tub.

"About time you got back," grumbled another maid, wiping her hands on her apron as she moved to join Sera. "I'm not doing that lot all on my own."

Sera paused. Hugh was waiting for her. But it seemed rude to leave the maid with such a mountain of pots. "How do they use so many?" she murmured as she reached for a scrubbing brush.

"I've seen some of them piss in 'em," the maid replied as she dropped in the bar of soap.

It took them some time to work through the pile of pots, and she hoped Hugh wouldn't storm the palace looking for her. As they worked, they traded gossip about the nobles. Sera learned a few more interesting titbits about her so-called peers.

A footman burst into the kitchen. "You want to hear the racket up there. The king is worse and was hollering. All those mages and doctors and not one can help him."

The master of the household, dressed in black, stared at the footman. "We do not speculate on the king's health. Get back to your job."

"I feel sorry for him. It's like some demon is inside his head," the maid whispered to Sera.

"We should pray that he finds peace." Sera scrubbed hard at something burned to the bottom of the pan.

It was an hour before she could slip away. Her hands were red from lye soap and hot water. The flour in her hair to make it appear grey had congealed with sweat and the steam rising off the water. Once outside, Sera peeled the uncomfortable cap off her head and shoved it in her apron pocket. With a plain cloak around her shoulders, she lifted the hood so that it veiled her face in shadows. Through the gates, she hurried, and along to a corner cast in dim light by the nearby trees.

Hugh paced along the wall. Elliot lounged nearby, smoking a clay pipe.

"At last! I thought they had captured you. Kitty sent Elliot to look for both of us as we have been so long." Hugh grabbed her in a bear hug.

"Sorry. In a way, I was captured. I couldn't leave the kitchen until I had washed a stack of pots." Sera kissed Hugh, a quick peck to reassure him she was fine and because she didn't want to start something they couldn't finish while loitering outside the palace.

Elliot laughed. "Your disguise worked a bit too well, then."

"Yes. But I am armed with more information." She shivered and rubbed her hands up her arms as she recalled the dark touch of the amulet.

"The amulet is cursed?" Hugh asked, taking her hand in his as they headed back to the pub.

"Yes. And it's a dark thing, too." To think Lord Rowan considered her line *tainted* when he was using something far worse.

TEN

THEY LOST no time in returning to the Apothecary's Poison, a place Sera considered a safe harbour from the harsh winds buffeting London and the malicious eyes trying to spy her out.

When they pushed into the cosy pub, Kitty was perched at the bar talking to Imp. Or cross-examining him about his background, more likely, given the keen interest she had focused on him. On hearing the door, her friend turned, and her eyes widened.

"Sera!" Kitty leapt off her stool and hugged her. "What took you so long?"

"I was scrubbing pots." Sera returned the hug, refilling her soul with her friend's love.

Kitty chuckled. "Only you would stop to help a scullery maid while we all worry about you."

Sera turned her hands over. The red from the hot water had changed to the slight blue tinge of cold. "You wouldn't believe how dirty they were."

"Mission accomplished?" Kitty asked as they retreated to their corner.

"Yes. Lord Tomlin was attending the king. Hugh took care of him," Sera murmured as she slid onto the seat and left room for Kitty to join her.

Kitty arched a dark eyebrow at Hugh. "Poison?"

The surgeon blanched. "No. A strong sedative."

Kitty snorted. "Pity."

"Wasted opportunity," Sera muttered at the same time.

Elliot glanced from one woman to another. "You two are scary when you get together."

Kitty's expression changed to an open, wide-eyed, innocent one. "Why, Mr Brynn, *you* have nothing to worry about...so long as you never cross us."

"Nobody is being murdered by my hand. Nor was inflicting harm on Lord Tomlin part of our mission." Hugh nodded his thanks to Evie as she placed full tankards on the table.

Sera took a sip. The malty flavour of ale was growing on her. Especially the lighter brews that were safer to drink than the disease-laden water from the pumps. "The tonic worked. The king became lucid and allowed me to examine the amulet."

"And?" Kitty prompted.

Sera hesitated, recalling the unnerving sensation that had engulfed her when she touched it. "It looks like a polished stone with dark-green veins running through it, but when I touched it...a dark void washed chills over me." She shuddered at the memory, her spine tingling with residual dread. "I've never encountered magic like that before, and it's certainly not something crafted by Lord Rowan. It could be Fae, perhaps Unseelie—the Seelie cannot channel such darkness."

"Poor old King George. All that power and money and he's as miserable as any wretch stuck in Bedlam." Genuine concern for the monarch momentarily overshadowed Elliot's usual insolent charm. "Did you take the thing off him?"

"No. The king cannot remove it. He said that when he tries, the chain seems to shrink, suffocating him, and his mind is attacked by demons." Sera wondered if that was part of the ensorcellment in the stone or if there was another spell upon the chain. In the horror of the moment, she hadn't thought to consider them as separate things working together.

Hugh's brow furrowed. "We must find a way to break the curse and restore the king's mind. That is our best hope of having the edict against Sera revoked."

"My father is searching legal texts, but he is not hopeful there is any legal way to reverse the order imprisoning you in that odd Repository. The king's good grace, once lost, cannot be restored except by himself." Kitty traced a pattern on her tankard with her thumb.

Sera blew out a long sigh. It had been a faint hope that Mr Napier might have been able to champion her cause through Parliament, just as he had done with the Mage Act. "You know I appreciate his trying. But this pendant is something insidious that has had years to alter the king's mind."

She considered options and weighed potential solutions and avenues of enquiry. "First, we have to figure out the sort of magic contained in the amulet. If it truly is Unseelie, then perhaps there are otherworldly methods we can employ to counteract its effects, or Elowyn might be able to offer advice from the Fae realm."

"What about finding someone who knows more about such things? Is there an expert in dark magic?" Elliot suggested with a wry grin.

"The only one I can think of was Lord Dewlap. And even then, he only seemed to dabble." Not to mention the slight problem that the old mage had died and his power was reborn in Sera. If he were alive to ask about dark magic, that would mean Sera didn't exist...and that created a spiral of interlocking problems with no solutions in her head. "There are whispers of such mages in Europe, but we don't have the time to hunt one down, even if they were inclined to help."

As they debated potential courses of action, Sera basked in the warmth of camaraderie that surrounded her and the unwavering loyalty of her friends. Kitty always said that two heads were better than one, and Sera had four with which to come up with solutions. Though with four heads, she couldn't be Cerberus. Perhaps their group was more like a hydra.

"Oh!" Kitty slammed down her tankard. "Why don't we ask Warin to take us back to...you know where?" She lowered her voice on the last words. They might have been safe in the pub, but they still refrained from mentioning out loud a secret magical library.

"He's going to think I am as troublesome as Nat already does." It seemed Sera's life relied heavily upon gargoyle protection and assistance. *Gargoyles in all their forms*, she thought as she met Hugh's warm gaze.

"That's because you *are* troublesome." Elliot toasted her with his drink. "I doubt you know how to be...ordinary. Besides, it would be blasted boring."

Ordinary did sound boring to Sera. But the constant obstacles and adversities to overcome were exhausting. She could do with a few days of *ordinary* in which to recover before the Fates dumped the next problem on her.

"Back to the church, then, and hope he is there and in an agreeable mood," Hugh said.

"Do gargoyles have an agreeable mood? Both Warin and Natalie always look so sombre. At least you can smile, Hugh, but then, there are generations of human in you diluting the gargoyle seriousness," Kitty mused out loud.

The descending sun cast an orange-pink glow on the cobblestone streets that relieved the usual sombre grey of London, as the friends made ready to find Warin. Sera and Kitty donned male attire once more, ensuring they could move about the city without attracting unwanted attention.

"Elliot should have what we require outside," Kitty

said. She had dispatched the footman to procure horses for them from the local mews while they went upstairs.

As they left the cheerful warmth of the pub and stepped out into the chilly winter evening, they found Elliot holding the reins of three horses.

"I'm glad I'm not going. It's bloody cold and only going to get worse," he grumbled as he gave Kitty a leg up onto her horse.

Kitty cast a sharp look at the footman. "Don't think you will be sitting by the fire getting drunk just yet, Mr Brynn. You have my letters to deliver to Father."

Elliot heaved a sigh as he stood back and thrust his hands deep in his pockets. Sera bit back a laugh. He acted put out, but secretly he loved his unconventional employment.

Sera gathered the reins. "Don't wait up."

With a nod to each other, the group set off through the city towards the derelict church. They walked their horses in silence as they navigated the narrow roads and were often single file to leave room for the people hurrying on foot to their homes.

On reaching their destination, they dismounted and tethered their horses to a nearby post, its lamp unlit. Sera huffed and pointed a finger at the wick, and a flame burst into life and cast a flickering glow.

"That's better," she murmured.

They squeezed through the broken door and ventured inside, where damp air and the musty scent of decay once again filled their nostrils.

The friends made their way through the darkened

church, guided only by the faint light filtering through the brightly coloured stained-glass window. Rustling came from above, like a hundred bat wings. Then a shadow swooped upon them.

Warin landed with a soft thud before the altar, his wings momentarily blocking the light through the window until he folded them back. Mimicking the action of his wings, he folded muscular arms across his chest and narrowed his gaze. "I did not realise you would be back so soon. Delacour said you were bothersome."

"I also reunited you with your family and gave you a reason to keep existing," Sera replied in a firm voice. It wasn't *all* trouble and strife for those associated with her. She also brought light and warmth back into cold, lonely lives.

"I promised Meredith I would help you." The gargoyle huffed, as though he regretted that now.

Kitty smiled as she approached. "We don't have the luxury of spacing out our social calls, and the king's deterioration is most pressing."

Sera stood beside her friend. "There is dark magic attacking the king's mind. We seek knowledge in your library as to what it might be and how to remove its influence."

"Very well," he said in his rumbling voice. Then he took flight and disappeared into the shadows cast by the collapsed beams.

"How does he get out, do you think? There's no hole in the roof large enough to let him through." Hugh stared at the ceiling, trying to figure out where the gargoyle had gone.

"Ask him later." Kitty prodded Hugh in the kidney and made him move his feet in the right direction.

Outside, they climbed back into damp saddles, fat drops of rain staining the leather a darker colour. Turning their horses towards the old cemetery, they trotted on. The streets cleared as people sought to avoid the increasingly heavy rain.

By the time they reached the cemetery, their cloaks were wet, the damp seeping through to the skin. Thankfully, her friends didn't complain. Sera couldn't cast a protective sphere around them. Any mage in the vicinity would feel her enchantment, and it would have been equivalent to painting a giant, glowing, pink pointing hand over her location. They rode all the way to the deserted corner of the cemetery before dismounting and leaving the horses to shelter under the trees.

Warin had already opened the mausoleum and leaned against the granite, waiting for them. Once in the cold dark of the tomb, Sera again cast a small orb to light their way. This time, it seemed a quicker journey to the imposing stone doorway. Or perhaps they now knew what to expect.

Warin didn't speak until he uttered the words for the door to reveal itself.

Moments later, Sera, Kitty, and Hugh stood in the middle of the oval room, gazing at the shelves.

"Where do we even start?" Hugh said.

"Let the shadows of the past guide your way," Warin intoned, then flew up to be swallowed by the shadows near the tapered ceiling.

Kitty stared up at the dark corner. "If he's only going to be cryptic, I'd rather he stayed silent."

Sera cast more hovering orbs while she considered Warin's words. "*Shadows of the past* could mean old, hidden history."

"It doesn't get much older or more hidden than this." Kitty gestured to the ancient books surrounding them.

"*Shadows* could also imply the dark nature of the magic you felt," Hugh suggested.

"Let's just make a start. Look for anything about old, powerful stones. If Warin's words make more sense to anyone or he decides to come down from his high perch and be more helpful, we can change what we look for." Sera picked a direction and walked to the shelves. If she were a dark magic stone, what sort of book would describe her?

"I'll look for anything about the Unseelie." Kitty picked a spot further along from Sera.

"I'll look for anything forbidden," Hugh called from his chosen position.

Sera's fingers brushed the dusty spines of the books. Some tickled with the residue from long-ago spells. Somewhere within these pages lay the answer they sought; she was certain of it.

At random, she pulled a heavy tome from the shelf, its leather cover cracked with age. As she flipped through the brittle pages, her keen gaze scanned the ancient text for any mention of amulets or dark magic.

"Nothing," she muttered and returned the book to its place. She continued her search, pulling another tome from the shelf. And then another. And another. Each book seemed more impenetrable than the last, filled with cryptic symbols and complex diagrams that made her head swim.

As her frustration grew, Sera had to resist the urge to kick the shelves and pout. She gathered up a selection of books and took them to a round table that, rather annoyingly, didn't sit in the middle of the room and threw off the visual symmetry of the place.

Kitty and Hugh joined her, each with their own stack of heavy tomes to study. The dimly lit secret library seemed to breathe. Its ancient walls pulsed with the whispers and moans of the dead, an ever-present reminder of the bones embedded in the earth surrounding them. Shadows danced at the edge of Sera's vision as they pored over brittle parchments and crumbling grimoires.

"Curse this handwriting. This script is harder to read than that of a physician in a hurry," Hugh muttered, his broad shoulders tense as he squinted at the text before him.

"A shame that trace of gargoyle doesn't give you better eyesight, rather than size." Kitty smirked, her gaze darting over her pages like a kestrel soaring over a meadow, able to spot its prey no matter how hidden.

Sera sympathised with Hugh. Not every scribe had

a clear and concise hand. Some books seemed to have been written while a battle raged around the author. Her fingers traced the delicate lines of ink, the parchment crumbling beneath her touch like the fragile wings of a moth.

The library was a labyrinth of knowledge, if only they could navigate it. Towering shelves groaned under the weight of countless ancient tomes and scrolls. The air was thick with musty scents, the mingling odours of old leather and forgotten magic clinging to each breath. From somewhere deep within the shadowy recesses, there came a distant fluttering of something smaller and more agile than Warin.

"Listen. Do you think they are trying to tell us something? The dead might be the shadows that Warin referred to," Sera whispered, straining to decipher the faint moans and sighs that echoed through the library. The constant murmuring of the dead enveloped them, a ghostly chorus that seemed to rise and fall with each turn of the page.

"Or they might simply lament their eternal confinement. If I were trapped here for all eternity, I'd moan as well." Kitty looked up from her book to follow a shape that ghosted over the shelves.

A shiver rippled over Sera at the haunting cacophony. They were close. The dead hadn't been this vocal the last time they visited the library.

"Here! I have found something. This book speaks of something called *entropy magic.*" Hugh pointed at a passage in the grimoire open before him.

Sera frowned and pushed her book away. "Entropy magic? I've never heard of it."

Hugh's eyes shone with excitement. "Listen to the description. *Dark entropic forces sap the very essence of life from those caught within their icy grasp. Invisible tendrils of morose energy coil around the mind, eroding rationality and mental faculties over time.*"

Kitty let out a low whistle. "That sounds eerily similar to what is happening to the king."

Hugh's enthusiasm was infectious. Sera left her seat to peer over his shoulder. His finger followed the text written in a cursive hand with extravagant flourishes. She took up the reading. *Powerful forces can embed entropy magic in objects, particularly porous materials like stone. When those objects are worn or carried, they infect the bearer with the dark energy and fracture both mind and spirit.*

"Like the amulet the king wears," Kitty said.

"We have found it." Sera draped her arms around Hugh's solid neck and kissed his cheek. No wonder she had never heard of such a thing as entropy magic, with its dark and monstrous effects. "That would explain the cold void I brushed against."

"How do we remove the thing from around the king's neck if he cannot take it off without suffering unbearable pain—to say nothing of demons?" Kitty asked.

Hugh continued reading. "The scholar doesn't mention anything about that. Although this bit contains a warning, as if the description wasn't enough. *Beware the touch of the dreaded entropy stone, for it will consume your mind and render all reason null."*

Sera felt a shudder pass through her as the words seemed to echo ominously around the dimly lit chamber. Her grip tightened on Hugh's shoulders as she leaned against his broad back. "That confirms it, then. The king is being slowly infected by the dark power of an entropy stone."

"Good. Now we know what sort of dark magic we face. How do we counter its effects?" Always practical, Kitty saw the silver lining. They had named the shadow that consumed the king, which would help defeat it.

Hugh shook his head. "It doesn't say. It just mentions that it takes an enormous force to bind the dark spell to the object."

The words ricocheted around Sera's head. "Enormous force...like something that caused a rupture in the Fae realm and trapped their guardian?"

Hugh's breath left him with a whoosh. "The Nereus."

Kitty looked from Sera to Hugh. "You think *that* being created the entropy stone the king wears?"

"That would certainly be a shadow from the past." Sera stared up into the dark as she repeated Warin's words.

Eleven

"We need to learn more about the Nereus and what happened when it was destroyed," Kitty said.

"He—" Sera murmured. Her hands trailed along Hugh's arm as she returned to her chair at his side. "He was a ten-year-old boy."

Kitty's mouth opened and closed a few times before she could speak. "A child? You never said it...*he* was only a child."

"Elowyn said his parents realised what they had done and laid the trap that captured him. He wasn't killed, but his magic was transmuted into something else." The story tugged at Sera's heart as she imagined the long-ago battle. All the Mage Council, or druids as they were back then, supported by the might of the Roman army as they faced one small boy.

Kitty drew herself upright and closed the volume before her. "No wonder the Mage Council covered it all up. They didn't want anyone knowing their horrid secret. What became of the child if he wasn't killed?"

"I don't know. Elowyn said he was imprisoned. Not in the Repository—before you ask—but near where it all happened in Scotland." Sera turned her memory back to the conversation with the dryad in the wild-flower meadow.

"At least we have a direction now, and a time period. We need to find anything in here about the Nereus." Kitty stood and surveyed the expanse of books and parchments.

First, they put the discarded books and scrolls back where they'd found them. Kitty wouldn't let them create chaos in the library, even if it only had a visitor once a century. Or longer. She seemed to have appointed herself head librarian, and she scolded Hugh when he tried to slide a rolled-up parchment into the wrong compartment.

"How do you remember where they all came from?" Sera asked her friend as she pushed the last volume back into place.

Kitty tapped the side of her head. "All this capacity is in need of a task, and I refuse to waste it on silly seating plans for society events."

Next, they turned their attention to finding the older parts of the library. Ideally, Sera wanted first-hand accounts from any druids who had been involved. But she suspected any such reports were being hoarded by the Mage Council in parts of their library she couldn't access.

"What about Roman soldiers writing accounts for their families?" Hugh suggested as he pulled delicate scrolls from their resting place.

"Or a Roman scribe—they were fond of recording every moment of every day," Kitty said as she gently teased open an old scroll and glanced at the text. "We seem to have gone too far back in history. This looks Egyptian."

Sera selected another and slowly unwound the rough paper. "I will never complain again about your making me learn Latin."

"Did any of it stick? You were a horrendous student and, as I recollect, were more interested in making up naughty Latin rhymes." Kitty walked a few paces and tugged another scroll free of its companions.

Hugh's shoulders shook in silent mirth as Kitty recalled the lessons she'd insisted both of them learn as children. They both received a classical education as good as any man's.

"I enjoyed learning. It was all the sitting still I couldn't tolerate." Sera defended her antics in the classroom.

As they delved deeper into the secrets kept by the library, the bond between the three grew stronger. Each book and scroll they plucked free brought them closer to their goal. Shadows lurking in the corners seemed to retreat before their united purpose.

Sera's fingertips followed an ancient hand as she struggled to interpret the shaky letters. She did, of course, cheat and murmured a spell to alter the words to English as her finger stroked over them. The air in the library was heavy with the scent of old parchment, the stillness broken only by the soft rustle of scrolls being unrolled and the occasional murmured conversation among the friends.

"I have found something." Kitty's voice cut through the silence and drew Sera and Hugh to her side. She unfurled the scroll more and then laid it out on the table. Sera and Hugh each held a side down as Kitty translated. "A soldier found a stone on the shores of the loch. He placed it in his pocket but soon after became maudlin. When another tried to take the stone from him, he fell into fits of rage."

"Did they link the stone to entropy magic?" Sera peered at the shaky hand. The scribe had either been old or in a hurry when he wrote the account.

Kitty muttered under her breath as she first read the Latin and then translated it. She stumbled over a few words until she found the right interpretation. Then she continued. "A druid was summoned, and while three soldiers held the man, the stone was prised from his grasp. The druid said it contained the vastness of the night sky and demanded to know where the soldier had found it." Kitty glanced up at Sera. "What does he mean by the *night sky*?"

"The dark void. It was never-ending, like a winter's starless night. Or like standing at the edge of a deep well in that instant before you tumble in. It's the pull of the entropy magic." Sera shivered as she recalled the sensation that had passed over her from only a brief touch of the stone.

"Then what happened, Kitty?" Hugh pointed to the remainder of the text.

Kitty hummed as she read ahead. "The druids journeyed to the loch where they had battled and found two more stones that they say were imbued with the strange and compelling cold magic. They took all three of them away to study. After that, the scribe goes on to complain about the state of the latrines at the camp." Kitty stood, hands on hips. "The stones ended up in the mage tower, didn't they?"

"Most likely, yes. There are many dangerous magical artefacts kept in specially reinforced safes. When he was Speaker of the Council, Lord Rowan would have had full knowledge of everything hidden in the tower and the secret history of mages in England." Sera could imagine what had happened. Lord Rowan had learned of the hideous effect of the stones and crafted one into the amulet he'd placed around the neck of King George.

"He certainly played a long game. It's rather impressive when you think of all the pieces he had to place on the board and the moves he has made." Kitty rolled up the scroll.

Hugh stared at her. "You admire his evil plot to seize control of England—and Sera?"

Kitty waved a dismissive hand. "Certainly not. I meant his forward planning. To think decades in advance of what had to be put into play. The patience to wait for a woman mage to be born." Here, Kitty gestured to Sera with the scroll. "And he had to sow the seeds to incapacitate the king in a way that would never cast suspicion on himself but left him ideally situated to step in as regent."

"What a shame he didn't think far enough ahead to realise he needed a *compliant* woman mage." Hugh reached out and took Sera's hand, placing a kiss on her knuckles.

"You said the druids found the stones on the shores *where they had battled*. They defeated the Nereus on the shores of a loch in Scotland. If Elliot were here and taking bets, I would say it's a safe one that the defeat of the little boy created the entropy magic, the rift in the Fae kingdom, and the other ripples that were felt throughout the land. I can only imagine the despair of a mother in that moment, amplified by the betrayal and confusion of her child, and it attached to the stones near them." As the glowing orb hovered above them and it cast a soft glow over the table, a chilling realisation crawled up Sera's spine.

The meaning behind Warin's cryptic words about *shadows of the past* dawned on her. He must have been referring to the Nereus.

She stared up into the gloom, sensing the gargoyle on his perch, but unable to see him. She spoke into the shadows. "You meant the Nereus, didn't you, Warin? He is the shadow in my past that has decided my path."

Once she made the connection, more bloomed in her mind. Everything was connected, forming an intricate web of events and consequences that spanned centuries. The Nereus, whose defeat had forged the entropy stones, was a spectre from the distant past—yet the child's legacy lived on in the very substance that Lord Rowan sought to harness for his sinister purposes.

The rustle of wings stirred the scroll on the table as Warin dropped from above. "There is some knowledge that cannot be given. It must be earned."

Kitty snorted. She'd obviously had enough of cryptic pronouncements. "You mean there are some things so dangerous, it's best not to talk about them in case people get ideas."

The gargoyle turned his pale gaze to her and nodded. "Yes."

"That's why you couldn't help us," Hugh said.

"It's almost like an ouroboros." Sera imagined the mythical snake devouring its own tail, the circular symbol that guarded the mage library. "Long ago, two mages created a Nereus. When the boy was defeated, the blast of his magic created the stones. Which Lord Rowan wants to use to bring about another Nereus."

"You have thwarted that part of his scheme. Now we need to find a way to release the king from the other part," Kitty said.

"How do you remove the stone from the king and release him from the curse?" Hugh asked of both Sera and Warin.

"The boy did not leave a curse without a cure." Warin crossed his arms over his chest. He seemed to prefer his stone form with its chiselled clothing and only rarely adopted his human appearance.

"Like the box that contained Ebonfyre's essence and a way to release them." Sera's thoughts raced. "That was found near the fracture. Which means any cure for the entropy magic will be somewhere near where the stones were found."

"We're off to Scotland, then. To find this loch." Hugh crossed his arms, unconsciously mimicking the gargoyle's stance.

Urgency gnawed at Sera. "Time is not on our side. Every day, the king grows weaker and Lord Rowan grows stronger."

"We shall leave no stone unturned," Kitty added, humour glinting in her eyes despite the gravity of their situation. "Or, more appropriately, no page unturned."

Sera managed a smile at her friend's quip despite the circumstances. "Let's see if other scrolls in the same compartment might contain details of the battle or its location."

They gathered most of the rolled-up parchments in the same area and set them in a row on the table. Working methodically, each took one to read, and when finished, placed it back in its home. That way they ensured they didn't miss one or examine the same one twice.

"I have one here that speaks of a remote loch, guarded by ancient spirits and shrouded in an impenetrable mist." Hugh turned his scroll around for Kitty to verify his translation.

"Someone had a poetic bent," she murmured over the old vellum. "The writer describes the loch's ethereal beauty, the great oaks that stand sentinel on its shores, and the soft cries of the wind as it whispers through the trees. It sounds like a place of enchantment and wonder but also one of darkness and danger."

"What we need is a map of Caledonia from Roman times so we can match the ancient location names to their current ones. Are you able to assist with that?" Sera asked the library's guardian.

Warin didn't reply but stalked to a particular section of the library and plucked a roll free from its companions. He returned and handed it to Sera, then he retreated to his perch above the shelves. Sera laid out the map, and as Kitty read, she traced old Latin place names and rivers until she found an approximate location for an abandoned Pictish fort named in the scroll.

"It looks like it's not far from Inverness," Hugh said.

"So off to Scotland, then, to find a cure for the king." Kitty took Sera's hand and worry now tempered her earlier curiosity and excitement. "That's a journey of over five hundred miles—and every mile an opportunity for Lord Rowan to snare you."

"I will find a way." Kitty's concerns wormed their way through Sera. Her friend was right. To journey to the loch and back gave the wily old mage a thousand miles in which to set his traps, *if* he knew of her intention. Staying in the shadows and not revealing her hand would provide some protection. Her thoughts turned to

Kitty's comments about Lord Rowan playing a long game and how he viewed Sera as a pawn. But her opponent had forgotten one crucial thing.

If a pawn makes it all the way across the board, it becomes a queen.

"I wonder if I should go at all." More thoughts assailed Sera.

Hugh's eyes widened. "Of course, you must. We need to seek a cure for the king. You cannot leave him in such torment."

Sera touched his arm as she paced before the shelves. "I meant if I should go *now*. It is a journey that will take two weeks. Meanwhile, Lord Rowan's grip on this country grows stronger every day."

"I did not want to tell you, but Lord Rowan has been officially endorsed by the House of Lords as Regent of England," Kitty murmured.

Sera glared at her friend.

Kitty shrugged. "Father sent news last night. The old mage had been acting as regent while the queen and her son fought over it, and neither saw his wily move for power sneaking up on them. Now they have both lost."

"Then it is even more important that I confront Lord Rowan first. Otherwise, who knows what further chaos he will unleash in the next few weeks?" Sera resumed pacing, magic flaring over her knuckles as her loyalties were torn in different directions.

"As a physician and a humanitarian, I argue that easing the king's mind should be paramount. If—*when*

—you defeat Lord Rowan and the king is still not himself, you will still be considered a traitor, to be seized and incarcerated at the Repository."

Kitty tapped her chin with a fingertip. "Hugh raises a legitimate concern. You need the king to reverse the proclamations Lord Rowan made him sign. Unless you want to go back to that place?"

A shudder worked through Sera. "As a prisoner? Of course not. I did wish to return as a visiting scholar to unpick its secrets. But I cannot afford to leave Lord Rowan to spread his poison."

Kitty snorted. "I am going to change my answer and agree with Hugh. Cure the king first. As much as we love the queen, her power is limited. If the king is lucid once more, it may stop the other mages from siding with Lord Rowan, thus reducing his number of allies. Besides, winter still has us in her grip. We all know no one engages an enemy until spring."

Sera still paced as the internal dilemma raged inside her. Kitty raised a crucial point. If the king loudly denounced the previous proclamations and sided with her, she might only face one or two of the mages, rather than the entire council.

Decision brought her to a halt. "We journey to Scotland and find a cure for the king."

Twelve

When they returned to the Apothecary's Poison, which would forever have a place in Sera's heart for how quickly it had become their safe haven in a dangerous city, they gave Elliot two tasks. The first was to steal the livery for Buckingham House again. The second was to find a way for Sera and Hugh to journey to Scotland without attracting the attention of Lord Rowan and his soldiers.

"I suppose my family's travelling coach might be a tad obvious," Kitty mused with a glint of mischief in her eyes.

"You are enjoying every moment of this, aren't you?" Sera nudged her friend with an elbow as they plotted over ale and a meal.

"Of course I am. Life as your friend is like having a crucial role in a rather exciting novel. Do you think we could insert a thrilling encounter with dashing pirates before the end?" A rare sigh heaved through Kitty, and

Sera wondered what sort of thrilling encounters she was imagining.

Later that evening, Sera once more donned the livery of a footman, and Kitty drew a rakish moustache and goatee with a piece of coal. Through the quiet streets, they made their way to Buckingham House and the smaller gate that allowed staff in and out.

Becoming accustomed to the bustle of palace kitchens, Sera stood silent a moment to watch the choreographed dance among maids and footmen as their superiors issued them instructions. Spotting an opening, Sera inserted herself, plucked a tray bearing a tea set from a table, and whirled out the other side.

With a determined stride, she walked the opulent halls. The scent of beeswax and wood polish filled the air, mixing with the delicate fragrance of roses that drifted from vases filled with fresh hothouse blooms.

As she had in St James's Palace, she kept to the edges of the hall, to avoid any magical traps that might linger in the weave of the expensive runners. She nodded to another footman carrying a tray of empty crystal goblets as they passed.

Her footsteps were silent as she navigated around ornate side tables laden with precious curios, careful not to disturb a single object. Each step brought her closer to the queen's private chambers. What guards she saw appeared bored, and one even lounged against the wall with his eyes closed.

At last, Sera stood before the door to Queen Charlotte's sanctuary. She glanced over her shoulder, ensuring the coast was clear before she laid her palm over the lock and let a tendril of magic weave its way through the mechanism. When the click sounded, Sera took a steadying breath and pushed the door open with one hand, holding the tray with the other.

She approached the queen, seated on a sofa with a book open on her lap. Across from her, two of her ladies fussed with spaniels with glossy ears and silken coats. She paused, bowed, and placed the tray on the low table before the queen.

"Your Majesty," Sera murmured. Catching the queen's eye, she winked.

Queen Charlotte stared at her for a hard moment, and then she chuckled. "You two, leave me," she commanded her ladies.

The women scooped up the dogs and curtsied before gliding into an adjoining room and closing the door behind them.

"Lady Winyard. You had better have news for me, and stop locking the blasted door behind you when you leave. I will not be treated like a common criminal." Queen Charlotte tossed the book to the sofa.

"I shall ensure the door stays unlocked, Ma'am." Sera clasped her hands together behind her back. "I was successful in seeing the king, and my fears were confirmed."

"It is that amulet?" The queen's own hand went to her throat, wrapped in a necklace of rubies and diamonds.

"Yes. I brewed a potion that Mr Miles administered. It granted the king a brief respite from his affliction and brought a short-lived clarity to his mind." Had it been a cruelty to lift the king from the dark magic that tormented his mind, only to plunge him back into the festering pool it had wrought within him?

"George…" The name whispered past the queen's lips, and she turned her head for a moment. When she turned back, there was a determined glint in her eyes. "Why did you not remove the damned thing?"

"The king said that when he tries, the chain contracts and cuts off his air and the demons…tear his mind and cause him great agony."

If Sera had expected tears or the tremble of a lip upon hearing that, she did not elicit such a response. Instead, the queen's gaze hardened. "You will make Lord Rowan pay for this. As we shall."

"Such is my plan, Ma'am." The queen was a woman after her own heart. One of action and justice.

"How is this amulet depriving the king of his senses?" Queen Charlotte inquired, her brow furrowing as concern settled over her features.

"The pendant is a rare thing called an *entropy stone*. It is a dangerous and powerful artefact that feeds on the energy of its wearer, causing their mental faculties to decline. Over time, it has taken a significant toll on the king's mind," Sera explained.

The queen rose and walked to the fireplace. One hand curled around the exquisite marble mantel, as though she needed a substantial anchor for the turmoil inside her. Sera waited, unsure whether to proceed with her plans or not. While she had decided to seek a cure for the king first, the queen might prefer she deliver the old mage's head on a spike before she left for Scotland.

"Tell me plain, Lady Winyard," the queen said as she gazed up at the wedding portrait of herself and the king hanging above the mantel. "Is there a way to remove the amulet and cure the king?"

The Nereus didn't leave a curse without a cure; she reassured herself. "I believe, Ma'am, that one may be found in Scotland, where the entropy stones were formed. On the shores of a loch, I hope to find a means to counteract its malevolent influence."

The queen tapped the marble and paced to her writing desk. "You will do this. Leave immediately. In exchange, we will have these ridiculous edicts against you reversed. You are our true subject, unlike Lord Rowan, who has weaselled control as Regent for himself. This has been his plan all along, has it not? To have my George declared unfit to rule so he might snatch the crown for himself. But we shall ensure he fails."

The queen's growing rage matched Sera's own. "He will not triumph, Ma'am. Although Lord Rowan has impeded me. He has strewn London and the countryside with magical traps to ensnare me. They are also triggered by any aftermage with a trace of magic in their blood, and it is causing chaos as others are caught instead."

"You have done well thus far, then. Leave at once. I

will do what I can from the cage he has placed me in. When you return, Lady Winyard, you will cure the king, and Lord Rowan will be the one declared traitor. He will be stripped of his rank and wealth, and while we may not have him executed for treason, he and his family will be cast out from this court and all good society." The queen's tone softened as she studied Sera. "Your friend will be brought down with her grandfather."

Sera bit back the urge to scoff. "Lady Abigail Crawley is no friend of mine. She showed herself to be cut from the same cloth."

Queen Charlotte nodded. "Then we are agreed."

Sera bowed—since she was disguised as a footman it would have been odd to curtsy. The queen and king, once restored, would end Lady Abigail Crawley's precious reputation and prospects. The duke would insist that his son disentangle himself to stop his family from tumbling into the same treacherous waters that would claim Lord Rowan's kin. Revenge would be swift and complete.

Having made a pact with the queen, Sera slipped from the royal rooms and left the door unlocked. On the margins of the wide halls, she hurried back to the kitchens.

"I hope you have an idea, Elliot," she muttered as she dodged cooks with large pots and maids with stacks of plates.

Once out the last door, cold air enveloped her like a welcome embrace. Coal smoke hung heavy in the air, as few families could afford to heat their homes by magical means. That gave Sera the seed of an idea. The gargoyle library, held deep in the clutches of death and the earth, was temperate. Was there a way to funnel the warmth of the soil into a home?

By the stone wall, Hugh patiently waited. Scotland beckoned, its wild moors and ancient lochs holding the key to King George's salvation. Excitement tinged her words at what mysteries she might uncover in Scotland. "The queen wishes me to heal the king first. Then she wants Lord Rowan's head mounted above her mantel."

Hugh stared at her in horror.

Sera took his hand. "Well, she didn't exactly say those words, but it was strongly implied."

"I have wondered how so many men can be so wrong in believing women to be the weaker sex." He pulled her closer to his side, having theorised that the trace of gargoyle in his blood might cloak Sera from Lord Rowan's traps if she were close enough to him.

"Most men are not as intelligent as you, Hugh." A good mood wrapped itself around Sera. Something in her blood whispered that she had chosen the right direction.

The Apothecary's Poison tavern crouched in its triangular intersection like an old crone awaiting unsuspecting prey, its exterior at odds with the soft golden light inside and the welcoming atmosphere. Perhaps most strangers turned away after taking one look at it, which allowed the pub to remain a well-kept secret for locals.

Elliot and Kitty waited in their usual corner.

"We leave tonight. I cannot afford to waste a moment," Sera said before she even sat down.

"Well, isn't it lucky you pay me so handsomely for my many talents?" Elliot leaned back and crossed his arms, a smug look on his darkly handsome face.

"I assume from that look that you have a way for Hugh and I to travel to Scotland without ending up back at the Repository?" Sera stole Kitty's tankard and took a long drink to ease her parched throat.

Mischief shone in Elliot's dark gaze. "There's a troupe of travelling Daoine Sidhe camped outside London. They are returning home to Scotland. Their magic will shield you from prying eyes."

"The fairy folk?" Sera blew out a contemplative sigh. Putting herself into their care brought its own dangers, but the risks would be worth it. "Elliot, I could kiss you."

Sera jumped to her feet, and Elliot pushed himself back into the corner and raised his hands just in case she intended to carry out her threat. Instead, she grabbed Hugh's hand. "We have to pack and find them before they leave. It is a full moon, and the Daoine Sidhe prefer to travel by moonlight."

In their little room, Sera dug out her satchel and shoved in a change of chemise, stockings, and shirt. It took them less than fifteen minutes to prepare for the long journey. Anything they needed, they could acquire along the way.

Kitty and Elliot accompanied them to the outskirts

of London, where the sounds of people gave way to the whispering rustle of trees and the distant hoot of an owl. There, nestled to one side of a meadow, they found the Daoine Sidhe. Their camp was lit by the ethereal glow of countless fireflies that hovered over them.

"Miss Napier and I can't go any closer. Only you and Mr Miles can approach." Elliot halted and held out a hand to stop Kitty from following her friend.

Kitty snorted. "The next trip you take off into the unknown, you are absolutely *not* leaving me behind." Then she flung her arms around Sera and hugged her fiercely.

"I'll be back before you know it. We shall set everything to rights, and then, I promise, we will go on an adventure together," Sera whispered against Kitty's russet hair.

Sera took a moment to consider what to say as they stepped into the circle of light. "I am the mage Seraphina Winyard. I seek your protection and assistance to travel to Scotland," she called, her voice steady and strong despite the uncertainty that churned within her.

The fairy folk regarded her with a mixture of curiosity and wariness, their eyes glinting like emeralds in the moonlight. "Why should we aid you, mortal?" one man replied, without moving from his position on the ground before the fire.

Someone hushed him, and the fairy folk shuffled aside as an ancient figure approached, her face lined with the wisdom of countless years. A cloak of pale cream fell in soft folds around her diminutive form, as though the centuries had compressed her. "I am Liriel, seer of the Daoine Sidhe. Tell me, child, of the path you walk."

Taking a deep breath, Sera laid bare her heart and her mission, revealing the pact she had made with the queen, her determination to save King George from the clutches of madness, and her resolve to see the traitorous Lord Rowan brought to justice. As she spoke, the old woman's eyes seemed to bore into her, weighing the truth and sincerity of her words.

A hush fell over the Daoine Sidhe encampment as Sera awaited the old seer's response. The inky sky above seemed to hold its breath, the stars shimmering with anticipation. The scent of wood smoke and damp earth enveloped her, grounding her in the moment.

"Our paths are entwined, child. We will shelter you as we return to our homeland," Liriel said at last, her voice a blend of ancient wisdom and quiet power. "I foresaw your coming, and tonight was the last night we would have waited for you."

Sera glanced at Hugh, who stood at her shoulder. She had things to discuss with him, like what the seer had foreseen, but that would have to wait until they were alone. "Thank you. We are most grateful for the gift of travelling with you." Relief washed over her. "This is my—my cavalier, Hugh Miles. He walks with me."

"You will be hidden among our ranks. That fox Rowan will not sniff you out here." Liriel winked and gestured to her people. "However, our protection comes at a price. In exchange, you will be beholden to us for a task of equal measure. When we call, will you answer?"

"Yes." Sera didn't even hesitate or question what, precisely, they might want of her.

From the trees, where Elliot and Kitty watched, her friend uttered a soft gasp—her legal mind no doubt imagining the untold horrors Sera might have just agreed to.

Sera met the seer's gaze, determination settling in her bones. "I understand, and I vow to uphold my end of the bargain." She swiped a tendril of magic across her palm, drew forth a drop of blood, and then held out her hand.

Liriel laughed and pressed the sharpened nail of her left thumb into her right palm. Then she held out her hand to Sera. "You know of our ways. Good."

They joined hands and made a blood pact—one to protect the other. The surrounding air crackled with energy as the Daoine Sidhe murmured their agreement, their collective magic swirling through the camp like a tempestuous wind. Then Liriel slammed her staff to the ground. While it made no sound, an odd *whump* rolled up through Sera's body.

"The moon is high, and we have lingered close to London overlong," Liriel said. "Let us depart."

Sera turned and waved one last time to Elliot and Kitty, then let the fairy folk guide them to the wagon they would travel in. The wagons had rounded tops.

Some had windows with wooden shutters. Stove pipes poked through the roof. At the rear, each had a sheltered porch and steps that could be pulled up when travelling.

The horses had the metallic sheen of Fae mounts, coats gleaming silver, copper, and bronze under the moonlight. Sera and Hugh climbed up on a seat next to a slight Daoine Sidhe lad.

"I am Yarrow. Liriel is my grandmother," he said as two women helped the old seer climb the steps into the wagon.

"I am Sera, and this is Hugh. Will it take us long to reach Scotland?" Sera asked.

The boy grinned. "Not as long as it would take mortal folk. Our horses are much faster than yours."

"Hugh and I have ridden Fae horses when we rode out with Queen Deryn's warriors." Sera met the boy's amber gaze.

Yarrow clucked his tongue, and the horses leaned into their harness as the lead wagon rolled away. "There is a tale I wouldn't mind hearing if you are inclined?"

Sera narrated their adventures at the Seelie court as the shadowed countryside passed by. The rustle of leaves filled the air, melding with the soft murmurs of conversation among the fairy folk. Someone began playing a flute, and the haunting tune accompanied them throughout the long night.

By the time dawn roused the birds in the surrounding trees, Sera's innate connection with the earth told her they were a long way from London. Much further than a rider on a galloping horse could have covered in a single night. Smoke rose in the distance from the many chimneys of a large town.

"Where are we?" Sera asked Yarrow as they climbed down. Her muscles protested, and she shook her limbs.

"Manchester," the boy replied as he tended to the horses.

"We have travelled two hundred miles overnight. How is that possible?" Hugh stared at the plumes of smoke.

"They are the Daoine Sidhe," Sera murmured. "Elliot is going to be unbearable when he finds out how perfectly his plan has worked."

Thirteen

THEY RESTED the horses near a forest, and the men ventured into the shadows to hunt. Around a campfire, they shared a meal and relaxed for a few hours before continuing their journey. Hugh bombarded Yarrow with questions about how they could travel faster than a galloping horse and yet only a gentle breeze touched their faces. Apparently, if they could achieve such incredible speeds of a hundred miles in a couple of hours, Hugh hypothesised the air would be sucked from their lungs and they should all have died from asphyxia.

Yarrow didn't know how it worked, other than something about the land moving faster under the horses' hooves, rather than the equines setting a gruelling pace. When they were on their way once more, Sera left them to discuss the mechanics of travel and time and sat with Liriel in the swaying interior of the wagon.

Within was a cosy room complete with a lush, velvet-covered bed built into one end, a tiny stove, and a table under the window. The old seer told Sera stories of the fairy folk and their journeys around England. They always returned to Scotland, their ancestral home, for spring and to celebrate the renewal of the earth.

"I wish I could stay and join the celebrations with you." Sera sighed and leaned her cheek against the curved wall of the wagon.

Liriel chuckled. "Another spring, mage. Our paths will cross many times yet. You were born to walk a darker path, and many eyes watch to see what you make of it."

That was an intriguing pronouncement from a seer, but no matter how Sera phrased her questions, the old woman refused to be drawn any further.

As the sun rose on the second day, the Daoine Sidhe crossed the border into Scotland. The enchanted horses moved with an eerie grace, their hooves barely making a sound on the rough terrain. As they reached the foothills, the fairy folk halted their procession.

"Wait," Liriel said, her eyes glinting with ancient knowledge. "We must perform a ritual to honour our ancestors on our return."

Sera exchanged a glance with Hugh, and they watched, fascinated, as the Daoine Sidhe formed a circle, their voices rising in a haunting melody. The air around them shimmered, as if the very fabric of reality bent to their will. With each note, a sense of peace settled over the assembled group, connecting them to the land and the spirits that dwelled within it.

As the Daoine Sidhe completed their ritual, a soft glow enveloped the group, infusing them with a warmth that radiated from the earth itself. The moment lingered, suspended in time, until at last the sun shook off its slumber and climbed higher in the sky, heralding the change from dawn to morning.

Scotland's rugged beauty unfolded before them, its wild landscape a testament to the fierce magic that ran through its veins. Towering mountains loomed over deep lochs, their surfaces as still and reflective as mirrors. Heather-covered moors stretched out like a purple sea. It was a country steeped in myth and legend, where every rock and tree held a story of its own.

Sera spread her arms wide and welcomed the wild magic. "I wish you could feel it, Hugh. The very air is charged."

They journeyed another hour with the fairy folk before Liriel called a halt near a dense forest where the treetops were shrouded in mist.

The old woman took Sera's hand in her gnarled ones. "We must part ways here. You cannot follow where we go."

"We thank you for your hospitality. It will not be forgotten, nor will I forget the promise I owe in return," Sera said.

A smile tugged at the corners of Liriel's mouth, her wrinkled skin crinkling like ancient parchment.

"Good, child, for our memories are long." Letting go of Sera's hand, Liriel reached into her robes and produced a roll of parchment. Unfurling it carefully, she revealed a map covered in intricate symbols and swirling patterns.

She placed the map in Sera's hands. "This is a map of the fairy rings that will speed your return to London. Step into one ring and it will transport you to the next."

"Thank you, Liriel," Sera whispered, marvelling at the delicate beauty of the map.

"But be warned, each fairy ring can only be used once," Liriel explained, her voice barely audible above the rustle of leaves. "After you have stepped through, the ring will vanish from the map, leaving no trace behind. Choose wisely, for once a ring is gone, you cannot return to it."

"Travelling by fairy ring." Hugh blew out the words in an excited and awestruck tone.

Sera's fingertip traced one of the circles on the parchment. "I understand." She rolled the map up and secured it with a strip of leather, then tucked it into her satchel for their return journey.

"Go, my child, and may the spirits of this land guide and protect you both." With both hands on Sera's shoulders, Liriel touched her forehead to Sera's. Then she did the same to Hugh, after indicating he should bend at the knees.

Yarrow waved as the Daoine Sidhe turned into the forest for the last leg of their journey to their hidden realm. After the trees had swallowed the wagons, Sera took Hugh's hand. "I suppose now we walk towards Inverness."

The wind whispered through the trees, carrying the promise of adventure and the lingering scent of ancient magic. It also brought stinging-cold rain. Before long, Sera and Hugh were trudging along a muddy track, rivulets of rain trickling down their faces. The wild beauty of the Scottish countryside brought with it a sense of isolation. The rolling hills were shrouded in mist. Or Sera assumed they were still there—they had disappeared behind the haze.

"By god, I didn't think it was possible for the rain to get any harder," Hugh muttered as he pulled his coat tighter around his throat.

Sera couldn't help but chuckle despite her sodden state. "Welcome to Scotland."

She cast a small enchantment to keep the worst of the rain from them, but the determined droplets squirmed through, and soon she couldn't hold up the shield and have enough energy to walk at the same time.

Just as Sera gave up trying to stop them from being drenched to the bone, an old farmer driving a rickety cart pulled by a stout horse came up behind them. He slowed to a stop as they stepped onto the verge and cast a curious glance at their dripping state.

"Where are you two wet sheep headed?" he called over the patter of raindrops on the cart's canvas canopy.

"Inverness," Sera replied, trying to keep her teeth from chattering.

"Ah, well, ye're in luck," the farmer said, a grin revealing the gaps in his yellowed teeth. "I'm goin' that way meself. Hop in. I'll give ye a ride."

"Thank you, sir, we are grateful," Hugh said as he helped Sera up into the cart before climbing in himself. Four sheep lay on the straw and regarded them suspiciously. As they settled on the dry bedding, the farmer flapped the reins, and they were off.

"Name's Fergus," he said conversationally as they bumped along. "If ye don't mind me saying, ye look a long way from home. What brings ye to these parts?"

"We have a relative who is terribly sick. We have come here in search of a cure." Sera stayed as close to the truth as possible, without revealing the full extent of the harebrained scheme to save the king.

"Ah, well, ye've come to the right place." Fergus gestured at the breathtaking vistas that surrounded them. "There's magic in these hills. Our land is full of old secrets." He winked at Sera and then chuckled to himself.

Hugh shifted closer, draping an arm around her shoulders for warmth.

Sera found that, yet again, she was fantasising about a hot bath. It seemed to happen a lot in her battle against Lord Rowan. Perhaps it was a sign that she needed to lure him to Bath for their final encounter, where she could take the heated waters afterwards.

Fergus dropped them off on the outskirts of Inverness and carried on his way. At least the rain had subsided, becoming little more than a chilly drizzle.

They walked the streets, looking for somewhere to dry off and have a warm meal. Locals they passed were wary, their eyes narrowed with suspicion as they watched the strangers in their town.

"Not exactly a welcoming place," Hugh murmured, his brow furrowed in concern.

They found an inn that appeared clean and set back off the main roads, which Sera hoped meant there would be more locals than travellers.

The barkeep watched them with a stern expression. His hands slowed as he poured ale from a keg on its side into a large clay pitcher. "Can I help ye? Are ye lost?"

"We're looking for a room for the night and a meal, please." Hugh leaned on the bar.

"We can do that," the bartender said, placing the pitcher on the bar, where a man pounced on it and took it back to his table. "We don't get many travellers here. Wouldn't you be more comfortable among others who are breaking their journey at Inverness?"

Sera rested her forearms on the bar. "No. My father is terribly ill in London. We have come in search of a cure that we are told might be on the shores of a loch. I was hoping someone might point us in the right direction."

The man stared at her and then *tsk*ed under his breath. "Shouldn't you consult a doctor, or a mage if you're able?"

"Doctors cannot help. He is afflicted by a curse. We were told by a mage to find a magical cure here." Sera spoke the truth. A mage had sent them to Inverness to find a way to reverse the entropy spell. And that mage was herself.

The barkeep huffed. "Glynis will show you to a room. Come see me when you want a spot of supper."

Their room was smaller and not as well kept as the one they'd shared at the Apothecary's Poison.

"It will do. Hopefully, we'll not be here long." Sera dropped her satchel on the table.

"At least there are towels." Hugh tossed one to Sera, and they both dried off as best they could.

They kept their ears open over a substantial supper (Hugh had missed several meals, by his calculations), but conversation was subdued around them. The locals were guarded, and they cast many glances in their direction.

"Perhaps their tongues will loosen after a few pints," Sera said as she sipped an ale.

They spent the evening in the pub as the rain resumed and pounded the roof. Rivulets ran down the thick glass of the windows. Every time someone opened the front door, loud grumbling came from the patrons as the warm air escaped.

At least Sera's clothing dried out. They agreed to approach people separately. Sera tried to engage the few women in the pub in conversation, but they glared at her, and one went so far as to say she couldn't under-stand her accent.

With growing frustration, she surveyed the room, wondering who to try next. A group of men huddled in a corner; their voices lowered to conspiratorial whispers that ceased the moment they noticed her gaze. Hugh leaned against the bar, attempting to engage the barkeep in conversation, but it was clear by the man's tight-lipped expression that he wasn't getting far. The only thing Hugh seemed to get from the man was a refill of their pitcher.

"Any luck?" Sera asked, hoping the publican had whispered the location of the loch when no one was looking.

"None," he said with a sigh, shaking his head. "It's like trying to coax secrets from a stone wall."

"Perhaps they only need to get used to seeing us about. We shall try again tomorrow." Sera poured an inch more ale into her tin mug.

"Or perhaps there's a reason they're not telling us," Hugh said quietly, scanning the room.

Sera bit her lip, considering his words. She had noted the unusual atmosphere in the town, but then, to her, the whole of Scotland vibrated, every breath infused with the faint trace of magic. Was there more to it than the fairy folk being more prevalent here? Had the entire region been affected by the Nereus?

"Given the rupture we saw in the Fae realm, it is possible there is still a trace of the Nereus here. Such unimaginable power must have scarred the land where he was defeated." Even thinking of it made the hair stand up on Sera's arms. Elowyn hadn't said what had happened to the boy or how the land had been affected where he stood. If it could create the entropy stones, what other dangerous magical artefacts might litter the loch? The locals might have a good reason for keeping quiet.

As the evening drew on, someone pulled out a fiddle and struck up a lively tune. A few men danced a sort of jig, and laughter rang out around the room.

Eventually, aware that their presence stifled the usual atmosphere among the patrons, Sera and Hugh climbed the stairs to their room.

After a solid night's sleep and a wash, Sera was ready to find someone who would talk. If no one would, she wasn't above a little *witchy stuff* (as Elliot would say) to loosen a few tongues. She didn't have time to wait twenty years or more until she was no longer considered an outsider.

Stepping out into the watery sunlight, they headed along the road towards a market. Sera approached a woman selling bread. "Excuse me, could you please tell us how to find the loch where a mighty battle happened centuries ago?"

The woman held out a delicious-smelling roll. "I dinna ken what you mean. Bread?"

Hugh passed her a few coins and took four rolls in exchange. Giving one to Sera, he slid one into his coat pocket and ate the remaining two simultaneously.

No matter who they stopped and asked, they were met with confusion, denial, or rudely told to go back to England.

"I'm not too surprised they aren't welcoming of nosy Englishmen. Culloden is only a few miles from here, and many would still remember." Hugh finished his bread rolls and eyed up the stalls for one selling hot drinks.

Sera chewed her bottom lip as Hugh purchased hot chocolate in carved wooden mugs. They sat on a bench in the sun as they drank the rich brew. Sera watched children playing. Some threw a stick for shaggy dogs. Girls gathered in groups to throw knuckle bones in the air and see how many they could catch while swiping others from the ground.

"Culloden. It seems so long ago." Sera sipped her drink and flicked through her memory for what she had learned of the rebellion by the Scottish. One that the English had brutally suppressed.

"A long time to you is but a moment to the Fae or fairy folk. Many here would have lost family. Now think how long ago the Nereus was, yet we are trying to hunt out that battleground while walking past one that still bears open scars." Hugh's attention turned to a young lad with an obvious limp. He shook his head at a badly set leg that would plague the boy for life.

"I think we should find stables and hire a couple of horses. It would be more productive to search for ourselves. There is a chance I will be sensitive to any residue despite the passage of time." Sera would rather do something than wait on the off chance someone would answer their questions.

Having decided, they finished their breakfast and returned their mugs. Hugh asked where they could hire horses, a question the woman could answer—since it involved coin.

As they walked along a muddy lane, the shrill sound of distant screams made Sera's heartbeat surge. The urgency in the cries pulled them from their path. Hugh paused only long enough to take a bearing before he ran towards the noise.

"Help!" a young woman screamed, dropping to her knees in the mud. "Please, someone must help my father!"

Locals gathered around her. A man helped the woman to her feet. Her hands and the cuffs of her sleeves were covered in blood.

"What happened, Innes?" the man asked.

"A wild boar, while we were tending the fields near the forest. It—it gored him," she sobbed, her voice shaking. "He's bleeding so much. I fear he won't last long."

"Fetch the doctor!" someone yelled, and a boy broke away and took flight back along the road.

"I'm a surgeon. Take me to him," Hugh instructed, his voice steady and authoritative.

His gaze was determined, lit by a fire that kindled whenever he faced a challenge that demanded his skills as a surgeon. Sera stayed by his side. She had helped him perform surgery before, and her skills might be needed.

Innes, the young woman, leaned on a man as they led the way through the streets to a cottage near the outskirts of the town. Inside, a man aged around fifty lay on a straw pallet, his clothes torn and stained with blood. Innes fell to her knees beside him and pressed a hand to his head. "I have brought a surgeon, Da."

Hugh knelt beside the injured man and methodically assessed the wound, his fingers gently probing the edges of the deep gash in the man's side. "I need bandages, hot water, and alcohol," he said. "Help me get him on the table." Hugh gestured to the other man to assist.

The injured man cried out as he was moved and laid on the table, the breakfast dishes hastily shoved aside to make room. Hugh drew his field kit from his pocket and unrolled the leather to reveal his tools.

"If you wouldn't mind, Sera." He gestured with a tilt of his head to the moaning man.

Sera warmed her palms and then placed them on the man's chilled face. Then she murmured in an ancient tongue a spell that could have been a lullaby.

"What is she doing?" someone else demanded.

"Taking away his pain and sending him to sleep," Hugh replied as he sliced the man's shirt open to reveal a scrawny torso.

"Witch," Innes whispered, her eyes wide.

Sera winked in return.

FOURTEEN

INNES HELD a bowl of hot water, and Hugh wrung out a cloth and cleaned the wound as best he could.

"He's asleep," Sera said as she took her place next to Hugh.

He worked carefully, dousing the wound with alcohol before he began, carefully slicing a thin layer from the torn flesh. "This edge wouldn't heal properly," he explained to Sera and those watching. "It is better to make a clean incision before stitching such a wound closed."

When asked, Sera passed him the threaded needle and dropped the scalpel into the bowl of water to clean it. Hugh worked with a steady and confident hand despite the gravity of the situation. When he was done, he trickled more whiskey over the neat line of stitches.

"A few cobwebs would help it heal, if the spiders could spare any," Hugh said as he wiped his hands.

Sera walked to the corner of the room where a spider had spun a marvellous web. "I am sorry," she murmured to the arachnid, "but we need your home."

Using a magical touch, she pulled the web free of its corner, the spider scurrying along the ceiling to avoid being caught up in it. Sera kept it outstretched before her as she approached the prone man.

"Over the stitches, please," Hugh murmured.

Sera brushed her fingers through the air, and the web obeyed. It re-shaped itself into a rectangular strip and dropped over the wound, adhering to the stitches. Only then was a bandage passed around the man's torso, and he was gently moved to a bed. His daughter tucked a blanket around the sleeping patient.

"Keep him warm and change the dressing daily. If you can, keep applying a web. I have found they help stave off infection, although I have yet to explain how." Hugh dried his hands and then cleaned his tools before putting them back in the leather roll.

"Thank you, sir. I cannot thank you enough," Innes whispered, tears streaming down her cheeks as she threw her arms around Hugh's middle and hugged him.

"Well done, Hugh. Let us see if saving a life makes anyone more talkative," Sera murmured as they walked back to the tavern.

As word spread through the village of the life-saving procedure performed by the mysterious outsiders, the atmosphere shifted. The wary, uncooperative locals softened, their eyes now holding a mix of curiosity and respect when they regarded Sera and Hugh.

That evening, Sera found herself seated before the crackling fire with Hugh and the tavern patrons. A sense of camaraderie now infused the air as the locals opened up and shared stories and laughter with their newfound friends.

"Ye did a fine job savin' old Angus," said a gruff man, clapping Hugh on the back. "I've nae seen such skilled hands in all me days."

"Thank you. I'm just glad I could help," Hugh replied, his cheeks flushing slightly at the praise.

"Help?" the old man chuckled around his pipe. "Ye damned well saved his life!"

The locals murmured their agreement. Sera couldn't help but smile as she watched Hugh's discomfort at the attention. He didn't like being in the spotlight, but for once, she was grateful for it. His skill meant the people trusted them and might open up in ways that hadn't seemed possible earlier that morning.

"Are ye a witch, that you could take away his pain?" a wide-eyed woman asked Sera.

"Yes." She didn't see the point of lying. Besides, if history was correct, the Scottish had more respect for magical women than the English.

Murmurs ran through those assembled, and the curiosity in their eyes deepened.

"You're not here to harm us, are ye?" another man asked. He had an enormous bushy beard that could have hidden a kitten.

"No. I'm here seeking a cure for a curse. Somewhere near Inverness is a loch that saw a terrible magical battle over a thousand years ago. That is where the curse was born, and I am hoping the same spot also holds a cure." Sera spoke with her hands, creating the image of a shimmering body of water. Next to it, she placed the Roman soldiers and a semi-circle of druids as they fought the shadow before them.

"Most folk hereabouts keep their lips sealed when it comes to matters o' magic," the pipe smoker said. He blew a series of rings that drifted towards the rafters. "We hold their secrets, and they keep ours."

Which was rather what Sera suspected and confirmed her nagging suspicion that magic did indeed linger at the loch. "We're not here to cause any trouble or breach any agreements with the Daoine Sidhe. I only want to help someone who is much tormented by a dark spell."

"No one here will tell you what you want to know," he replied. Before Sera could rally a reason why they should, he continued. "But if you ask Old Eithne, she might. She is the keeper of such tales, if ye ken."

Sera didn't ken, but at least they were making progress of a sort. "Where do we find Old Eithne?"

The man gave them rough directions to the woman's cottage on the northern side of the town. Not wanting to wait another day, Sera and Hugh set out in the dark.

As they moved through the town, the cobblestone

roads gave way to dirt tracks, lined with twisted trees that seemed to lean inwards, as if sharing whispered secrets. The air grew colder, and a chill ran down Sera's spine—but whether from the temperature or anticipation, she couldn't quite discern.

Finally, they reached a cottage that sat by itself, nestled in the embrace of the trees, which seemed to have broken away from the forest to gather around the building. A vegetable patch enclosed with a willow-withe fence lay dormant to one side, waiting for spring to warm the earth.

Flames flickered on the other side, where a figure sat on a bench before a fire. A shawl was drawn around thin shoulders. A massive black hound lay at her feet. The dog lifted its shaggy head and uttered a single *woof* before lying down again.

"Eithne?" Sera asked as they approached.

"Aye, milady. You took your time to find me." When she met Sera's gaze, her eyes were white with no irises.

Hugh held out a hand and waved it before her face. "Blind," he murmured.

"But not deaf," she snapped.

"I did not mean to offend," Hugh said.

The woman seemed ancient and ageless at the same time. Her form was slender and frail. Hair of pure silver was wound in a tight plait around her head to make a crown. The shawl she clutched was made from a tartan of deep blue and green.

"You know who I am," Sera said.

Eithne gestured to a blanket set out beside her. "Sit."

Sera did as instructed, Hugh lowering himself to the earth beside her. The dog cast them a weary look but seemed content so long as they didn't get between him and the fire. Or make any sudden moves towards his mistress.

"The earth feels your steps. For too many years has our mother had her daughters taken from her." Eithne tossed a stick onto the flames, and they flared a pale lilac for a moment.

Sera considered the woman's words—a reference to her being the first woman mage since Morag. "You're not human."

Eithne cackled. "I have walked these lands for far longer than either of you have been alive. I have seen the rise and fall of kings, and I have heard whispers of ancient magic that even now still echo through the ages."

To be so old, she had to be one of the Fae or the Daoine Sidhe. Sera took a guess as to which, as there was a familiar shape to the woman's face. "You wouldn't happen to know Liriel, would you?"

Another laugh. "She is my younger sister."

Sera glanced at Hugh, who wore an expression of realisation. One seer must have told the other to expect them. The world beyond their little circle faded away, leaving only the crackling of the fire and the occasional rustle of leaves caught in the gentle breeze.

"Do you remember the battle fought on the shores of the loch?" Sera referenced the loch in case Eithne thought they wanted to know of Culloden.

"I am not quite *that* old. But my grandmother told me the tale. She saw what they did that day. When a mother grieved the fate of her child...a fate she had brought about." Eithne's voice softened, as though she shared the mother's pain.

Gooseflesh erupted along Sera's arms. She was on the cusp of uncovering knowledge that could change the course of history and save their beloved king.

"Long ago," Eithne said solemnly, her voice taking on a melodic quality as she wove her tale beneath the starlit sky, "there was born a child of two druids. The boy possessed magic that surpassed even the most skilled druids of his time. As he grew, so did his power. His magic was raw and untamed, and it frightened his parents. When the boy was angry and he lashed out, he felled forests, and great storms thundered across the land." She leaned forwards slightly, her voice lowering to a hushed whisper.

Sera could see it all in her mind's eye. The fierce determination of the druids as they clashed with the boy's overwhelming ability. She pictured them forming intricate sigils in the air, weaving spells of protection and attack. Their robes billowed around them like storm clouds gathering on the horizon, each druid a tempest of arcane energy battling an unstoppable force.

"As the boy grew older, it became clear his mind could not contain the arcane forces. His parents tried to reason with the child and the council of elders, but something had to be done. In fits of rage, the child unleashed terrible devastation. Many became fearful that he would destroy everything and everyone who walked this land." Eithne sighed and leaned back on the bench. The dog looked up, and she dropped a hand to his head.

Sera knew what happened next, but still, she bit her lip, waiting for Eithne to go on.

"Despite their best efforts, the druids found themselves unable to tame the child. They could not instruct him on how to use his magic. Their desperation grew, and they made a fateful decision—one that would alter the course of history forever." Eithne's voice was tinged with sadness.

Sera's heart ached as she imagined the weight of the impossible choice pressing on the boy's parents like a crushing tide. At the same time, a tendril of anger wormed through her. Because of what they'd done, fear had driven the Mage Council to implement their abhorrent policy. So many gifted girls had been deprived of the basic right to draw breath.

"His mother lured the child to the shore with a promise that she had found a way to harness his magic. Surrounded by a thousand Roman soldiers and the druids, a terrible battle took place. Throughout the day, it raged. Men lay slaughtered. Druids were drained to empty husks. Yet they could not defeat the boy." Eithne paused and gestured to a pot that nestled in the embers at the edge of the fire.

Sera took a cup sitting on the bench at Eithne's side. Wrapping her gift around the handle of the pot so she didn't burn her fingers, she poured a fragrant and steaming brew into the mug. Then she placed it in Eithne's hands.

In Sera's mind, the battle raged on, the air crackling with energy as the druids chanted incantations, their hands weaving desperate patterns in an attempt to subdue the boy's immense power. The sky darkened overhead, storm clouds swirling as the distant ocean itself roared in response to their call.

The old woman sipped before continuing her story. "Since the druids could not defeat the boy, they sought instead to turn his own magic upon him and bind him. Tethering him to something powerful enough to contain his raw potential. The loch passes underground to the sea, so they chose the sea itself, hoping its vast depths would be strong enough to hold him."

"Along with his parents, a Nereus is the child of Mother Earth and Old Man Sea. If the source of his power was the ocean, it makes sense to use that against him." Sera's mind raced with ideas about how the child could have been subdued.

The flames of the fire altered, and the battle played out against them. The loch appeared, and the forces arrayed against the boy held their ground among the bodies of the fallen.

"Look!" Eithne cried. "The sea answers their pleas!"

A monstrous wave rose from the depths of the loch,

its crest reaching towards the heavens. It towered above the battlefield, casting a dark and menacing shadow over the druids, soldiers, and child. Power emanated from the water, rolling away from it with the heat of flames. Old Man Sea himself had been summoned to claim his son.

The boy's expression turned to one of terror as he sensed the impending doom that threatened to engulf him. Against the backdrop of the flames, he shimmered as he raised his hands, attempting to conjure another barrier of magic, but it was in vain. The force that now encircled him was too great, and his strength waned against the unrelenting tide.

"Please," he whispered, his voice choked with fear. "Please don't—Mam—"

But there was no mercy to be found that day, even from the woman who had borne him. With a final incantation, the druids redirected the boy's magic back upon him, using his own power to bind him to the terrible fate they had devised.

Hugh gripped Sera's hand, as entranced by the scene playing out before them as she was. Pain speared through Sera as the woman druid dropped to her knees and bowed her head, salt tears running down her cheeks.

"By the sea, thou shalt be bound," intoned the boy's father, his voice carrying over the roar of the waves. "An immortal creature thou shalt become, forever cursed to wander these depths."

And then, as Sera watched in horror, the boy's

body began to transform. His limbs twisted and contorted, elongating into sinuous tendrils that writhed and coiled around him. His youthful face warped into a visage of anguish, eyes pleading for an end to the torment that tore apart his young form.

"Thus was the Nereus captured," Eithne whispered, her words heavy with sorrow. "A being of great power and eternal suffering. Condemned to a watery prison by those who sought to save their world from his magic."

In the instant the boy's sentence was enacted came a clap of thunder so loud it burst eardrums, accompanied by a flash of lightning that blinded those nearby. People fell to the ground, clutching their heads.

"The fracture," Sera murmured. Here was the blast that had torn into the Fae realm and trapped Ebonfyre. Here was the explosion of concentrated despair and anguish that had created the entropy stones.

The Nereus disappeared beneath the churning waves, his mournful cries echoing through the storm as a chilling reminder of the price they had paid for their victory.

Sera's heart ached as the weight of the Nereus's tale settled upon her. Over the crackle of the wood drifted the anguished cries of the boy, now an immortal creature forever trapped beneath the waters of the loch. The sound faded into the surrounding night.

Just before the image vanished, Sera glimpsed something dropped on the stones. A wooden horse.

The toy of a child. All that remained of a beloved son and the most powerful being to ever walk the earth.

Eithne's voice softened, sorrow lacing her words as she continued the story. "The Nereus still roams the depths of the loch, his heart filled with remorse for the destruction he caused as a boy and sorrow for the pain he caused his parents. It is said that when the moon casts its silvery glow upon the loch that clasps hands with the sea, the Nereus rises to the surface, staring longingly towards the land he once walked."

To think Lord Rowan believed he could harness and control such a being. What a nightmare he would have unleashed on the world. Sera had stopped him, but only a few would ever know of what terrible destruction she had averted.

"It is said that when he cries under the full moon, his tears contain all the magic of his lost humanity," Eithne whispered, her eyes glistening with unshed tears of her own.

"Lost humanity," Hugh repeated, his gaze thoughtful as he turned to Sera. "A dose of that might help our particular patient."

"The tears of a Nereus." Sera's mind raced as she made the connection ignited by Hugh. "Capturing those tears might reverse the effects of the entropy curse."

"Your task will not be an easy one. The loch is vast, and you must lure the creature close to the shore." Eithne pointed to Hugh with her mug. "This strong man of yours will still need to row you out deep enough to reach him."

"How do we compel such a dangerous aquatic creature to come close to shore?" Hugh asked.

"We don't. We reach out to the boy. The one who dropped his wooden horse and who cried for his mother." Sera needed to appeal to the child within...if any of him remained after fifteen centuries.

FIFTEEN

THE OLD SEER's words had woven a tapestry of mystery and destiny. The flames cast shadows upon her weathered face, accentuating each line etched by time. Echoes of the past lingered in the air, along with a haunting melancholy.

Sera leaned in closer to Eithne's campfire. "He killed so many and caused such destruction, yet I can't help feeling pity for him," she whispered to the last tiny piece of the scene as it was consumed by the fire.

"Do you think his parents had any idea how their magic would combine in their child?" Hugh asked.

"I doubt it. I'd prefer to think his parents created him out of love and ignorance. If there had been others before him, I think people would have remembered. This Nereus caused scars that remain on the land centuries later." Sera broke up a twig and tossed fragments into the flames as her thoughts roamed through time. Elowyn's words haunted her, of how childish tantrums had drained lakes and set fire to forests. How many animals and creatures had died in a moment of his anger?

And what had happened to the two druids who had created the Nereus? Sera let out a sigh and tossed the rest of the stick into the fire. "Every action and decision we make causes ripples throughout the world. Even if we don't see those consequences or realise they are there."

Hugh laced his fingers with hers and then gazed at their hands, lost in his own thoughts. "Sometimes all we can do is make the best decision we can at the time."

Sera leaned in closer to his side and closed her eyes, letting his love wash over her. Whatever journey they took in life, she would always have his strength at her side. And his calm temperament would remind her to take a breath when she wanted to lash out in anger.

"Where do we find him, Eithne?" Scotland seemed to have an abundance of lochs, and they needed to find the right one.

"The loch you seek is some fifteen miles southwest of here. Follow the River Ness upstream and you cannot miss it," Eithne whispered, her voice barely audible over the crackling fire.

"Thank you, Eithne. I have learned more here with you than I did in weeks of reading books in the mage library." A storyteller who brought words to life taught her more than a pile of dusty books. Sera rubbed her chest. The mother's anguish at luring her son into a trap still lingered under her skin.

She rose to her feet, now barely eliciting a half-opened eye from the hound. The duo bid farewell to the old woman, and the warmth of the fire was replaced by the chill of the Scottish night. But determination coursed through Sera's veins like molten steel.

Above them, the moon hung heavy in the sky.

"The moon is waxing. We have two, maybe three days until it is full and the Nereus will emerge from the depths," Sera murmured, her words frosting on the chill air.

"Even with the slowest horses, we should make fifteen miles in three days." Hugh grinned, his belief in their success undiminished.

As they returned to the bustling tavern, shadows cast by the moon slid along the cobblestone streets. Silver wisps danced a haunting ballet that mirrored the turmoil within her heart as a tiny, niggling doubt assailed her. What if Lord Rowan's horrible idea was the best choice? A Nereus wrapped in magical chains from birth, its power drawn off by others, would never unleash destruction upon the world.

She shook her head, chasing the foul idea away. Better the phantom child was never born at all than be created for such a monstrous purpose. She glanced at Hugh and, for a fleeting moment, wondered what sort of father he would be. A most patient and gentle one, she imagined.

As they entered the tavern, the noise of laughter and clinking glasses enveloped them and momentarily dulled the urgency gnawing at Sera's mind. Boisterous conversation echoed off the low-beamed ceiling, while the rich aroma of roasted meats mingled with the acrid tang of pipe smoke. The room was alive with energy as patrons huddled around tables, their faces illuminated by flickering lanterns.

Sera drank in the atmosphere. She had found many such places along her journey. Ordinary folk who, once she won them over, welcomed and sheltered her. Offering what little they had, with no expectation of anything in return. Who laboured in obscurity, and yet without them, there would be no grand homes for the nobles to live in. No magnificent feasts spread on their tables. No skilled artisans to clothe them.

These were her people and, whatever happened, she would keep them close in her heart and mind. The Fates had made her a mage for a reason—to become the champion of the people. She curled her hands into fists, and magic crackled over her knuckles.

I'm coming for you, Lord Rowan. "Three nights, and we return to London," Sera murmured, half to herself and half to Hugh. She surveyed the crowded room, searching for Gordon, the barkeep, amidst the sea of bodies.

Hugh, being taller, spotted him first as he returned to the bar with his hands full of empty pitchers. They pressed between bodies to find a space at the bar and some supper.

The burly owner caught sight of them and waved, his eyes crinkling in a warm smile. "Did ye find what ye were after?"

"Yes—Eithne told me the tale I needed to hear." Sera rapped her nails on the polished wood, thinking of what she might need for the encounter in three nights' time.

Gordon huffed a laugh and wiped his hands on his apron. "She's a canny one, for sure. Will you be off, then?"

"We leave in the morning. Could you recommend somewhere to hire horses?" Hugh asked.

Gordon said he would have horses sorted by morning, and so after they had eaten, Hugh and Sera climbed the steps once more. They would rise early and leave with the first hints of dawn. Rather than keeping her awake, Sera found the raucous noise from below helped her fall asleep. As though her mind knew she was safe with the patrons below to guard her slumber.

———◇———

THEY ROSE EARLY while the dark blanket of night still lay heavy over the town. In hushed voices, Sera and Hugh dressed, packed the few items they'd brought with them into their satchels, and crept down the stairs.

They found Gordon in the kitchen, red-eyed and clutching a mug of coffee. Silently, he poured from the pot into two mugs and handed them to Hugh and Sera. When he spoke, his voice was rough-edged with sleep.

"Horses are out back. But there's something you should know. An Englishman came in late last night, asking after a dangerous woman and showing a sketch that looks a lot like you, lass."

Sera swore under her breath while her mind raced. "How could he have found us so soon? We were protected by the Daoine Sidhe. He can't have known we came to Scotland."

Hugh set down his coffee and took Sera's from her hand before it spilled with her jerky, panicked movements. "He doesn't know. Not for sure. But think about it for a moment. You have been searching for more information about the Nereus. Lord Rowan knows exactly where that stone was found, so it is logical he might have sent someone here in case you learned about the loch."

Sera drew a shuddering breath and let Hugh's calm steady her. He was right. Lord Rowan knew she was a curious student, and it was a lucky guess that she would travel to where the Nereus had been defeated. She kissed Hugh's cheek and murmured her thanks.

"You are right. But the fact remains that one of his men is looking for me, and I am indeed here." She picked up the mug again but couldn't drink the potent brew with her mind galloping in different directions.

"We didna tell the English bastard a thing. You saved Angus's life and eased his pain. We'll no' forget that." Gordon leaned on the bar and gulped down his coffee.

"Thank you, but it is all the more reason for us to

leave. I'll not bring trouble to your doorstep." As Sera's thoughts calmed, she could drink the coffee. Although it was so strong, her heart gathered speed once more.

"We'll make sure the horses are returned to you when we have found what we seek," Hugh said. He had downed his coffee in a few large gulps and poured himself more.

Before they left, Gordon handed them some bread and cheese wrapped in cloth. "May the old gods watch over ye," he said.

They left him to return to his bed while they walked out to the stables. Dawn wasn't far off, as the inky dark of the sky lightened at the horizon. A young lad sleeping in the hay woke with a start when he heard their voices. He rubbed sleep from his eyes and grabbed bridles from their hooks. It was only a matter of minutes before both horses were saddled and led out to them.

As dawn broke over the horizon, Sera and Hugh rode out from Inverness, their horses' hooves clattering on the cobblestone streets as they left the slumbering town behind. The air was crisp, laden with the scent of dew-soaked grass and the faint whispers of wood smoke from the early-rising households.

"It's such a beautiful place. I'd love to return one day." The River Ness flowed beside them, its surface reflecting the dawning sky above.

"I'm developing a liking for haggis," Hugh said.

Sera grimaced. She didn't know how Hugh could

eat the thing. "That is *one* thing about Scotland I can live without."

As the day warmed, shadows retreated, and the world came alive with birdsong. As they followed the river, a peculiar sensation prickled at the edges of Sera's consciousness. Furrowing her brow, she glanced around to find the source.

"What is it?" Hugh asked as they pulled the horses to a halt.

"Something isn't right." Glancing around, she noticed a crow perched on a nearby branch. The bird's dark gaze seemed to bore into her very soul. She passed her reins to Hugh and then leaned forwards until she could wrap her arms around the horse's sun-warmed neck. "I'm going to see what lies behind us."

Closing her eyes, Sera extended a tendril of magic outwards as she sought the mind of the crow. Caressing its glossy feathers with a ghostly touch, she asked its permission to use its form. When the crow consented, Sera blended her mind with that of the bird. Then they took flight, soaring through the skies. As she circled the trees and river, the crow sighted three riders. They galloped along the dirt road, bent low over their mounts. The crow dived, flying close enough that Sera recognised the emblem on their cloaks—that of the Mage Council.

She thanked the crow and disconnected her mind. She experienced a moment of discomfort as her limbs became heavier and she settled back into her body.

Pushing off the horse's neck, she sat up and gathered the reins.

"Three of Lord Rowan's men are behind us. Someone in Inverness must have talked of the witch and the doctor who saved Angus's life." Sera's voice was tinged with urgency.

"It is not much of a leap to conclude we headed this way early this morning." Hugh ground his teeth. It seemed not all the locals had been impressed by his surgical skill if someone had given them up.

"We have one advantage—we know they are there. But we need to pick up our pace," Sera said.

Together, they urged their horses into a swift gallop, hooves thundering along the banks of the River Ness. As they raced onwards, Sera took in the treacherous terrain around them. The river's waters churned and roiled, crashing against the rocky shoreline with a ferocity that mirrored the urgency of their flight. Moss-covered boulders protruded from the earth like the jagged teeth of some ancient beast, while gnarled roots threatened to ensnare their horses' feet at every turn.

"Keep to higher ground. The riverbank is loose footing!" Hugh shouted, his voice barely audible over the roar of the river. He guided his horse around a treacherous outcrop.

Sera followed suit, her thoughts racing almost as fast as their steeds. Fear coiled within her, but she refused to let it overwhelm her. Instead, she channelled it into action, thinking out what to do if the men caught up to them.

As they navigated the dangerous landscape, she drew on her magic to bolster her senses and sharpen her reflexes. When they had a clear stretch before them, she reached up to the crow that had followed them and used its eyes to judge how far behind the men were.

Sera's heart pounded as they galloped along the rocky riverbank, the wind whipping through her hair and tugging at her cloak, her ears straining for the distant beat of hooves behind them.

"They'll not lay their hands on you," Hugh yelled as he glanced over his shoulder.

"Trust me, I have no intention of letting that happen," she replied, an edge of determination creeping into her tone. As she urged on her horse, she mentally ran through the different spells she knew, preparing herself for a fight if it came to that.

Hugh's horse stumbled on the uneven ground, and in the blink of an eye, he was thrown to the earth with a jarring thud. Sera pulled her horse to a halt, her eyes wide with concern as she watched Hugh struggle to his feet, wincing in pain. His horse whinnied and pawed at the ground with its front foot. It had caught the shoe and ripped off a chunk of hoof.

"Are you all right?" Sera asked both man and horse. Her voice was thick with concern as she dismounted and hurried to Hugh's side.

"Mostly," he grunted, grimacing as he rotated his shoulder. "A few scrapes and bruises, nothing serious. But the horse needs that shoe fixed before it can go on."

The sound of their pursuers grew louder, drawing ever closer, like a storm cloud on the horizon.

"We shall make a stand here, then." Sera held out her hands, a soft, ethereal light dancing over her skin as she prepared to face their adversaries head-on. The familiar hum of magic coursed through her veins, ready to be unleashed in a devastating torrent.

Twigs snapped in the forest beside them.

"Someone's there!" Dropping his horse's reins, Hugh drew the short knife he kept in his belt.

Sera sent a blast into the trees, but the orb of wind hit something and blew apart. Bits of leaf and twig were spat back at them.

"Impossible." Sera frowned and constructed another orb. This time, she laced it with electricity. When it crackled between her palms, she prepared to throw it, but Hugh grabbed her arm.

"Wait. We don't know if they are friend or foe," he said.

Sera paused as a cloaked figure emerged from the shadows. As she prepared to blast it, unconvinced by Hugh's assertion it might be a friend, the man pulled back his hood.

Relief washed through Sera. "Lord Pendlebury! Whatever are you doing here?" She shook her hands and dispersed her lightning orb, turning it into fireflies that scattered into the sky.

The older mage was a friend. The Mage Council had sent him to Scotland some months ago on a mission. She had no idea he was still lurking in the

Highlands and assumed he had returned to London before Christmas.

"I have been engrossed in my studies with the Daoine Sidhe and quite forgot the passage of time. I sensed another mage nearby, and curiosity drew me here. Why on earth are you galloping through here, Lady Winyard?" He clutched a gnarled staff and squinted down the track behind them.

"Lord Rowan had me declared a traitor, and his men are in pursuit. We sought to outrun them, but Hugh's horse has come up lame." Even as she spoke, the lead rider rounded a distant bend in the path.

"Well, I am sure we can sort them out between us." Lord Pendlebury winked. Then he raised his staff and summoned a thick veil of mist, pulling the tendrils from the river. Dense fog that rivalled the notorious pea soups of London soon muffled the sound of horses' hooves and left them draped in a clotted cream miasma.

"That will slow them down a little while we create a larger distraction," the older mage said.

"Perhaps a version of me they can chase in a different direction?" Sera suggested.

Lord Pendlebury's eyes sparkled with mischief. "An excellent idea. Shall we?"

He whispered an incantation that took form before him. Sera let her magic flow into the spell. Their power swirled together, and the image grew stronger and larger. They added layers, and the illusion became solid and lifelike. Then they created another to resemble Hugh.

The replica Sera took up the reins of her ethereal horse. The phantom Hugh did likewise. Keeping them obscured by the thick fog, they pushed the spirit riders through the mist. Voices shouted as they were sighted. Adding to the spell, Sera and Lord Pendlebury sent their creations along a different path, drawing the pursuers through the forest and away to the north.

As the sounds of pursuit faded, Sera allowed herself a moment of relief. They had bought themselves some time.

Sixteen

"That should keep them busy for at least a day. Two, given they will have to retrace their steps." Lord Pendlebury chuckled. "Now, I have a camp not far away. We can trade horses, Mr Miles, and I will ask the Daoine Sidhe if their farrier can put that shoe back on."

With a wave of his staff, Lord Pendlebury released the thick mist back to the surface of the river. They led the horses through the forest until they came across a clearing where Lord Pendlebury must have spent the night. His campfire still crackled. A horse was tied to a tree, and it lifted its head to nicker at the newcomers.

"Now that you have a little time, perhaps you can tell me why, exactly, you are a traitor to the crown?" Lord Pendlebury invited them to settle around the fire, his gaze intent upon her face.

Sera hesitated, her heart heavy with the weight of so many secrets. But she trusted Lord Pendlebury. Taking a deep breath, she recounted the horrifying details of Lord Rowan's scheme. How years ago, he had placed the amulet around the king's neck that tormented his mind and allowed Rowan to seize power as regent. Licking dry lips, she added his vile idea to have Lord Tomlin abuse her body to breed another Nereus so that he might use its power to be young again and wield unimaginable magic that would make him invincible.

When Sera finished, the polite and mild-mannered Lord Pendlebury swore in such a creative fashion that even Hugh blushed. Then the surgeon frowned, and Sera suspected he was considering whether such things as Lord Pendlebury wished upon Lord Rowan might be anatomically possible.

"I—I—" Polite words wouldn't form on Lord Pendlebury's tongue. He shook his head and rubbed his hands through his hair before he could speak. "I did not know. This is more ghastly than anything I could imagine. All this time, it has been dark magic wielded by Lord Rowan that has plagued the king?" He blew out a sigh.

"He has fooled many, all while he waited for me to grow to maturity as the final piece in his hideous scheme." A coldness grew inside Sera. She had once thought Lord Rowan a kindly mentor and had even wished that he could have raised her. Now she thanked the Fates that Lord Branvale had been appointed her guardian instead.

Lord Pendlebury stirred the fire with a long stick. "This would also explain the stories about the monster in the loch. I wonder why someone has locked away and kept so much of our history from us. When we consider knowledge dangerous, we create more dangers by limiting who knows about such things. You have my word, Lady Winyard; I will help you in whatever way I can."

"Thank you," she whispered, her gratitude fierce and heartfelt. "I fear the Mage Council is under his control and I have few allies left."

"Ah," he murmured, a sly smile playing on his lips, "you might have more allies in the council than you realise. There are those who still value loyalty, justice, and the greater good above all else. Even if they think you are a troublesome girl."

Sera snorted. He couldn't possibly mean Lord Ormsby. The man despised her. Didn't he?

"Will you share a meal with me before we go our separate ways? I have plenty for us all, and the loch is only a few miles away. You'll reach it by dusk." Lord Pendlebury rose and retrieved the items set beside his bedroll.

One of them was what appeared to be a frozen block of something brown and orange that he dropped into a pot. Soon they all had a bowl of nourishing stew with chunks of carrot—which explained the orange blobs—warming their hands.

The flicker of the campfire warmed Sera's face as she sat between Hugh and Lord Pendlebury swapping tales. The heat from the fire seeped into her bones, providing a comforting respite from the chill of the damp air. Their laughter rose in harmony with the crackling flames, filling the stillness as they talked.

"I assure you, Lady Winyard, I was a horrible child. Did I ever tell you about the time I turned Lord Rowan's robes into a flock of pigeons?" Lord Pendlebury had a distinct twinkle in his eye as he recalled the memory.

"I refuse to believe it, my lord. You are far too kind to have done anything like that." Sera couldn't reconcile the badly behaved lad with the very proper mage who sat across from her at their council table.

"It was quite the spectacle," he began, grinning widely. "You see, he had been terribly condescending that day, lecturing me on the importance of restraint in magic. So, naturally, I decided to prove him wrong."

Hugh leaned in, his arm resting against hers, offering the steady presence she had come to rely upon. "What happened next?" he asked.

"With a flick of my wrist, I transformed his robes into a flurry of feathers and beaks," the older mage recounted, his voice tinged with pride. "It took him hours to round them all up and restore his dignity. Not to mention the droppings everywhere!"

As the laughter died down, Lord Pendlebury's expression grew serious, and his gaze met Sera's with an earnest intensity. "I am fully committed to your cause. You have shown extraordinary courage and resolve. I will do all I can to ensure this curse is lifted from the king."

"Thank you, my lord. Lord Rowan thought to

isolate me, but I am gathering friends to my side," Sera said, her voice thick with gratitude.

Lord Pendlebury reached out and squeezed her forearm. "If we are done here, I shall pack up and start for London immediately. Once I have taken the horse to the fairy folk, I shall summon a willing kelpie to carry me south, making my journey quicker."

"Won't you get wet? Or drown?" Hugh was clearly pondering the many ways a person could die out in the rough seas.

The older mage winked. "I have a handy spell for when I travel by kelpie. It adds a waterproof layer around me and contains air to breathe."

Hugh moved his saddlebags to Lord Pendlebury's horse, and they helped the mage break camp and store everything in the bags now carried by Hugh's lame mount.

"We shall meet again, Lady Winyard, in London. Lord Rowan will not succeed, and I shall have a quiet word with Lord Ormsby." With one last look, he gathered the reins in one hand, then mage and horse walked deeper into the forest.

Sera and Hugh led their mounts through the dense growth until they reached open ground beside the river. Only then did they climb into their saddles and carry on their way. As the gloaming settled over the landscape, they reached the place where the River Ness flowed into the loch.

"Now where?" Hugh asked as they paused and marvelled at the beauty and size of the loch.

Sera rubbed her hands up her arms to dispel a chill. "A little further. If you lead my horse, I will find the right spot."

She passed the reins to Hugh and then closed her eyes. As the horses picked their way along the shore, Sera let her magic drift away from her like ripples in a pool. With arms spread wide, she let her other senses explore their surroundings.

When a prickling sensation erupted along her arms and jolted down her spine, she gasped and called, "Stop!"

Hugh turned around in his saddle, a question in his eyes.

"Here. It happened here." She dismounted and walked over the rocky ground. The forest huddled not far away, leaving only twenty to thirty feet of rocky shoreline before reaching the water.

Hugh watched as she walked back and forth, staring at the still loch.

"Silly, I know, but I thought I would *see* something. A great magical battle occurred here that created a fracture in the Fae realm and turned a boy into an eternal aquatic creature. And yet...nothing remains except a chill down my spine." She stared at the stones under her boots. Many of the pebbles looked like the one set in silver and worn around the king's neck. Picking one at random, Sera curled her fingers around it. It did not attempt to draw her into the cold, black void of the entropy stone.

"Let's make camp here and wait for the moon to rise." Hugh led the horses up to the sheltering trees.

"We will need a boat, too, to row out to the Nereus." Sera gestured to the vast expanse of the loch. She could hardly collect tears from here on the shore if the creature swam out there in the middle of the loch.

"Why don't you start a fire, and I'll go for a wander and see what I can find. There looks to be something on the rocks further down." Hugh tied the reins to a low-hanging branch and then set off.

Sera removed the saddles and rubbed the horses down with handfuls of grass. Then she gathered wood for a fire. By the time she heard splashing, she had a pot of water heating over the flames.

Hugh rowed into view, pulling the oars of a battered dinghy. Once close to shore, he hopped out and hauled the boat up onto the stones.

"Where did you find that?" Sera asked as he dropped to the ground next to her and stretched out wet boots to the fire.

"There were three boats further along, and what looks like an abandoned cottage in the trees. The other two were holed, as though they had been dashed on the rocks. I tried my luck with that little one and can report that for all its decrepitude, it didn't spring a leak." He unlaced his boots and wriggled his toes in damp socks.

Sera held her hands over his legs and encouraged the water to leave the fabric of his trousers and sink into the earth.

As evening fell, the soft lapping of water provided a soothing backdrop to their wait. Sera leaned against the trunk of a tree and let her thoughts swirl in anticipation. Would they be able to form a connection with the ancient aquatic beast, or would they be met with unyielding hostility? Her certainty of a successful outcome was now as insubstantial as the shadows dancing around the campsite.

She opened her eyes. "I need a horse."

Hugh gestured to the ones dozing under the trees. "We have two."

"No, a toy horse. Help me find a suitable piece of wood." It took them another hour to scour the forest floor and find a fallen branch that met Sera's requirements.

Hugh hauled it back to the campsite for her and startled the horses with the slithering noise it made as he emerged from the trees.

Sera laid her hands on the thick end of the branch and closed her eyes. She whispered to the earth goddess, asking for her help to shape the timber. The wood shimmered and shook under her fingertips, and she hoped she wouldn't get splinters in her palms. In her mind, she kept the image that Eithne had shown of the boy with the precious toy at his feet.

When the hunk of tree stopped moving, she opened her eyes. She now held a horse, approximately ten inches high. Its mane was carved in exquisite detail. The horse possessed a noble head, and all over its body were tiny Celtic knots and other symbols.

"I say, that is marvellous work. Have you ever

considered leaving the council and becoming a toy maker?" Hugh reached out and traced a swirl on the horse's rump.

"I'm hoping it will show the Nereus we mean him no harm and perhaps remind him of who he used to be." Sera caressed the horse's side, the wood warm, as though it were a thing of flesh and blood.

"That reminds me, I have something for you." Hugh pulled a leather object from his jacket. Unrolling one side, he revealed small vials all snuggled into leather compartments. Tugging one free, he held it out to Sera. "For catching the tears. Although I'm not sure what quantity of tears a Nereus sheds. Perhaps we should have taken a tankard from the pub or a bucket."

Sera took the little stoppered bottle. "I suspect he does not cry many if they are such a rare and valuable thing."

Night pulled her midnight mantle over the river and land. Sera nestled against Hugh, their hands intertwined as they waited for the moon to rise and illuminate the wide expanse of the loch.

"Are you nervous?" Hugh asked softly, his voice barely audible above the gentle lapping of the water.

"Terrified," Sera admitted, her gaze fixed on the dark sky. "But also...exhilarated. Imagine, Hugh—we will see the Nereus. A child born centuries ago and transformed into a creature. And, the Fates willing, we will find a cure for King George."

As the stars emerged, their pinpricks of light reflected on the surface of Loch Ness. Sera's thoughts turned inwards. If she could form a bond with the Nereus, it would set their mission on a path to success. But if they failed…

Slowly, like a shy woman removing her clothing on her wedding night, the moon peeked over the horizon. Dancing behind clouds, the glowing orb ascended, casting its silvery light across the landscape.

Sera and Hugh walked to the water's edge, peering at every ripple. Shadows glided over the surface, each movement playing tricks on her imagination, until—

"There!" Hugh exclaimed, pointing.

Sera's breath caught in her chest, her instincts screaming at her to flee at what rose from the water. In size, it was comparable to the dragon Ebonfyre but more snake-like. As the figure swam, it revealed a sinuous form that cut through the water with grace and power. It was unlike anything Sera had ever seen—a mixture of beauty and terror that left her in awe.

As she watched the creature glide back and forth in the moonlight, Sera felt an inexplicable pull, as though she were being drawn into its ancient, mysterious world. A shiver ran down her spine, cold and electric, igniting a fire within her that burned away all traces of doubt about what she had to do next.

Her fingers tightened around the wooden horse, its intricately carved form pressing into her flesh as she clutched it to her chest. She had intended for the toy to be a symbol, a reminder of the innocence that the fearsome creature had once possessed. Now it seemed tiny, like a fly compared to an elephant.

"What happens now?" Hugh whispered, his gaze locked on the enormous creature making lazy circles out in the cold depths.

"I try to lure it closer to shore." She drew in a breath, filling her lungs with the cool night air, and then sang.

The haunting melody of the lullaby danced across the stillness of the night. Each note reached out, seeking the heart of the Nereus, urging it to come closer, to remember, to trust.

Sera sang an ancient lullaby taught to her by Liriel on the trip north from London. Reverence filled her as the Nereus moved through the water, its body undulating across the surface. It was a living legend, a creature spoken of in hushed whispers and depicted in ancient myths. Sera could hardly believe she was serenading the lost child.

"Don't stop. It's beautiful." Hugh's hand found hers, giving it a reassuring squeeze.

Sera let the eerie song continue to flow from her lips, each word resonating through the creature to reawaken its lost humanity. The Nereus paused, its great luminous eyes fixed on her as though it searched her soul to judge her sincerity and purpose.

Only then did it swim nearer to shore, its immense presence casting a shadow over the water like a living eclipse. Sera's heart raced, beating faster with every inch the creature advanced. The wooden horse seemed to grow heavier in her grasp, as if it, too, understood the gravity of this moment.

Some thirty feet from shore, the Nereus halted. Its gaze never left Sera's face. Reaching out with her magic, she found a mixture of curiosity and loneliness shimmering around the creature.

"Hello, I have brought you a present," Sera said, her voice clear on the still night air. She held out the wooden horse. The Nereus arched its head closer, and then it blinked.

"Will it be safe to try the boat?" Hugh murmured.

"There is only one way to find out." She wanted to make a quip about being a mage and able to defend them. But the creature before them had nearly defeated all the druids in England before they turned his power against him. Sera didn't want to find out if the boy deep inside could still wield magic or not.

Hugh helped her into the small, weathered dinghy he had found earlier in the day. Its wooden planks creaked beneath their weight, and a musty scent hung in the air. Sera settled herself on one of the damp bench seats, her gaze fixed on the Nereus. Hugh pushed the boat into the water before he hopped in and took up the oars.

Sera clutched the wooden horse so tightly against her chest that the carved details dug into her skin. Her blood thrummed in her ears, joining the hoots of an owl that carried on the cool evening air. The silver moonlight illuminated the Nereus, its majestic form reflected on the mirror-like surface of the loch.

At her nod, Hugh rowed them out to where the creature waited.

SEVENTEEN

SERA SAT in the prow and held the toy horse before her like an offering.

The oars slid through the water like silk, the only sound in the otherwise tranquil night. Ripples spread out around them. Stars were reflected in the inky water, and Sera imagined they glided among them in the sky.

As they ventured further from the safety of the stony shore, the vast expanse of water stretched out before them, offering no escape should the Nereus prove to be hostile. Sera's breathing grew shallow, and her pulse quickened as the creature loomed ever closer. It was immense—far larger than she had first perceived from the shore.

"Good god. It's the size of a cottage," Hugh muttered, his oars pausing in mid-stroke as he took in the Nereus's size.

A rather comfortable cottage with at least two storeys, Sera thought.

As the boat drew alongside the colossal creature, it turned its attention to them, its silver eyes piercing the darkness. The air crackled with tension, and fear clawed at Sera's throat like an icy hand. Would they be destroyed or accepted?

As the Nereus towered over them, it cast a shadow that seemed to swallow the world. It lowered its enormous head towards Sera and Hugh, a curious glint in its ancient eyes. In that moment, Sera's heart swelled with hope as she glimpsed beyond the creature's intimidating exterior to the soul hidden beneath.

"I imagine it has been a long time since anyone sang to you," she said, her words tinged with sadness.

The Nereus regarded her with an air of cautious acceptance, its nostrils flaring as it caught the scent of the wooden horse clutched tightly in her hands. The toy seemed almost comically small compared to the magnificent beast before them. Sera glanced at Hugh, whose eyes were wide with awe, his jaw hanging slack and open.

"I made this for you. Do you remember having one?" Sera extended the wooden horse towards the Nereus.

The air was heavy with anticipation as the Nereus's face drew closer to the wooden horse. Sera held her breath even as her heart thumped faster. As the creature's massive snout nudged the toy, a shiver raced down her spine. Her magic entwined with the soul of the Nereus, and they established a connection. Intrigue rippled over the creature as it examined the horse with its nose.

"Once, you were a little boy who played with his wooden horse." Sera spoke in a soft tone. "I know you've suffered for a long time. I would help you if I could."

The Nereus studied the wooden horse. The creature's huge eyes glistened with a mixture of curiosity that turned into sorrow. A shimmering veil dropped over its gaze as an inner eyelid blinked.

"It's for you." She held the toy aloft.

The Nereus hesitated for a moment, as if unsure what to do. Then it extended a massive flipper and cradled the wooden horse against its side with a tenderness that belied its fearsome appearance. The creature arched its sinuous neck and emitted a heart-wrenching cry that filled the night and echoed across the loch. It was a sound of pure despair, as long-forgotten memories resurfaced and filled the ancient beast with both joy and pain. Sera shivered, struck by the raw vulnerability that radiated from the Nereus.

She kept her connection with the creature as its mind spiralled back through millennia to when it was a boy. One who had been loved and innocent. Before he had stained his soul with the lives he had taken. A time when he had been free, unburdened by the weight of centuries imprisoned in the dark depths of the loch.

As its cry reverberated through Sera's body, the

Nereus's tears began to fall. Fat, crystalline droplets that shimmered with an ethereal beauty.

She reached for the glass vial in her pocket and pulled out the stopper. Leaning out of the dinghy, she placed one hand on a wet but warm side and held the vial aloft.

"Could you lower your head, please?" she asked.

Its eyes closed, and the Nereus bent its head towards the sound of her voice. Sera caught the tears in the vial, each like a glistening pearl, the next melding into the previous droplet, until the bottle held a universe of emotions within it.

Once it was full, she stoppered the vial and passed it back to Hugh. Then she placed both hands on the blunt snout and pressed her cheek to that of what had once been a boy. "Thank you. I promise that if there is a way, I will have your sentence ended so that you can live out a mortal lifespan."

Perhaps Sera imagined it, but she thought the soul of the boy's mother settled over her. A mother who mourned a child who had been too powerful to allow to live. She pressed a kiss to the scaled face, and her lips touched the soft, rounded cheek of a child.

The Nereus opened its eyes and blinked away the last few tears, which fell into the water like diamonds dropping into a bottomless well. Slowly, so as not to create a wave that would capsize the little dinghy, the Nereus turned and swam a short distance before slipping beneath the surface and vanishing from sight.

Sera stood with her hands curled around the edge

of the dinghy long after the Nereus had returned to its watery home. "Poor child," she murmured. "Punished for what he did, and yet...it doesn't sit right with me."

Hugh rowed them back to shore. "Blaming the boy seems like raging at a storm or earthquake that steals lives."

"Yes. What he did was more like a terrible natural disaster, not the actions of a cold-blooded killer or a mage using dark magic with evil intent." What had happened to his parents? Had they been punished for their actions, or was losing their child the worst thing that could have befallen them?

There were many secrets Sera would hunt out in two very different hidden libraries when she had the time. When she was no longer deemed a traitor.

Moonlight played upon the gently undulating water as Sera's heart ached with a bittersweet mix of hope and sorrow. The icy tendrils of the wind teased at her hair, but she barely noticed, for the warmth of Hugh's presence before her was enough to banish the chill from her bones.

"Nearly there," he murmured. His broad shoulders rippled beneath his coat as he rowed with steady, powerful strokes.

Sera hopped from the little vessel as they ran up on the gravel, the wooden hull scraping against pebbles with a gentle rasp. She helped Hugh drag the boat up to higher ground. The owner might return and look for it and wouldn't appreciate having to retrieve it from the middle of the loch.

Standing at the water's edge, Sera gazed out over the rippling surface. She had the tears and a way to reverse the effects of the entropy curse that tormented the king.

"I never thought I'd help you catch the tears of a mythical creature," Hugh mused, his eyes on the horizon where the Nereus had disappeared minutes earlier.

"And you have not known me for an entire year yet. Imagine what adventures we will have in the years to come." Sera reached out and took his hand.

Hugh caressed her cheek and cupped her nape. "I'm imagining things we could do right now," he murmured before placing a heated kiss on her lips.

Their love for one another ignited like a spark in the darkness. The world around them fell away, leaving only the heat of their connection and the overwhelming sense of belonging to each other.

Sera's heart raced, her breath coming in shallow gasps as she gazed into Hugh's eyes, shimmering with desire and longing. Amidst the chaos and danger, what a gift it was to steal a moment for themselves.

"It makes sense to stay here tonight. But what should we do until dawn?" She sucked in her bottom lip, swollen from Hugh's kisses.

With a grin that made her heart flutter, Hugh swept Sera into his arms and carried her effortlessly towards their camp under the sheltering trees. Her body was weightless as he cradled her against his broad chest and strode confidently through the shadows.

Hugh gently placed her on a blanket beside the fire. Their bodies entwined as they surrendered to their desires. The warmth of his skin seeped into her own, banishing the chill of the night air as they explored each other with reverent touches and whispered endearments.

The full moon bathed them in an ethereal light as they exposed as much bare skin to the cold as they dared. Time seemed to slow. The world beyond their embrace faded into insignificance, leaving only the two of them moving together in perfect harmony. The whisper of leaves and the murmur of lapping water provided a gentle accompaniment to their passion.

Eventually, spent and breathless, they collapsed onto the blanket, limbs still entangled, hearts beating in unison. For a while, they lay in silence, gazing up at the stars that glittered like diamonds in the velvet expanse of the sky.

"Look, there." Sera pointed to a constellation she recognised. "That's the Archer, guiding us by his bow."

As they lay there, the world held its breath, waiting for dawn to break and herald a new day. Rolling in Hugh's arms, Sera stared into his eyes and was struck by the depth of devotion that shimmered there, a fierce and unwavering loyalty that sent shivers down her spine. She only hoped she deserved such love and wasn't about to lead him to his doom in a battle she couldn't win.

"Stop worrying," he murmured as he wound a strand of her hair around his fingers.

"How do you know I'm worrying?" She flung herself across his chest.

"I suspect a part of you never stops. Concern for others and this country always simmers in the corners of your mind." He tapped the side of her head with a gentle touch.

"Are we not the same in that way?" With her cheek pressed to his chest, she listened to the steady beat of his heart.

"I worry about my patients *singularly*. You seem intent on worrying about everyone." He huffed a soft laugh that made her head rise and fall.

"I was made this way for a reason. I will help as many people as I can while I walk this earth." She rolled back over and grabbed the other blanket, pulling it over them to shield their sleep from the chill bite of lingering winter. Then she cast a warming bubble around them.

Inverness was significantly colder than London.

THE SUN BEGAN its ascent and painted the sky in hues of orange and pink. Sera's eyes fluttered open, and the sight of Hugh's peaceful profile greeted her, his chest rising and falling gently with each breath. A pang of reluctance tugged at her heart as she considered rousing him from sleep. However, their journey to

London could not be delayed. With great care, Sera disentangled herself from Hugh's embrace, her fingertips lingering on his warm skin for a moment longer than necessary.

Standing, Sera watched as the morning light kissed the surface of Loch Ness, leaving a trail of sparkling ripples in its wake. Where did the Nereus go when the sun was high in the sky? Did the creature have a lair somewhere in the depths, or was local lore right, and it had a way out to the greater freedom of the ocean?

They broke camp, rolled up blankets to secure behind their saddles, and stuffed items into saddlebags. Sera's gaze skimmed over the flattened grasses, a fleeting reminder of their passionate union. Even now, the blades sought to stand upright once more.

Before they set off, Sera pulled out the map Liriel had given her. Its edges were worn and creased, as though it had guided countless travellers before her. Sera's fingers brushed against the soft parchment. The intricate lines and symbols wove a story of ancient pathways and hidden gates. She could sense the whispers of magic imbued within the very fibres of the paper.

She determined a path for their journey, jumping between rings that were as close to each other as possible. A trip south that normally took a week might be achieved in a day or two. The last jump landed them a distance from London, but there would be more traffic, and some farmer might offer them a ride in his cart. Or Kitty could send Elliot with fresh horses.

"Where to?" Hugh asked, peering over her shoulder, their bodies pressed close together as they stood beneath the sheltering boughs of a great oak.

"Here." She tapped a small mark on the map with her finger. "It's the closest ring to where we are now, and in the opposite direction to where my ethereal doppelgänger sent Lord Rowan's men."

Hugh's brow furrowed momentarily. "What will happen to the horses? Can they travel by fairy ring?"

"No. Probably not." It would be cruel to leave the animals tied to a tree. "I can sense the Daoine Sidhe all around here. I will ask them to send the horses back to Inverness." Closing her eyes, she focused on the words she needed, shaping them into a magical message, asking the fairy folk to please take care of the equines. Then she dispersed her note so that it filtered through the trees.

Once done, Sera placed her foot in the stirrup and swung up into the saddle. She kicked her horse into a trot as they rode along the shores of the loch for a distance. Then they veered into the forest. Branches reached for them and snagged on their clothing. Sera had to stop and glare at the trees, in case they uprooted themselves and advanced, like the magical ones in Bumblefoot Forest.

The horses navigated narrow paths, the dappled sunlight filtering through the canopy above, casting playful shadows across the forest floor. From time to time, she pulled out the map and checked their bearings. A star on the map that represented them moved across the parchment.

"It's not too far now," she said.

Taking the lead, Sera nudged her horse onward, stepping over fallen trees and around others. Hooves crunched softly on the leaf-strewn floor. The surrounding forest seemed to hush, as if the very trees leaned in to listen to their conversation.

Always they followed a narrow track, worn into the earth by hundreds of feet, of all sizes and varieties, over time. As they ventured deeper into the forest, the shadows lengthened, their fingers reaching out to brush against Sera's skin. She shivered, though not from cold; there was an otherworldly energy pulsating through the air, as though the very fabric of reality were thinning. They were close to the portal.

The trees opened out into a grassy clearing. In the middle grew a perfect circle of mushrooms. Their spotted orange caps glistened like pearls in the sun and seemed to beckon them closer. There was no denying the magic that emanated from this ancient formation, its power resonating within her very core.

Sera dismounted and tied her horse to a nearby tree. Hugh did the same. Then they took the saddlebags and blankets and swung them over their shoulders.

Hugh stared at the mushrooms. "I promise not to eat these ones."

As they approached the circle, a figure stepped from the shadows. A boy no older than fifteen, with wild, unkempt hair and eyes of such a startling blue they seemed to pierce straight through Sera.

"I'm here for the horses," he called, his voice surprisingly deep despite his youthful appearance. He unlaced the reins and held both sets in one hand.

"Thank you. We are grateful for your assistance," Sera said.

With a last glance at their equine companions, Sera took Hugh's hand and approached the gateway. A strange energy pulsed through the air. The hairs on the back of her neck stood on end, and a shiver ran down her spine. They stepped over the mushrooms, and the surrounding air shimmered and rippled, like water disturbed by a thrown stone. A tingling sensation enveloped their bodies, as if a thousand tiny sparks danced upon their skin. Sera took a deep breath, drawing in the heady scent of damp earth and dew-kissed grass, her heart pounding with anticipation.

Holding the map in one hand, she kept a tight grip on Hugh with the other. She focused on the next spot that would jump them down the country. Then she whispered the incantation Liriel had taught her.

Sera closed her eyes and uttered the ancient words, her voice barely audible above the rustling leaves of the glade. The syllables slipped over her lips like water tumbling across smooth stones, resonating with a magic that was far older than the words of mortal men.

As the final syllable left her mouth, the air crackled with electricity, and then a cloud dropped over them and the world went dark.

Eighteen

Their bodies were weightless, suspended in an otherworldly space where time itself seemed to hold its breath.

"By Jove, it's like flying," breathed Hugh, his voice echoing strangely in the void.

Sera grasped his hand tighter. At least travelling by fairy ring didn't involve the choking, dirt-filled whirlwind of stepping across Shadowvane. They whooshed through a night painted in shades of black, deep ocean blue, and granite grey. Suddenly, as quickly as it had begun, the transport came to an abrupt halt.

Sera's body was dumped onto solid ground in an untidy pile of limbs and luggage. Pushing Hugh's thigh off her legs, she found her satchel. Then her feet, her legs oddly heavy. They stumbled, disoriented and breathless, out of the fairy ring. They exited an identical circle of mushrooms surrounded by greenery that was lush in comparison to that of their entry point.

Sera steadied herself against a nearby tree trunk and laid a hand on Hugh's arm. "Are you unscathed?"

"That was incredible," he replied, his eyes sparkling with exhilaration.

Sera drew out the map from under her stays and unfolded the worn parchment. Her fingers brushed over the markings of the fairy ring they had used. A moment later, the ink seemed to vanish like smoke, leaving behind only a faint trace of their magical journey.

"Is that supposed to happen?" Hugh peered over her shoulder.

"Yes. Liriel said each ring can only be used once. The map will erase our path as we travel." Sera squinted at the map to make out their new location. The tiny star that represented them had shot south when she unfolded the map, and now it settled in one spot. "We appear to be near Edinburgh."

Hugh let out a low whistle. "We have travelled over a hundred and fifty miles in a few heartbeats. But we are still in Scotland."

"We have a bit of a walk to the next fairy ring, which should take us to north Yorkshire." Sera checked her bearings and the direction in which they needed to go, then folded the map and tucked it away again.

"I assume we won't be going into Edinburgh." Hugh gazed at the distant spires that pierced the horizon. Perhaps he was thinking about the city's reputation for medical discoveries.

"No. But we might pass a village on the way where we can buy something to eat," Sera said.

They set off, walking in comfortable silence. Sunlight coming through the bare trees dappled their faces. The countryside was alive with the twittering of birds and the gentle whisper of the wind through the trees. It was a symphony of life that sang in harmony with the magic coursing through her veins.

Scotland, she thought with a smile, was truly a paradise for those who could sense its wonders.

They skirted the edges of the city, where brick homes became smaller stone cottages clustered together. Edinburgh might be a haven for women like Sera, but it was also a place where shadows lurked, and danger waited just around the corner.

Past the cottages, the land opened out in meadows where sheep grazed quietly.

Hugh paused and drew a deep breath, then let it out in a sigh.

"Whatever have you caught the smell of?" Sera asked, laughter tinging her words.

"Apple pie." He grinned and drew her closer to the sheep.

A river cut through the field, and a farmer sat on the bank. His weathered face broke into a grin as he waved them over. "Ye look weary from yer travels," he called out. "Come share my wife's pie. There's more than enough for all."

Sera's stomach rumbled as she eyed the steaming

pastry the man had set out. "We would much appreciate such a kindness, sir."

As they sat down beside the man, Hugh murmured his thanks, his eyes darting to where the farmer's sheep were grazing nearby. The animals seemed content, their woolly coats keeping them warm from the winter snows. Yet, as Sera studied them more closely, she noticed something amiss. Mounds of dung clung to the wool around their hindquarters, causing discomfort and irritation.

The farmer sliced the pie and handed pieces to Hugh and Sera.

She bit into the buttery pastry, and tart apple exploded across her tongue. As she chewed happily, savouring each mouthful, Sera focused on the grazing sheep. Between mouthfuls of pie, she murmured ancient words under her breath. Bit by bit, dung detached itself from the wool and dropped to the ground. The sheep bleated in surprise and relief, kicking up their heels as if to thank her.

"By the heavens, lass!" the farmer exclaimed, his eyes wide with amazement as the sheep bounced past him, all with tidy bottoms. "Ye've saved me an entire afternoon's work of dagging. Thank ye!"

"I am merely repaying one generosity with another," Sera replied before she took another mouthful of pie.

As they chatted about the weather and local gossip, Sera's heart warmed. A simple act of kindness between strangers was a reminder of why she fought so fiercely for ordinary people. Lord Rowan would crush them under his boot and turn them back into serfs if his horrid vision came into being.

With their bellies full, Sera and Hugh bid the grateful farmer farewell and continued on their journey. The forest soon closed around them, a silent witness to their passage. Sera's senses were alert, her magic reaching out for the next fairy ring.

"Here," she whispered as they stumbled upon a circle of mushrooms nestled in a grove. The air hummed with energy, ancient and potent.

Hugh made sure the saddlebags were comfortable around his shoulders. Then he reached for her hand. She squeezed it gently as they stepped into the circle. Once again, the air rippled with electricity around them. Holding the map in her hand, Sera concentrated on the next jump point and whispered the incantation.

The world dropped away from under their feet, and they were suspended, weightless, as the country shifted around them. Then they were tossed to the ground once more, their bodies once again seeming heavier than usual. The sensation took a few moments to disperse, time Sera used to check the map and visualise the next fairy ring.

When they left the embrace of the forest and followed a packed earth road, they came upon a tiny village, its buildings huddled together like newly shorn sheep seeking warmth.

"Welcome to Middlesbrough," Sera murmured, scanning their surroundings. A wary undercurrent drifted through the air, and whispers seemed to echo from every corner.

As they ventured deeper into the village, Sera couldn't shake a sense of foreboding that danger lurked around the corner. She kept muttering *Middlesbrough* under her breath, the name nagging at her as she tried to dredge up a memory. When she did, she stopped in her tracks and grabbed Hugh's arm.

"Lord Dench," she whispered, scanning the buildings for any locals listening to her words.

Hugh frowned, then recognition lit his features. "He's a mage?"

Sera nodded. "He has an estate around here and is an ally of Lord Rowan."

"We are travellers passing through, like any other." With his hand at her elbow, Hugh kept them walking along the main street.

What villagers they passed whispered behind cupped hands and cast furtive glances at the newcomers. Sera gripped the edges of her cloak tightly as a shiver that had nothing to do with the cool breeze ran down her spine.

Up ahead appeared a tavern, a tired-looking sheep painted on the sign swinging over the door. But it wasn't the peeling ewe that caught Sera's attention, but the large handbill nailed to the door.

Bearing a picture of her. And underneath, in large bold letters: TRAITOR!

"Oh," was Hugh's only comment on seeing it. Then he squinted. "It's quite a good likeness."

Sera glared at him. "No wonder the locals are treating us like thieves. Let's move on. The sooner we are out of here, the sooner we can reach the next portal."

The tension in the air was thick as they walked past shuttered windows and closed doors. From beyond seeped the murmur of uneasy voices. A crowd formed in their wake, following at a distance, but clearly intent on keeping them under watchful eyes. Fear and hostility were etched on their faces, and the villagers seemed poised to pounce at the slightest provocation.

"We most definitely want to be gone before things escalate." Hugh rested a hand protectively on her shoulder.

"Lord Dench has poisoned these people against me," she whispered. Were these handbills posted in every town in England?

With each step they took through the village, the weight of the locals' suspicion grew heavier, pressing down on Sera like a physical burden. But she couldn't blame them for their mistrust. They were simply pawns in a game far beyond their understanding.

As they reached the end of the main street, a door slammed shut. Then came a thud as a bolt was rammed into place. The people were locking their families inside for whatever came next. A crowd of men blocked the path behind them. They could only go forwards into what was feeling like a trap.

Then horses trotted up, pulling a carriage that halted and blocked the road. A portly man stepped down. Lord Dench. Clad in his blue cloak adorned with stars and a matching pointy hat, he was every inch the storybook mage. His cold eyes seemed to bore into her soul, the mask of civility he wore at the council table now stripped away.

"Well, well, well. Look what rabbit ran into my trap. The traitorous Seraphina Winyard," Lord Dench said with a sneer, his voice dripping with disdain. "My people informed me of your presence here. At first, I couldn't believe you'd be so stupid as to cross my lands, yet here you are."

Men stepped from the shadows and nearby trees to form a group before the mage. All of them were armed with farm tools and makeshift weapons. A militia drawn from those who worked the land. They eyed Sera and Hugh warily, their hands gripping their weapons.

Sera's magic surged within her, crying out for her to use it against those who dared threaten her and Hugh.

"Step aside, Lord Dench. We are merely passing through on our way to London," Sera said, her voice level and calm despite the danger crackling in the air.

"I'll not step aside. Not when I can take you to London myself and claim the pretty prize your head will bring." An ugly sneer twisted Lord Dench's features.

He took a menacing step forwards. Sera held her ground. Her anger flared, and she instinctively raised her hands, ready to unleash her fury upon him. But Hugh's hand on her arm stopped her short.

"Do not become a Nereus," he whispered in her ear, his breath warm against her skin. "These people are innocent."

Sera clenched her fists, her nails digging into her palms as she struggled to keep her magic in check. Hugh was right. Lashing out in anger would have unintended consequences on all those around her. To harm these people would make her the very monster she sought to defeat.

Sera forced herself to remain composed despite the tremors of anger coursing through her. "I have no wish to harm your people, Lord Dench. We will leave this village peacefully, or I will remove you if you stand in my way."

"Is that so?" Lord Dench replied, his eyes narrowing as he regarded her with an air of malevolent amusement. "Very well then, *girl*. Show me what you can do."

With a theatrical flourish, Lord Dench raised his arms and summoned a torrent of crackling energy that surged towards Sera like a violent storm. Her breath caught in her throat as she watched the writhing tendrils of magic draw nearer, but she refused to be cowed by his display of power. Drawing upon the wellspring of her own magic, she deftly wove a protective barrier around herself and Hugh. The mage's blast hit her shield and bounced up and over them.

"Is that all you've got?" she taunted, her voice steady despite the adrenaline coursing through her veins.

"Ha! You think you're so clever, witch!" Lord Dench's face twisted with rage. "Let's see how you handle this!"

He unleashed a barrage of magical attacks, each more powerful than the last. Sera met them head-on, dismissing them with a flick of her wrist or a whispered incantation.

"You will not beat me, you pathetic worm!" Lord Dench bellowed, his voice shaking with fury. He lobbed an orb of swirling metal towards Sera.

She swiped it sideways. The blast hit a nearby cottage and tore off its thatched roof. A woman screamed from within, then came the cries of children, their terror piercing the air like shards of glass.

"Stop this madness, Dench, before someone is hurt!" Sera yelled. It pained her to think of innocent people caught in their crossfire. As much as she longed to soundly thrash the man, she couldn't risk causing more harm to those who had no part in their dispute.

"Look at you," Lord Dench spat, his eyes gleaming with malice. "Pretending to care about these people when all you want is to save your own skin."

"Leave them out of this!" Sera shouted, her voice cracking with emotion.

"Come quietly, and no one needs to be hurt," Lord Dench said, his lips curling into a sinister smile.

People had rushed to the cottage with the collapsed roof. Lord Dench didn't even look as two children were carried out. One had blood dribbling down his leg. Their mother close behind was covered in dust and had a gash on her arm. Hugh was torn, wanting to stay at Sera's side but needing to tend the injured.

Sera realised what she must do. She feigned exhaustion, allowing herself to collapse to her knees as if drained of all energy. The crowd behind Lord Dench surged forwards, their makeshift weapons clutched tight as they moved to apprehend her. She offered only weak resistance as two men bound her wrists behind her back.

They treated Hugh more roughly. He was knocked to the ground as men hogtied his hands to his feet. Typical. Sera could cast magic, but they thought the muscular man the bigger threat.

"Pathetic. I always knew you were no match for me," Lord Dench said with a laugh, his voice dripping with scorn.

"Underestimating a woman will be the downfall of men throughout the world," Sera murmured, mostly to herself and Hugh. But even as the words left her lips, she couldn't help but wonder if she had made the right choice in surrendering. Had she just condemned herself and Hugh to a fate worse than anything they had encountered so far?

The rough hands of Lord Dench's men gripped Sera and Hugh, hauling them towards a rickety, covered cart. They and their belongings were uncere-moniously thrown on the hay-strewn floor and the canvas dropped. The scent of damp hay and stale sweat permeated the air, making it difficult to breathe.

"I assume you have a plan?" Hugh whispered as he struggled to find a comfortable spot on his side.

"Of course I do," she replied, even as a thread of uncertainty gnawed at her. "But I want to wait until we are away from the village."

The cart lurched into motion, jostling its occupants with every bump.

"I feel like a hog being taken to market," Hugh grumbled, unable to sit upright with his feet and hands tied behind him.

Sera peered through a hole in the canvas. At least they were heading in the right direction for the next fairy ring. "All I have to do is get out of these ropes, untie you, and defeat all the men riding beside the cart."

She grinned at Hugh, refusing to let him see the worry that gnawed at her. Yet again, she was being held captive. She wriggled her hands, seeing if she could slip them loose without having to use magic. Whoever had tied her had some familiarity with knots, and the ropes held fast.

Magic would be needed. Probably best not to try burning the rope in case she set fire to the hay. Holding her hands as far apart as possible, Sera summoned an invisible blade to saw at the fibres, hoping that she didn't slice herself in the process.

"What will you spend your share of the prize money on?" one man asked his companions outside.

"His will all go to the Frolicking Ewe," another said to much laughter. That must have been the name of the pub they'd passed. At least, Sera hoped it was the name of a tavern and not a special friend of the man.

The cart continued to jounce along the road. The wheel hit a bump, and Sera gasped as a stab of pain dug into her palm from the magical knife.

"What is it?" Hugh cast her a worried glance.

"I cut myself with that bump." She ignored the burn of the cut, closed her eyes, and took up the scalpel made of air once more. As she sliced at the thick rope, sweat trickled between her shoulder blades. It was taking longer than she liked, and if they travelled much further, the cart would draw them away from the next fairy ring.

"Come on," she murmured. She was reluctant to use too much magic or too big a phantom blade in case Lord Dench sensed what she was up to—or she took her hand off. Finally, her bonds came apart with a pop. Grabbing her left hand in her right, she examined the heel of her hand. "Not too bad, considering I was working blind." She had a small nick, about an inch long but, thankfully, shallow. Only a single drop of blood welled up in one corner, and she licked it away.

"Now you." She turned her attention to Hugh, murmuring to the knots to undo themselves. Soon they were both free of the ropes, and they crawled on their stomachs to the back of the cart so their guards wouldn't see their movement.

Nineteen

Sera peered through a gap in the canvas. Two men rode behind them, hands relaxed on the pommels of their saddles as they discussed how they would spend their share of the reward.

"We need a distraction," she whispered to Hugh.

Sera loosed a tendril of magic, letting it drift up into the darkening sky. Above, a sparrow flew with its friends, intent on reaching their night-time roost. With a gentle touch, she merged a tiny portion of her consciousness with that of the bird. Then she surveyed the scene below.

Lord Dench's carriage travelled in front of the cart. More men rode beside them. She counted a total of ten mounted guards.

Thanking the sparrow, she let it go to hasten to its home. Her fingertips tapped on her chest as she pondered what to do.

"I have always found that when you and Kitty are

silent, you are at your most devious," Hugh muttered from her side.

Sera flashed him a grin. "Lord Dench is in front of us. I am going to use him to make the guards behind us ride up front. That will give us a few moments to climb out unnoticed and run for the trees."

She refused to knowingly harm an animal, particularly one just doing its job. But Sera needed the horses pulling the carriage to bolt. To achieve that required their cooperation. Horses were trickier than birds. As prey animals, they took fright easily. Especially when a mage tried to tap into their heads. Instead, she used a different type of motivation.

In her mind, Sera constructed a marvellous stable. The stalls possessed the freshest straw to roll in. A hot meal of barley steamed in a feed bowl. The water was crystal clear. She placed the imaginary stable off the road. Then she did something only a little bit cruel. She wrapped wafts of magic around the ears of the two lead horses and roared like a tiger, giving them the impression the predator was right behind.

The horses did the logical thing. They bolted for the safety of the phantom stable, the carriage bouncing madly along behind them. Shouts went up as men kicked their horses forwards.

Hugh lifted the canvas an inch, enough to see that the rear guards had galloped to their lord's rescue. Sera didn't need to say a word. They snatched up the saddlebags, scrambled out of the confining cart, and sprinted towards the sheltering darkness of the forest.

They had to get as far off the road as possible before the men realised they had escaped. At the same time, Sera didn't want to run in the opposite direction to the next fairy ring.

As they plunged deeper into the woods, the shadows grew darker and more menacing, swallowing them whole. The ancient trees stood as silent sentinels. Gnarled branches reached out as if to ensnare them but, thankfully, stayed rooted in place.

"Are you certain we're running in the right direction?" Hugh muttered between laboured breaths, tightening his grip on her hand.

"No. But we need to get far away from that cart first before I dare to stop long enough to take my bearings." She tugged him onwards, deeper into the forest.

At least the men would be forced to dismount to pursue them. The terrain was too rough for their horses. But they also knew the area, an advantage Hugh and Sera lacked. Nor did she want to use her magic and send up a beacon for Lord Dench to follow.

Instead, Sera let her gift attune to their surroundings and absorb the subtle ebb and flow of life around them. She whispered a plea to Gaia, to guide her steps in the direction of the fairy portal made of mushrooms. When a subtle tug made her want to veer off the path, Sera followed it and trusted in the earth goddess.

When it was nearly pitch-dark, Sera and Hugh huddled in the hollowed-out roots of a tree perched over a bank. Sera caught her breath and eased the old map out from under her stays. Risking the tiniest light of a firefly, she traced the intricate lines and symbols etched onto the parchment, her eyes scanning for any hint of a fairy ring within the forest.

The star that marked their position zig-zagged across the page and, at one point, doubled back on itself, as it traced where they had fled. Finally, it settled in one spot.

"Find it?" Hugh asked, his voice low and cautious, mindful that other ears might be listening in the dense forest.

"It's hard to see, and I don't dare make a larger light." The inked lines on the parchment seemed to dance and shift beneath her gaze. Finally, a small, glowing circle appeared, indicating the location of a fairy ring nearby. Sera exhaled, relief flooding through her. "Found it. It's not too far from here. We just need to head east." She tapped a spot on the map.

"Let's get moving. We don't want them to catch up." Hugh held out his hand to help her stand on the unstable ground.

They moved more slowly now. Every few minutes, Sera asked a firefly to illuminate the map clutched in one hand. As they made their way through the thick underbrush, Sera focused on every rustle of leaves and snap of twigs.

"Did you hear that?" Hugh pulled her to him as he pressed his back to a large beech tree.

Sera strained her ears, searching for any sound that could betray their pursuers. But the only noise she heard was the steady thump of her own heart. "Probably just a deer," she reassured him. And herself.

At length, they came to an area where the trees thinned, and the star on the map butted against a circle.

"Here it is!" Sera exclaimed, her voice barely more than a breath, their feet on the edge of the mushroom ring. The dim moonlight filtered through the canopy above, casting an ethereal glow on the delicate fungi.

"Finally. It feels like we've been on our feet for hours, and I could do with a good sit." Hugh sighed, his relief palpable.

"Ready?" Sera asked, reaching for his hand. He took it without hesitation, his grip firm and reassuring.

"Always," he replied.

As one, they stepped over the mushrooms and into the centre of the ring. Sera focused on the next portal in the east of England and uttered the ancient words. The now familiar flare of lightning tingled over their bodies moments before they became weightless. The land moved beneath them, then snapped back into place with a jolt.

Sera dropped to her knees, hands flat on the lush grass as her body and senses oriented themselves after the journey. "We should be in Shrewsbury," she said as they stepped out of the ring and the used portals erased themselves from the map.

"Two hundred miles." Hugh shook his head in wonder. "Lord Dench won't be covering that much ground overnight."

"We have two fairy rings left. The last one will take

us to Oxford. I'll let Kitty know." Sera had been keeping her friend abreast of their movements when she could, dashing off quick notes on the ensorcelled paper.

This time, they were at the edge of a wooded area, where short grass ran back into the lusher meadow beyond. Heading across the field, they soon found the road. Sera studied the map and pointed along the track. "That way."

Hugh sighed. "I'm assuming we'll avoid any villages that might have warm taverns?"

"Sorry. But I think that might be best." They walked hand in hand under the watch of the moon. At least they didn't have to run. For now.

They approached a cottage with a riotous garden, as though spring had warmed the earth early for the resident. Light flickered in the windows, and a delicious aroma wafted from it. The door opened, and a woman emerged to take a few steps along a path overgrown with lavender plants.

"Oi! You two. Come on in," she called.

Sera turned around, assuming there were others behind them or perhaps children who had run off to play in the longer grass.

When they hesitated, the woman walked to the bottom of the path. Her long hair was pulled back in a loose knot, and she had kind eyes that were etched with laugh lines. "The Sight told me two weary travellers would appreciate a meal and somewhere to rest their bones."

"You're a seer." Sera rested one hand on the willow withes that enclosed her garden. "You should know it is dangerous to harbour us."

The woman snorted. "As if I've ever listened to what a man told me to do."

Sera laughed. "We seem to have that in common. We would be grateful for your hospitality."

They followed the woman inside. She lived alone, reading the fortunes of those who sought her out, and she offered them a hearty stew and strong tea. Then she provided a place before the fire to sleep.

Sera woke at first light and made her way to the vegetable garden at the rear of the cottage. There, only a few winter-hardy plants grew. Placing her hands on the frigid ground, Sera reached down and pulled forth warmth and nutrients to ensure the seer had a bountiful crop in summer.

Then she collected Hugh, and they thanked the woman for her kindness.

"You have allies in unexpected places, milady. They will rally when you need them most," the woman said with a wink.

They continued along the road, enjoying the weak sunlight that melted the late frost. Houses appeared in the distance, smoke from chimneys making lazy spirals in the morning air.

"Oh, that smells good." Hugh tilted his chin and struck off to the right.

Sera trotted behind him as the cottages gathered together around a square where a market was being held. Conversation and the scent of freshly baked bread filled the air. Sera found a coin in the corner of her pocket and purchased a loaf of bread.

Another vendor had cheese, and she bought a lump. Then she tore the bread into uneven parts—two-thirds for Hugh, a third for her. Sera shoved a piece of cheese into the soft centre of her bread. They chewed as they strolled through the market, so different from their experience in Middlesbrough. Here, the people were curious. Many called out friendly greetings.

Sera stopped; her blood suddenly chilled as she spied the handbill tacked to the back of a stall. The one bearing her likeness and offering a reward. Except someone had crossed out TRAITOR! and written OUR DEFENDER instead.

She heaved a sharp, emotion-laden breath and caught the eye of a man standing by a cart.

"Would you like coffee to wash that down with, milady?" He gestured to the pots on the back of his cart, kept warm by small flames in metal stands.

"Yes, thank you." She struggled to say the words.

He poured two mugs of a potent brew and handed them to her and Hugh. "There's two wights in the forest here that terrify the children at night. Rapping on windows and scratching at those caught outside. It would be much appreciated if you could deal with them while you are here. We've asked the Mage Council, but they tell us it's not important. But I tell you, it's darned important to the parents around here."

"Point me in the right direction, and I shall have a

few words with these wights for you," Sera said as she blew on the hot drink.

The man showed her where the malicious spirits lingered while they finished their breakfast. Sera handed back the empty mug. "In the future, send such problems directly to me. I will help where and when I can."

"Thank you, milady!" he called as they headed out the other side of the market.

Other locals offered their thanks and pressed small items on them. An apple for Sera, a substantial Cornish pasty for Hugh that warmed his hands.

By the time Sera approached the woods that harboured the wights, her heart was lighter. People noticed the good she had done. In the years to come, she would do more, she silently promised them.

The wights were easily dealt with. Perhaps they were bored now that the parents were keeping their children inside at night. They rushed out of the gloom, thinking Sera and Hugh would be easy to terrify. Sera ensnared them and then bound them to a hornet's nest dangling from a tree. For decades to come, they would provide a soft blue light to guide travellers.

With that problem sorted, she pulled out the map and set off for the last fairy ring that would push them straight to Oxford. They found it hidden within a copse of trees, close to the new blue light. As they stepped into the circle, Sera felt the familiar pull of magic tugging at her core. With a deep breath, she took Hugh's hand and focused on their last landing point.

When she uttered the words, fairy magic swept them up, and the world around them dissolved into a whirlwind of colours and sensations before spitting them out in the middle of a paddock full of grazing cows. One bovine looked up and mooed at Hugh.

"Someone is making calf's eyes at you." Sera laughed as the cow licked the side of his face with a long black tongue.

"The last leg. We are nearly back in London and can get that cursed stone away from the king." Hugh repositioned the saddlebags over his shoulder and held out a hand to Sera.

After the last two fairy rings on the map disappeared, Sera tucked the parchment into her satchel and took Hugh's hand. They walked as the sun rose higher in the sky. People passed them as they travelled along the main route from Oxford to London, but either none had room for two weary bodies or they were going in the wrong direction.

Up ahead, Sera spotted two riders, each holding the reins to a spare horse. When she recognised the figures, a surge of relief and joy coursed through her veins, revitalising her weary limbs.

"Kitty!" she called.

The riders halted before them, and Kitty swung her leg over the pommel of her saddle to jump to the ground. She threw her arms around Sera, and the friends hugged tight.

"We set out last night. Mr Brynn prefers travelling

in the dark over an early start," Kitty said with a mischievous glance at Elliot.

"You keep turning up like a bad penny," Elliot said as he handed a set of reins to Sera.

"What news? Has Lord Pendlebury made it back to London?" Sera glanced from friend to footman.

"Not that I have heard," Kitty said. "How was he travelling?"

"By kelpie. I believe he was going to get one to swim him right up the Thames." Sera would love to hear that tale over a cup of tea, tucked up in the older mage's tower office.

Kitty stared at her, as though undecided whether Sera were jesting or not. "Let's head back immediately. With most of the peers in their country homes for the winter, Lord Rowan is acting as though he is Emperor of England. He has seized control while the lords enjoy their figgy pudding."

"He stands unimpeded, then," Hugh said as he swung himself up into the saddle.

Sera snorted. It sounded as though the old mage had committed to his treasonous course of action even without her. She settled in the saddle and turned her horse to face back the way Kitty and Elliot had come.

She grinned at her friend. "He is about to meet a very thorny obstacle."

TWENTY

THEY PUSHED THE HORSES, and themselves, hard, stopping only to water their mounts and stretch their muscles. The sun travelled across the sky and dropped to the horizon as the horses' hooves clopped rhythmically against the packed earth road. Exhaustion pulled at Sera's limbs, but determination kept her focused on the road ahead.

"We should change horses at the next inn," Hugh said, his breath visible as he spoke. Despite his broad shoulders, even he showed signs of weariness. His usual confident posture was slumped, and dark circles shadowed his eyes.

Kitty, ever composed, appeared to be faring no better. Her cheeks were flushed from the biting wind, and her usually sharp wit had dulled under the strain of their journey. Beside her, Elliot's charming smile had been replaced by a grimace, betraying the toll their ride had taken on him as well.

With the welcome sight of a public house ahead, Sera slowed her horse to a walk. "We need fresh horses if we're going to make it to London tonight."

On entering the yard, the group dismounted with stiff limbs, each one of them grateful for the temporary reprieve from the saddle. The public house was a modest, weathered building, but it offered them the chance to rest, however briefly, while they tended to the horses.

Sera approached the stable hand to tell him what they required. He gestured to another. Between them, the two men led the horses into the stables and quickly stripped off saddles and bridles. Then they tacked up four fresh mounts.

As they put their feet into stirrups once more, Kitty remarked in a dry tone, "I never imagined I'd be grateful for a change of horse."

"I could do with a change of company," Elliot replied, managing a grin despite his growing exhaustion.

With renewed vigour, they set off once more through the descending twilight, but the fatigue that clung to their bones was not so easily shaken.

They were a weary group by the time they finally reached the outskirts of London, the sprawling city opening up before them like a blackened labyrinth under the night sky. The air was choked with soot and the faint scent of decay from the murky waters of the Thames, the cobbled streets slick with an oily sheen from the day's rain.

The tired quartet made their way through the labyrinthine alleyways of the city's east end as they headed for sanctuary. Perched inside the triangle created where two roads merged, the Apothecary's Poison tavern was the most welcome sight Sera had seen in hundreds of miles. The potion bottle on the sign with its skull-and-crossbones warning waved gently back and forth as though it greeted them.

Jumping to the cobbles, Elliot took all the reins and headed to the mews along the road.

As they entered the tavern, they were immediately enveloped in warmth, both from the roaring fire in the hearth and from the convivial atmosphere that pervaded the room. The scent of bubbling stew filled the air, mingling with the smoky aroma of burning wood and the earthy undertones of ale. Patrons huddled around tables, their conversations animated and hushed.

"Knew you couldn't stay away," boomed the deep voice of Imp, Hugh's adopted brother. His muscular form towered over most in the room, his craggy features softened by a warm smile as he regarded them. He walked around the bar and enveloped Hugh in a bear hug, lifting him off the ground for a moment before releasing him. "I was getting worried about you. It's dangerous out there." Imp gestured to the door and the city beyond. "Common folk are being rounded up and sent to Newgate."

"Why?" Outrage surged up Sera's throat.

"Because they support you, milady. And because

Lord Rowan thinks the common folk are lazy. Apparently, we'd all be rich if we worked a bit harder." Imp snorted and went back behind the bar to fill clay pitchers.

Kitty rolled her eyes. "There are times I am ashamed of my noble blood and those who cannot recognise their privilege. People need help if they are to improve their lives. All prison does is make more criminals."

"We've had a long, hard journey, Imp. Could we trouble you for food and ale?" Hugh leaned on the counter as his adopted brother set out four tankards and a pitcher.

"And a bath? Please? Lord, what I'd do for a bath." Sera closed her eyes and fantasised for a wonderful moment about the enormous copper bath in the Fae palace.

Imp chuckled. "I'll have the women draw a bath for you while you eat."

Kitty held up two fingers. "Make that two, please. I have sweat in places a lady shouldn't."

Hugh carried the tray of drinks as Kitty and Sera led the way to their corner by the fire. With its high-backed bench seats, it enclosed them and felt as though it held tight to every secret whispered over the table.

It was only a few minutes before Elliot joined them. He dropped to the bench with a sigh, picked up a tankard, and drank deeply. After he wiped his mouth, he stared at Sera across the table. "I want to renegotiate my employment terms. I think I should be paid hourly."

Sera leaned back and stared up at the ceiling as she considered the idea. "So I will only pay you for the hours you actually work? And not for sitting at the kitchen table eating Rosie's cakes? Nor for lounging in the sun or sitting in a pub drinking ale while you wait for me to have something for you to do?"

Elliot coughed and drank more ale. "Yeah. Well. I might have been a bit hasty."

Kitty chuckled. "You missed your calling in life, Mr Brynn. You would have made an excellent solicitor."

"Except I don't like paperwork." He refilled his tankard and toasted his employer with it.

Sera let the warmth of the tavern seep into her bones. She took a deep breath as comfort spread through her soul. Here, safe among friends, she found respite. They had a small amount of time to reflect and decide what to do next.

As they waited for their meal, Sera studied the faces of her friends, noting the lines of fatigue etched into their expressions. They were all feeling the strain of their recent journey. But there was also determination in their eyes.

At last, the barmaid brought over a tray laden with plates of steaming food and set them on the table. She winked at Elliot and trailed a finger along his shoulder before she tucked the tray under her arm and wove through the crowd.

Sera savoured every bite of the hearty stew. Tearing off chunks of fresh bread, she swiped it through the rich gravy before popping it into her mouth.

"Right then," Kitty began, wiping her mouth with a coarse napkin. "We need to discuss our plan of action."

Hugh leaned forwards, resting his elbows on the worn wooden table. "I think it is clear. Sera and I will find a way into the king's chambers to administer the tears of the Nereus. Once he is healed, he can publicly denounce Lord Rowan."

That seemed the correct course, but Sera doubted Lord Rowan would relinquish power so easily. "Lord Rowan needs to be stopped. His power grows, and who knows how many of the mages have been turned to his side? I can't see him relinquishing power now, if all the king can do is issue a decree."

"Sera is right." Kitty laid her hand on Sera's arm. "The wily old man has waited decades for his opportunity, and he has seized it with both hands. Divisions are being drawn amongst the nobility, and Abigail has positioned herself as queen of the new court. You cannot counter their action with a writ."

"I must draw him out and strike him down before everyone," Sera murmured. Her mind whirled with ideas as to how.

"What of the king? Will you leave his mind trapped in its torment?" Hugh rapped his knuckles on their table.

"Of course not. We must split up. Lord Pendlebury

will not be far away, and you need a mage who can get you close to the king. Not one who will be seized on sight. You must find Lord Pendlebury, and with him, get the cure to King George." That part of the plan Sera fully trusted to Hugh and the mage who had come to her aid more than once.

Hugh ground his teeth, and his hand curled into a fist. "I'll not leave you to fight Lord Rowan on your own. You promised we would do this together, Sera."

Hugh's words rattled around in Sera's mind. *On her own.* Yes, that was exactly how she needed to approach Lord Rowan. Because he always underestimated her.

She reached across the table and took Hugh's hand. "We do this together, but sometimes, parts must move in different ways. I need you to remove the entropy stone from around the king's neck. Otherwise, all of this is for nothing, and I will have my own neck stretched as a traitor." Or worse, imprisoned and defiled in the Repository, breeding the Nereus Lord Rowan so desperately needed. But she kept that horrid thought to herself.

The surgeon drew a ragged breath and fixed first Elliot and then Kitty with his stare. "Promise me you'll not leave her side."

"Of course I won't. Quite apart from the risk of getting killed and losing everything my father has worked for over the years, I've never had so much fun." Kitty grinned and nudged Sera with her elbow.

"Has it ever occurred to you that your faith in me

might be misplaced?" Sera loved Kitty, but there were times she worried whether she could live up to her friend's expectations.

Kitty frowned and pursed her lips. "If my faith is misplaced, I promise it will be the last thought that flits through my mind."

Elliot shook a finger at them. "That...is not reassuring."

"What do you plan to do while I am sneaking back into St James's Palace?" Hugh's voice was laced with reluctance.

Sera stiffened her spine as she met his gaze. "I'm going to give Lord Rowan exactly what he wants. Me. Alone."

Kitty drew in a sharp breath of surprise. "You're going to set a trap and use yourself as bait?"

"It's the only way to expose his lies and show everyone what he truly is under that genial exterior." Sera rolled the tankard between her hands and cooled the liquid within.

"Are you certain that is the only way?" Kitty's voice carried the faintest trace of a waver. "Confronting Lord Rowan is dangerous. He has the support of the other mages *and* the king's soldiers. We have yet to discuss alternatives."

Hugh remained silent but clenched his jaw. At length, he spoke in a slow, cautious tone. "Perhaps we can devise another plan...one that doesn't put you so directly in harm's way? He has already captured you once. I doubt he will let you escape a second time."

"He didn't *let* me escape. My friends came for me. This will be different. He will think he has caught me, but I will have him in my grasp." In the quiet moments of the last few months, Sera had considered what to do about Lord Rowan. She had picked apart the spell he had used to cut her off from her magic and place it where he thought she could never reach it again. She was fairly certain she could replicate the enchantment. All she had to do was lay her hands on the old mage.

"Normally I go along with your hare-brained schemes, but I agree with Miss Napier and Mr Miles. Serving yourself up seems daft," Elliot said.

Sera listened to their fears, her heart heavy, for they spoke the truth. Confronting Lord Rowan was a risk that could cost her everything. Yet she needed to make a last bold gambit if the pawn was to reach the other side of the board. And she had a piece waiting to be played that the old mage knew nothing about. She drew the pendant from under her shirt and brushed a thumb over the silver disc, the physical manifestation of the first kiss Hugh had placed in her palm.

Next to it, she held up the scale that shimmered from black to deepest green, violet, then blue in the light. "You are forgetting...I have a dragon."

"Why didn't you lead with that?" Elliot grumbled, although worry still lingered in his eyes.

With a deep breath, Hugh squeezed her hand in silent support, acknowledging her decision.

"Since you are determined to dangle yourself as

bait, we shall do whatever is required of us," Kitty conceded, her voice soft but determined.

"Thank you. We can do this. Together," Sera whispered, grateful for their unwavering loyalty. "Tomorrow, I shall play my end-game move. Until then, I intend to have a bath and forget I have spent the last few days on the road, sleeping under trees without hot water."

"You're a mage. Why didn't you magic up a bath for yourself?" Elliot chuckled and leaned back against his seat.

Sera stuck out her tongue at her footman. In truth, she had been far too tired to expend the energy to conjure a bath and heat the water, nor had it seemed wise to alert Lord Rowan to her location by the use of magic.

After saying their goodnights, the friends retreated to their rooms above the Apothecary's Poison. Sera stepped into the room she shared with Hugh and turned her attention to the small tub set before the fire.

Disappointment dragged at her limbs as she eyed its less-than-ideal size, but nevertheless, steam curled from the surface. The maids had added lavender oil, and the fragrance drew Sera closer and helped her shoulders relax.

Stripping off her clothing and tossing it over a chair, she dipped one foot into the water before carefully lowering herself into the tub. It was shaped somewhat like a slipper, one end being higher to form a backrest. Sera closed her eyes and let out a sigh.

Warmth enveloped her and soothed her aching muscles. Water lapped at her shoulders. Heat seeped into her bones, chasing away the ache of their journey. Her fingers traced lazy patterns on the surface as droplets slipped back into the tub with a gentle plink. For a moment, she let mental and physical exhaustion overwhelm her.

The door opened and closed as Hugh entered the room. His footsteps crossed the floor, followed by the rustle of clothing as he shrugged off his coat and then pulled off his boots.

"Are you sure about this?" His concern reached through her half-slumber. A finger traced along her shoulder and then followed the line of her collarbone.

"I will be free. Once I defeat Lord Rowan, no one will ever dare to cage me again." She half-opened her eyes and reached for his hand, holding it against her cheek.

"That's a very small tub." He changed the subject with a grumble in his voice.

"You might fit, but we would have to be very close." She arched one eyebrow suggestively.

"I'm always keen for an anatomical challenge." He stripped off the rest of his clothes and dropped them to the floor.

Sera moved forwards, drawing her knees up until they were pressed to her chest. Hugh lowered himself into the tub behind her, then drew her against him. Their limbs tangled together like ivy, seeking solace in their closeness. The water sloshed over the sides, soaking the floor. It would probably rain on the room below, but they paid it no heed.

Hugh wrapped his arms around Sera. Safe in his strong embrace, she let go, surrendering herself to his touch. In a dreamlike state, Sera soaked up every caress and kiss. With a few banged knees, awkward moments, and one bout of giggles, they were able to satisfy the desire that flared between them.

Afterwards, they lay entwined in the tub. Sera's head rested on Hugh's chest. She drew patterns on his arm with a fingertip, letting a trace of magic illuminate the moisture clinging to his skin until his arm was covered in a glowing design.

A sense of peace washed through her soul. Or perhaps it was merely the calm before the storm. Tomorrow, she would face her puppet master. The man who, from the moment she was born, had manipulated her life.

They stayed crammed together in the small tub until the water cooled and their muscles protested the cramped position. Hugh stood and grabbed the towels, draping one around Sera's shoulders. After briskly drying themselves, they climbed into bed, the sheets cool beneath their heated bodies.

Hugh gathered Sera close, and she lay pressed to his side. In the silence, worry seemed to roll from Hugh's broad form.

Sera placed one hand over his heart and met his gaze. "He will not win."

Hugh placed a gentle kiss on the top of her head.

"Of course he won't. But I still worry about what will happen in the attempt. You are the air in my lungs, the blood in my veins. Without you, I would be nothing. I love you, Sera."

"I love you, and since I do not wish to see you reduced to an airless and bloodless bag of skin, I promise I will summon Ebonfyre when the time comes." To seal her promise, she kissed him.

TWENTY-ONE

THE NEXT MORNING, sunlight filtered through the thick glass of the kitchen window and cast an ethereal glow on the worn wooden table where Sera, Kitty, Hugh, and Elliot sat in silence, picking at their breakfast. The scent of bacon filled the air, mingling with the lingering aroma of stale ale from the night before. Sera's stomach churned as nerves gnawed at her insides and refused to be sated even by bacon. Whatever the day brought, in a few hours she would either be fully in control of her life or entombed once more in the Repository...with nothing to do but play ball with Lionel the lycanthrope and breed monsters for a madman.

"I'm not following you today." Elliot put down his spoon and faced Sera across the table.

She arched an eyebrow but held her silence. While technically he was in her employ, if he decided it was too dangerous to be involved, she wouldn't hold that against him. Part of her was simply relieved to know he would care for Rosie and Vicky, the two women who completed her little household.

Kitty glanced up. "Neither am I."

Sera set down her cutlery and stared at her best friend. They had their own plan afoot. That was the only reason Kitty would abandon her.

"The Crows will be here this morning. We're going out to Newgate with them. Lord Rowan has been rounding up the ordinary folk and cramming them like sardines into the prison. We're going to set them free." Kitty poured strong coffee into her mug and took a cautious sip.

"You two made your own plan. Why didn't you mention it last night?" Sera thought it was a sensible idea. Together, the three Crows were as powerful as a mage and could deal with any trouble the group encountered.

"Because we were all in dire need of a bath and some rest." Kitty met her gaze. "This is something practical we can do, and Mr Brynn and I will not be deterred. We arranged it with Mr Brynn's cousins while you were chasing aquatic monsters."

She would face Lord Rowan alone. It was what she had wanted all along, to ensure those she loved stayed safe and out of harm's way. And yet her throat tightened, and she struggled to swallow.

Kitty took Sera's hand and shook it. "Oh, for goodness' sake. Do not for one second think we are abandoning you. Mr Brynn and I, along with the Crows, intend to bring you an army of common folk who all support you. Once Hugh has reversed the dark spell affecting the king, he will strike down these ridiculous edicts of Lord Rowan, and the soldiers will once more obey their rightful monarch."

"We all have our parts to play, and we all struggle with leaving you alone," Hugh said in a soft tone.

"But I am not alone. I am a part of a larger machine. Each cog and wheel has its unique function that makes the entire thing work as intended." She saw it now, how they all moved independently but came together as a magnificent whole. Each of her friends used their strengths to aid the greater cause.

"What's life without a little excitement?" Elliot chimed in, then belched—he had eaten more than his fair share of the bacon.

Before anyone could respond, the kitchen door swung open with a bang, revealing the breathless young lad who was Imp's son. "Soldiers!" he gasped, his face flushed and his chest heaving. "In the streets! They're looking for—for *you*, milady!"

Sera shared a quick, worried glance with her companions. Since Lord Rowan's magical traps had failed—or rather, had worked too effectively and ensnared every person in London with a trace of after-mage blood—it made sense to send out the troops to physically search for her.

"Lord Rowan is growing desperate. Without the power of a Nereus, he cannot make himself young again. He is running out of time." Sera finished her coffee with a gulp and a grimace. No matter how much of the stuff she tried, it didn't become any more pleasant.

"And who wants to be a decrepit emperor when you can be an immortally young one?" Kitty murmured as they took their plates to the sink.

"Soldiers or not, there are things that need to be done. I have to see if Lord Pendlebury made it back to London. Otherwise, Hugh is on his own to gain access to the king." She had no idea how fast a kelpie could swim. Was it faster or slower than travelling by fairy ring?

"Won't the other mages sense you using your magic?" Worry pulled Kitty's eyebrows together.

"I shall only use a tiny bit. Just enough to find a raven and fly over the city to try to spot him." Sera closed her eyes and let her consciousness drift upwards. Many different types of birds flew over the rooftops, but she wanted one with more courage and intelligence. One with an innate sense of curiosity. A raven swooped over the walls of the Tower to answer her call. Sera merged a tiny part of her mind with that of the corvid.

Her vision shifted, taking on the sharp clarity of the raven. She soared over London, the city's familiar sights strange from the bird's perspective. The wind whipped around her as she flew, each gust carrying with it a symphony of scents—the tang of the river, the acrid smoke of coal fires, and the unmistakable aroma of fresh bread wafting from a nearby bakery. At times, the bird dived as it spotted something shiny and of interest. Then it would circle high again.

"Focus," she whispered to the raven. Lord Pendlebury would make himself obvious so they could find him. She just needed to know where to look.

"The Thames." Sera directed the raven, and it turned to skim over the brown water. As they climbed over London Bridge, not wanting to go under in case rubbish was thrown on them from the shops crammed along its length, the bird spotted an unusual sight.

A kelpie, its sleek form gliding effortlessly through the Thames, with none other than Lord Pendlebury perched atop its back as though he rode a horse along a forest path. He had one hand curled in the seaweed mane to keep his position.

He looked up and shielded his eyes from the pale morning sun, then waved to the raven and gestured to the foot of the bridge. The bird called out its understanding. Sera thanked the raven for its service and severed their connection.

Her mind slammed back into her body, plummeting like a thing without wings that couldn't stay aloft. How she envied Elliot's cousins—women able to shapeshift into crows and fly wherever they wanted. "I found him. He'll wait for you by London Bridge."

Hugh pushed back from the table. "Then I'll not waste time. The sooner we heal the king's mind, the sooner he can declare Lord Rowan the traitor."

"I love you," Sera murmured. Even though she refused to entertain the thought, a tiny part of her worried this might be the last time she would ever see him.

"You are my world," Hugh replied. Then he bent down and captured Sera's lips in a searing kiss. One that spoke of passion, fear, and the unbreakable bond between them.

As they separated, Sera could only watch as Hugh disappeared through the door, his form swallowed by the shadows that lurked beyond the safety of the pub.

Hugh

HUGH SLIPPED OUT of the pub and set off towards the Thames. Despite the calendar marching onwards to spring, a chill in the air made him tug his coat tighter around his body. The cobblestone streets were slick with a fine mist from an overnight drizzle as the city came to life around him. Patrolling soldiers marched along the roads, their red coats standing out like a glaring beacon. He kept his head down and avoided staring at them, but he wasn't their primary target.

As Hugh approached London Bridge, he had to push through a crowd that had gathered to stare at the kelpie. The Scottish water horse had never been seen before, except in drawings, and only then if one were lucky enough to have seen such a book. The creature glided through the water, its sinuous body reflecting the clear light of the morning sun. A mane made of seaweed billowed around the kelpie as though it were submerged.

Lord Pendlebury stood on the shore and answered questions from curious children. His boots were muddy from wading ashore, and his short hair was spiky with salt from the spray that had coated him during his travels.

On spotting Hugh, he turned to the water horse and waved. "Thank you, my friend. Your service was invaluable."

The kelpie dipped its head in acknowledgement before slipping beneath the surface of the river and disappearing from sight. Which made a disappointed cry rise from the assembled people. Most dispersed to carry on their day. Only a few children remained, hoping to spot some other aquatic marvel dancing on the Thames. Hugh wished them luck if they thought any self-respecting mermaid would cavort in the river's murky water. He advised his patients to stay out of it and to rinse their mouths if they inadvertently swallowed any of the filthy liquid.

Lord Pendlebury shook out his cloak and muttered a few words that made the water stains evaporate. Then he turned to face Hugh. "Mr Miles, good morning. I assume Lady Winyard was successful and we are off to see the king?"

Hugh tapped the inside pocket of his coat. "I have

what Sera gathered from the creature. Let us hope it restores calm to a tormented mind."

The mage turned to watch a group of soldiers march along the road. "Lord Rowan has reached too high," he murmured, a sad look in his eye for the man he had clearly once admired.

"With your help, I hope that by the end of this day, we will have restored King George's mind and broken Rowan's hold over him." Hugh fell into step beside the mage.

They joined the throngs of people moving about the crowded streets.

"Thus far, I do not believe Lord Rowan knows I assist Lady Winyard. He will assume that all the mages, or all the male ones, follow his lead. I should be able to gain access to the king without being challenged." Lord Pendlebury hailed a hackney, and when it rolled to a stop, told the driver to convey them to St James's Palace. Once the vehicle started along the cobbled streets, he continued. "There will be a mage at the king's side, I assume, not to mention his courtiers?"

In his pockets, Hugh still had a few vials of the sleep potion that Sera had brewed for him. Most of the courtiers were as timid as mice. "If you subdue the attending mage, I'm sure I can deal with the others."

The carriage rolled to a stop outside the palace, and a liveried footman swung open the door. Hugh walked behind the mage, as a servant might. When the guards blocked their way with their lances, Lord Pendlebury shot them a withering look.

"I am here at the direction of Lord Rowan to ensure the safety of the king. Get that thing out of my way." He pushed the lance aside with one hand, and under his touch, it turned into a python that slithered to the floor of the entrance hall.

The guard gasped in alarm and jumped backwards. The other flung his ceremonial weapon to the tiled floor in case it also turned into a reptile.

As they moved through the palace, no one tried to stop them again. Courtiers and ladies moved to the edge of the hall to get out of Lord Pendlebury's way. No one wanted to stop a mage who walked with determination and a fiery look in his eye. Clearly, the court believed they were all in league with Lord Rowan.

At the entrance to the king's chamber, Lord Pendlebury halted and looked down his nose at the courtier standing by the guards. The man stared back but didn't move.

"Well, open the doors. Or do you wish me to blast them off their hinges?" the mage said.

The guards exchanged looks and then one wrenched the door open and bowed as they passed inside.

Today, it seemed to Hugh that the king was more agitated than usual. He paced erratically, as though he followed an invisible chicken around the furniture. The courtiers clustered to one side with the attending physicians. Lord Tomlin stood by the expansive window, staring at the king. He narrowed his eyes on seeing Lord Pendlebury and Hugh.

"Ah, Tomlin. Lord Rowan wants you back at the mage tower. Some private matter he wants to discuss," Lord Pendlebury said after he had bowed to the king, who didn't seem to notice him.

The younger mage didn't move from his spot in a shaft of sunlight. "He made no mention of wishing to see me this morning. What sort of private matter?"

Lord Pendlebury huffed. "If he had told me, it wouldn't be private, now, would it?"

Lord Tomlin crossed his arms over his chest, his gaze flicking sideways to Hugh. Hugh walked towards the attending physicians, ignoring the two mages. It seemed they might have to change their plan. With the king's frenetic movements, they couldn't afford a magical battle. There was a risk one of them might inadvertently blast him with a thunderbolt.

As Hugh neared the physicians who stood by the food set out on the sideboard, Lord Tomlin turned to face the older mage. As he did so, he presented his back to Hugh. Taking the opportunity it offered him, Hugh darted forwards and grabbed Lord Tomlin from behind. With his forearm locked around the mage's neck, he cut off his oxygen supply.

Before Lord Tomlin could strike out with magic, Lord Pendlebury cast an enchantment over the younger mage. He threw a magical noose around Lord Tomlin's hands and snapped them together at the wrists, which prevented him from clawing at Hugh. Nor could he utter a spell, as his brain was rapidly being deprived of oxygen.

Lord Tomlin's body went limp in the surgeon's grasp as he lost consciousness. Hugh lowered him to the ground and placed two fingers against his neck. He didn't like the man, but he also didn't want to kill him.

"What do you think you are doing, Mr Miles?" An old physician strode towards them.

Lord Pendlebury cast a swirling orb of lightning that hovered between his palms. "I think everyone can stay exactly where they are. Unless anybody else would like to take a wee nap?"

The courtiers busied themselves pouring tea and slicing cake and steadfastly ignoring what went on behind them. The physician spluttered, then thought better of intervening. He plonked himself in a chair and glowered at Hugh. "Lord Viner will hear of this."

"I shall tell his lordship myself what transpires here this morning," Hugh replied.

With everyone behaving themselves and under Lord Pendlebury's control, Hugh turned his attention to the task at hand. He reached into his pocket and produced the small vial containing the precious tears of the Nereus. When he held the container to the light, the silvery liquid glinted as though Sera had captured the moon within its glass confines.

"I will need help with the king," he said to Lord Pendlebury.

Unaware of events in the room, King George muttered to himself as he stalked the confines of the room and climbed over chairs, rather than going around the furniture.

"Your Majesty, you must be tired after your walk this morning. Perhaps you would like to sit for a while?" Lord Pendlebury said in a quiet tone. He held out one hand to the king, while with the other, he gestured to the velvet-covered chair like a small throne.

Hugh wondered what magic he laced around the king as the monarch stilled, then yawned. "I am tired," King George said.

He walked to the chair and slumped into the seat. The king heaved a sigh, then his head rolled back against the deep-red velvet. He seemed to be asleep, yet his eyes were open and unstaring. The once-vibrant monarch was now a mere shell, ensnared by Lord Rowan's entropy curse.

Hugh knelt at the king's side, the vial curled within his hand. "Your Majesty, do you remember the tea I brewed that calmed the storm in your mind for a little while? I have another such potion that I hope has a more lasting effect." Hugh spoke in a low tone, not wanting the other physicians to hear the conversation.

King George uttered a noise that could have been agreement or a snore. Hugh reached out and pulled aside the king's robes. There, only partly visible under his shirt, lay the entropy stone—the source of the curse that had claimed his mind. Its surface seemed to writhe with shadows.

Hugh drew a deep breath to steady his nerves, such as he did before performing surgery. Then he uncorked the vial and angled it over the amulet so that a single droplet of the Nereus's tears fell onto the stone.

The moment the tear made contact with the polished surface, there was a sharp hiss, followed by an ethereal glow that radiated from the stone. It pulsed in a steady beat as a wave of light clashed with the darkness of the curse.

"By the old gods, it seems to be working," Lord Pendlebury uttered from Hugh's side.

Hugh carefully let two more drops land on the stone. The green veins glowed brightly as the remorse of the Nereus dissolved the object created in its moment of defeat. As the last remnants of the curse were neutralised, the stone emitted a single puff of dark smoke, then the surface became dull, the veins drained and grey.

"Now is the time to remove it," Lord Pendlebury urged.

Hugh reached for the chain that held the entropy stone around the king's neck and unclasped it. The stone was heavy in his hands, as if it contained the weight of all the suffering it had caused. Lord Pendlebury emptied a nearby pouch of the dice it contained and held it open. Hugh deposited the ordinary-looking stone inside, the chain slithering in on top. Then the mage cinched the bag shut and murmured a spell that raised the hairs along Hugh's arms.

At his curious look, Lord Pendlebury placed the pouch in his coat pocket. "A temporary seal until it can be properly disposed of. We don't know if it will resurrect itself or if the tears have neutralised it entirely."

Hugh turned his attention to the monarch, who

seemed oblivious to the amulet being removed from around his neck. That in itself was encouraging, as in his last moment of lucidity he had said the chain wouldn't allow itself to be undone. "There is one more thing to do."

He dipped his finger into the vial, allowing a single tear to cling to his fingertip before anointing the king's forehead with the iridescent liquid. As the droplet touched King George's skin, a soft glow radiated from the point of contact and spread across his brow like a ripple in a pond. His once-pallid complexion took on a healthier hue as the magic worked its way through his beleaguered body, revitalising him from within. And, Hugh hoped, restoring peace to the king's mind.

TWENTY-TWO

Seraphina

ELLIOT AND KITTY left the pub on Hugh's heels. Sera stood in the doorway until her friends disappeared around a corner. Then she scrubbed her hands over her face and told her hammering heart to calm down.

"I can do this," she whispered.

That morning, she had donned her Nyx outfit. The long-split skirt flared around her legs. The silver buttons on the double-breasted front were done up over a black shirt underneath. Her favourite long boots were laced up to her knees. All she needed were a few final touches for the performance she was about to put on for Lord Rowan and all of London.

She had left her hair loose, the curls tumbling down her back. Using a simple enchantment, Sera changed the dark brown to a colour bordering on midnight, with a smattering of stars. Straightening her spine, she stepped out of the pub and walked down the cobbled street. With each step, silver stars swirled loose from her hems. Winking and glinting, they trailed behind her like a comet's tail. It was as if Nyx herself, the goddess of the night, had descended from the heavens to walk amongst mortals.

People stopped to stare—some pointed, some waved in greeting. Others hurried along the road and refused to meet her gaze in case she cursed them. As she turned onto a busier street, two soldiers in bright red approached from the other direction. They stopped, jaws hanging slack for a moment. Then their grips tightened on their rifles. They aimed the weapons at her as people cried out and dived for shelter.

"Stop there!" one yelled.

She halted and let her lips curve in a slight smile.

"What do we do now?" the soldier loudly whispered to his companion.

"She has to come with us," the man answered.

"You are to come with us," the first soldier called.

"Actually, no. I won't. You may follow me, however-er," Sera replied.

The soldiers seemed confused by her refusal, and the quieter one gestured with his rifle. "You will follow us...traitor."

Sera held out her hands, palms upwards. From each burst forth a dark flame, dancing in shades of purple and inky blue. "Or what? Do you really think the two of you can command a mage?" She let her flames flare higher until she held two swords forged of midnight.

The men exchanged uneasy glances, the fear in their eyes betraying their bravado. Soldiers hadn't turned on one of England's mages since the turbulent Wars of the Roses. And even then, it took far more than *two* to have any impact.

"Lord Rowan said you didn't have magic anymore," said the quieter of the two with an uncertain quaver in his voice.

"Do I look powerless to you?" She crossed the flaming swords, and blue sparks jumped onto the road.

The soldiers made a decision. "You are to stay right there while we fetch reinforcements." With that, they turned tail and hurried down the road.

Sera spun the midnight blades and then let them dissolve into smoky mist as she shook her hands free. A few people laughed as the soldiers retreated, and Sera bowed to them. Then she continued on her way. She had a destination in mind and expected to draw quite the crowd before she reached it.

As she continued her path through London, people emerged from their homes and businesses, drawn to her like moths to a flame. The homeless rose from where they had sheltered overnight and followed in her star-strewn wake.

She also attracted more soldiers. Still, no man dared lay a hand on her. Instead, they surrounded her. Red uniforms made a barrier between her and the people she had helped when the other mages turned their faces away.

"It's Nyx!" People cheered, raising their fists in defiance of the soldiers who tried in vain to hold them back.

"We're with you!" cried an elderly woman, her eyes gleaming with the fire of rebellion that had been ignited within her by Sera's actions.

With each step, her confidence grew. She strode on, her chin held high and her gait steady despite the growing number of soldiers forming a wall around her. The throng of supporters grew larger and more boisterous, their voices rising in a deafening chorus of encouragement.

"Stay strong, Nyx! None of us are alone!" shouted a young man, his face flushed with excitement and hope.

Her eyes glistened with unshed tears. Their support meant more to her than she could ever express, and it gave her the strength to keep going.

She had a distance of about four miles to walk through London. Ample time for the soldiers to send up the alert, for Lord Rowan to be notified of her appearance, and hopefully, for the old mage to climb into a carriage.

Finally, Sera reached Charing Cross, the official centre of London. The bronze statue of Charles I astride his horse towered above her on its tall, ornate plinth. She touched the base as she passed. On the other side of the monument lay the Golden Cross inn. She hoped its patrons would stay safely inside.

Sera walked to the centre of the square. Then she brushed out her skirts and knelt gracefully, sitting on her heels. Placing her hands flat on her thighs, she bowed her head. The soldiers poured into the square and set up a perimeter around her. A hush fell over the crowd as they watched her, their breaths held in anticipation of what was to come.

"Keep back!" soldiers barked, brandishing their rifles to keep people from breaking through their ranks.

Surrounded by soldiers, Sera remained composed and resolute. She appeared to do nothing, but that was only on the outside. Unseen, she sent tendrils of her magic deep into the ground, like the roots of a sturdy oak. She sought the earth goddess, and when Gaia reached up to her daughter, their magic entwined. Sera became anchored to earth, her magic reinforced by the power of nature.

All she had to do now...was wait. And craft her revenge.

From the moment she'd awakened in the Repository, magic-less and alone, Sera had considered the sort of revenge to exact on Lord Rowan. She decided to stick with the Bible and its Old Testament *eye for an eye*. Or, as she'd learned playing games with Kitty as a child, tit-for-tat.

She would strip Lord Rowan of his magic. But unlike his spell, which left the seed deep inside her soul, she would make his recovery far more difficult and time-consuming. Since magic couldn't be destroyed, even by death, Sera intended to pluck his magic free of his very essence and cast it onto a beach, where it would form one grain of sand among millions. Or a pebble thrown into the Thames, where it would settle to the bottom with thousands of others just like it. The old mage would have to find the seed of his magic before he could even begin the process of nurturing it back into life.

Next, she had turned her mind to how to cast and then activate her spell. Lord Rowan had had her drink it in a tea brewed by Abigail, and her song triggered the magical trap. Sera chose a different method. Lord Rowan would, quite literally, walk into her trap.

While to those observing, she appeared to be at prayer, Sera was busy inscribing sigils into the ground under the cobbles. With the help of Gaia, she moved tiny pebbles to form the ancient signs. With care, she created each symbol and merged it with her unique shadow magic. It had to be perfect. She would only have one chance.

She remained a pillar of quiet composure, her head bowed as she knelt in the middle of the square. Around her, soldiers shuffled from foot to foot. Their uncertainty was palpable in the air. They had expected her to fight and to resist capture with every ounce of her strength. But she refused to engage.

Before long, approaching hooves rang out on the cobbles. The soldiers broke ranks to admit a glossy black carriage with the ornate purple-and-gold crest of the Mage Council. A footman jumped down to open the door and swing down the steps.

Lord Rowan emerged first, dressed like a nobleman out for a stroll on his country estate. Next emerged the stout and glaring figure of Lord Ormsby, the Speaker of the Council. Then Lord Gresham, dressed all in black, as was his custom. The colour made him appear gloomy and unwelcoming, like a puddle in the shadows. Lord Dench hopped to the ground last in his spangled blue robe and matching cloak. Apparently, he had found some way to make it to London from his estate in Yorkshire. Somehow Sera doubted he had skipped through the fairy rings.

She was to face four mages and hundreds of soldiers. That hardly seemed a fair fight.

Normally, Lord Ormsby would push himself forwards, but he deferred to Lord Rowan, who walked across the cobbles towards her. She noted his uneven gait and that he leaned heavily on his staff. Age consumed him, fuelling his abhorrent plan to make himself young again.

He stopped about ten feet away from her, the other three mages behind him. She needed him to come closer.

"At last, the traitor kneels before us," Lord Rowan called, speaking to his audience, not her.

Sera drew a breath and spoke quietly but used a waft of magic to project her voice to all those listening. "You call me traitor, but I am not the one who seized power from our king and who now commands England's soldiers."

A murmur of agreement went around the assembled crowd.

"You are a traitor because you refuse to perform your duty to this country." Lord Rowan adopted the tone of the patient teacher.

"Ah." Sera tilted her head and regarded him. "You mean I refused to let Lord Tomlin rape me so that I could birth a creature of extraordinary power? A babe you then intended to enslave so you could syphon off its magic to become young once more and establish yourself as the magical ruler of your own empire?"

Silence fell as her words filtered into the minds of those present. Some gasped. Others muttered, *That isn't right.*

Lord Ormsby let out a startled, "What?" He glared at the former Speaker. "You meant to *create another Nereus?*"

Sera swallowed a smile. It seemed Lord Rowan hadn't shared his plans with the others. Lords Gresham and Dench merely looked confused, as though they did not know what the other two were discussing.

"Dewlap's line was poured into your form for a reason. It is your duty to serve this country by birthing a powerful child. The Fates give us magic because we are meant to rule, not to be used like tools." Lord Rowan flung open his arms, and the orb on top of his staff pulsed a watery green.

More people flowed into Charing Cross, drawn by

the gossip that flew around the city faster than any raven. People lined the balconies of the surrounding buildings or hung out of windows. Some even climbed higher, to sit atop roofs.

"Yet you took my magic from me and bound it tight." As she spoke, Sera let her gift bubble inside her. Her skin tingled as it waited to pour out of her. She needed him closer. Just two more steps.

Another gasp raced around the square.

"It was the only way to teach you how to behave. Unfortunate that you had a gargoyle release you from your prison. I'll not make that mistake again." He took a step closer.

"I am tired of running." She met his gaze.

"Running is all she can do. She cannot cast. She cut her bonds with a knife and fled to escape my men." Spittle flew from Lord Dench's lips.

Sera allowed herself a moment to take in the faces surrounding her. The worried stares of the common folk, the calculating gazes of Lords Ormsby and Gresham, the uncertainty etched into the furrowed brows of the soldiers. They were all waiting, holding their breath to see what happened next. A wave of disbelief rolled off the Londoners. In their eyes, she was their protector. The mage who championed their cause and fought on their behalf. Yet here she knelt, admitting defeat.

"Alone and practically magic-less," Lord Rowan called out, his voice carrying effortlessly across the open space. "I will give you a task within the realm of your ability—that of motherhood."

She would have struck him down just for that comment. If women wanted, they could aspire to do many things besides, or instead of, motherhood. But these men would reduce her to a womb that they could control. Today, they would learn how wrong they were.

The tension in the air grew thicker as Lord Rowan took another step, his cloak billowing behind him like a dust cloud. The murmur of the crowd fell to a hush, leaving only the faint whisper of the wind and the distant clop of hooves.

"Today I face the consequences of my actions, as will you." Sera kept her chin raised, her gaze defiant as she met Lord Rowan's icy stare. How naïve she had been, having once wished he could have been her mentor.

Another shuffle of his feet and he was in position, exactly over the sigils she had created. Sera raised her arms and held out her hands, palms facing one another. A gesture of surrender.

A gesture to trigger her spell.

It seeped into the soles of Lord Rowan's boots and spread upwards, wrapping itself around his body. One tiny pebble wriggled free of the cobbles and jumped, throwing itself into his left boot.

The pieces were in place. Now she only had to get him to use enough magic to nearly drain himself, thus activating the last part of her revenge. How hard could it be to prod a man into displaying his superiority in a fight against a woman?

Lord Rowan stared at her outstretched hands for a moment, his eyes narrowing with suspicion. Then, he raised his own hand with fingers splayed, and a series of dark, shimmering chains materialised from thin air, slithering like snakes as they wrapped themselves around Sera's wrists. The enchanted bonds burned her skin, but she still refused to let her expression betray her inner turmoil.

She steadied her breathing to ease the blast of panic that surged through her. Never again would another strip her of her power. Gaia sent warmth along their bond. The goddess would protect her from below as Nyx watched her from above.

"You can bind me, but we both know who the criminal is here." Slowly, Sera rose to her feet.

The soldiers surrounding them watched the scene unfold with a mixture of emotions playing across their faces. Some wore expressions of triumph, their chests puffed out with pride as they witnessed the capture of the treacherous woman mage. Others, however, seemed less certain of which one was the traitor. Brows furrowed with doubt and confusion as they tried to understand what they had heard.

Sera's wrists ached where the magical chains dug into her flesh, their ethereal glow casting a cold, watery light upon the gathered crowd. The chains pulsated with an energy that was intended to both drain and restrain her, making any attempt at escape futile.

Still, the old mage didn't realise she wasn't a prisoner. She had led the soldiers here and allowed Lord Rowan to bind her. Things played out as she intended.

"Such a shame when you showed such promise. You could have had a place at my court, creating entertainments for our new queen, Abigail. Instead, you will be treated like the naughty grandchild you have shown yourself to be." Lord Rowan waggled a finger at her—likely in much the same way he had to his grandson right before he turned him into a tiny frog and imprisoned him in the terrarium in his study.

"What of the people you have taken away and imprisoned? Will they be released under your new reign?" Whispers echoing her comments rippled through the crowd.

Lord Rowan turned a slow circle to survey the grimy faces watching from behind the soldiers. "Thieves. Beggars. Murderers. You should thank me for cleaning them from the streets."

"Mothers. Children. The sick. The elderly. Veterans of war." Sera spoke in a clear voice. "What charity and compassion is there, usurper, under your reign?"

"Enough!" Lord Rowan shouted, his colour rising under his white whiskers. "Take her away!"

As five soldiers broke free and approached her, three crows dropped from the clouds and flew at the men. They raised their arms and batted at the birds. The crows only cawed and circled the soldiers. Then the birds landed on the ground beside Sera.

Feathers shook, and a shimmering light of purple and deep green enveloped the birds. Their shadows became taller and elongated. Then the light dropped away to reveal three women with raven-black hair wearing soft linen shifts the colour of a crow's feather.

"The Crows." Lord Rowan uttered the name of Elliot's magical cousins with disbelief.

While everyone stared in wonder at three crows turning into three women, they approached Sera and laced their hands above her bound ones. The women chanted a spell, and the magical chains writhed and slithered from Sera's hands. They fell as melted droplets that hissed and dissolved into the cobbles.

"Impossible. Unnatural creatures don't possess magic." Lord Gresham took a step closer as though he didn't believe his eyes.

"Descendants of a woman mage's union with a shifter do. It creates even more troublesome women," Lord Ormsby grumbled.

Sera rubbed her hands to remove the sting of the chains.

Lord Rowan laughed. "A fetching demonstration but pointless. Seize them." He gestured for the soldiers to carry out his commands. When the men hesitated, Lord Rowan slammed his staff into the ground, and a shock wave rippled outwards, slamming into everyone around him. "I am Regent of England, and I will be obeyed!"

TWENTY-THREE

Lord Rowan flung out his staff and his other hand at the same time. A swirling red ball appeared and blasted towards Sera. She raised her hands and created a shield; the ball bounced off and disappeared up into the sky with a bang.

The old mage narrowed his gaze at her.

Beside her, the Crows joined hands and merged their magic. Together, the three sisters wielded as much power as any mage.

"Did I mention that I have my magic back? And thanks to your little spell, I am stronger than ever." Sera touched the deep well of power far beneath her feet, then channelled it up through her fingertips. The air crackled around her, heavy with energy, as she thrust her hands outwards, releasing a powerful blast of magic that rippled through the air like a storm.

The force of her spell struck the advancing soldiers, knocking them backwards and sending them sprawling and tumbling to the ground. For a moment, the square fell quiet, save for the groans of injured men and the clatter of dropped weapons.

"No!" Lord Rowan took a step forwards, flanked by Lords Ormsby, Gresham, and Dench. "Not that it matters. You are a child with no battle experience. We shall soon have you and the birds in a cage." Lord Rowan gestured to the other mages, who promptly launched a barrage of attacks upon Sera and the Crows.

Sera's gaze locked onto Lord Rowan and Lord Gresham. They posed the bigger threat. The Crows deflected the magical attack of Lord Dench. Lord Ormsby seemed occupied with flinging weapons back into the hands of soldiers as they rose to their feet. The air crackled and flashed with energy.

As one, Lord Rowan and Lord Gresham released their spells, the force of their combined magic hurtling towards Sera like a tidal wave. She braced herself, drawing from her own reserves to counter their assault. The spells met in a violent clash of light and sound, the air thundering with the intensity of the duel. Blue, black, and copper lightning cracked across the square. Cheers went up from the crowd with every move Sera made, as though the mages performed an entertainment just for them.

As the soldiers regrouped and advanced, a horse barged through their ranks, followed by another. Kitty, lashing out with a sabre, ploughed through the red-coated men. Elliot rode at her side with what appeared to be some sort of truncheon or club, smacking heads as he went. An unruly mob of commoners surged behind them, armed with makeshift weapons—spades, hammers, and even brooms. Their faces wore a mix of anger and determination as they joined the fray, engaging the soldiers in a chaotic brawl.

"Perfect timing!" Sera shouted to her friend, her voice barely audible over the din of battle.

Kitty directed the commoners, her innate skill as a general evident in the way she barked orders and marshalled her makeshift troops. The tide of battle shifted, the soldiers faltering under the unexpected onslaught.

Lord Rowan's eyes narrowed, and his lips twisted into a snarl. Sera kept her wits about her as she countered every bolt and blast the mages threw. A whirlwind of magical energy engulfed the square. Sera and the Crows exchanged deadly spells with the male mages, each side trying to outmanoeuvre the other. Rain fell, as though the sky wept. Rivulets of water over the cobbles made their footing slippery and added chaos to the fight, but neither side showed any sign of relenting.

Sera's body strained from the sheer effort it took to counter the powerful spells launched at her by Lords Rowan, Gresham, and Dench. She risked a glance at Lord Ormsby, who seemed strangely hesitant to engage her directly. Why? Was there a shred of decency left in him?

The faces of the Crows paled, the women unused

to keeping up such a sustained attack against a mage. Sera needed to do something to end the battle before any of her friends were hurt. Reaching under her shirt, she pulled free the necklace she wore. Grabbing the shimmering black scale, she held it to her mouth and whispered the Fae phrase taught to her by Queen Deryn. The scale dissolved upon her lips like a wafer.

Not knowing if, or when, the summons might work, Sera returned to pushing back the advance of the mages. The rain ceased to fall as a gigantic cloud spread over the square. A woman glanced up and screamed.

Ebonfyre rose behind the Golden Cross inn at her back. With their wings spread wide, they cast a terrifying shadow over the battlefield.

"A toothless illusion, like the ones you cast to entertain the king," Lord Dench cried, referencing the event she'd put on with Lord Tomlin to entertain the nobles.

Sera pointed behind her. This was no mere illusion, but an obsidian dragon in all its fearsome glory. "This is Ebonfyre. They are like the Crows, only... bigger, and no illusion. They are guardian of the Fae realm, and they are here to aid me."

Ebonfyre roared, a deafening sound that shook the very ground beneath them. Then the dragon spewed black fire at the attacking mages. With a yell, the four men combined their magic to deflect the flames. Strain showed on their faces as two held aloft a shield while the other two tried to freeze the flow.

With the common folk of London engaging the soldiers and Ebonfyre taking the brunt of the magical attack, Sera and the Crows turned to the mages, who would drain themselves trying to defeat the dragon. Already, Lord Gresham seemed unsteady on his feet, so Sera concentrated on him.

She sent roots of magic racing under the ground and attacked the black-clad mage from below. With his attention split between the dragon and the force spearing up at his feet, he hopped from foot to foot. Then his knees buckled, and his face drained of colour. Staggering backwards, he threw himself at the soldiers. Two men caught him as he collapsed, and they dragged him away, propping up his form at the base of King Charles's plinth.

"Lord Dench!" Sera yelled to the Crows, pointing to the mage wearing the blue robes.

They nodded and peppered him with freezing orbs. Sera concentrated on Lord Rowan. She pulled his spells towards her, forcing him to use more and more magic against her. Each word he uttered, each ensor-cellment he cast, powered her trap.

With the back of her arm, Sera wiped sweat from her brow and kept up her constant stream against the old mage. Ebonfyre roared, and with a single flap of their wings, dropped to the square. People and soldiers alike screamed and scattered out of the dragon's way. Standing at Sera's back, Ebonfyre spread their wings and once more blasted the mages with fire made of inky shadows.

Lord Dench's knees gave out, and he fell to the ground. Lord Ormsby directed soldiers to carry him away, and they laid him beside Lord Gresham. It nagged at Sera that the Speaker of the Council didn't use his magic against her. Was the cunning man waiting until she was exhausted so that he could claim the credit of having defeated her?

The thunder of hooves and the blare of a trumpet cut through the chaos like a sword. A solid chestnut horse barged through the soldiers, closely followed by a second. Hugh and Lord Pendlebury!

The men jumped to the ground. Lord Pendlebury looked up at the obsidian dragon, and his eyes widened in surprise.

"Hugh!" Sera cried out his name. Had they been successful? Mounted guards wearing bear's fur hats pushed the other soldiers aside. They held their swords to attention as another rider came forwards, one with a regal bearing and a calm expression despite the turmoil surrounding him.

"Cease this assault at once!" King George commanded, his voice amplified by Lord Pendlebury so that it echoed across the square.

Ebonfyre sat back on their haunches and folded their wings against their sides. The soldiers hesitated, glancing between Lord Rowan and their sovereign.

"I am regent of this nation. Seize those women." Lord Rowan pointed to Sera and the Crows. Sweat trickled down the side of his face, and he had a bluish pallor.

"You were only regent when the king was inca-pacitated. As you can see, King George is quite capable of making decisions for this realm," Hugh called.

"Drop your weapons," King George ordered and clenched his jaw.

"Your king has spoken!" Lord Ormsby roared, showing at last which side he supported—the winning one. "Obey him!"

A clatter sounded as soldiers tossed their weapons to the ground. A cheer went up from the people. Sera twined her fingers with Hugh's. They had done it.

"What is this, Ormsby? We agreed to my new reign." Lord Rowan turned on the Speaker.

"Did we?" Lord Ormsby bowed to King George. "Lord Rowan has overstepped his authority, Your Majesty, and in doing so, falsely accused Lady Winyard of treason."

"That is not all he has done. This...person...has been poisoning my mind for many years. All so he might seize my crown." The king fixed his stare on Lord Rowan. "Take him into custody. Lord Rowan will be held accountable for his treason."

Lord Rowan's hand tightened on his staff, and he pulled himself taller. Magic sparked over one hand as he prepared to fight on, but it was a mere trickle—he had drained his reserves to near empty. "I am your superior in every way. I have waited a lifetime to rule!"

"It would seem Lady Winyard has scuttled your attempted coup. Better to go quietly, Lord Rowan, than add *indecorum* to your list of crimes," Lord Ormsby said.

Lord Pendlebury joined the Speaker. Together, they cast a magical barrier around Lord Rowan so that he could not lash out at the king or anyone else. Two soldiers took hold of the old mage and marched him towards his carriage.

Lord Rowan struggled in their grip, but with Lords Pendlebury and Ormsby focusing their magic on him, there was little the exhausted and drained mage could do.

"At least let me get this blasted stone out of my boot!" he grumbled.

The soldiers loosened their hold a little. With the two of them supporting his weight, Lord Rowan bent down and tugged off his boot. Turning it upside-down, he shook a small pebble into his hand. Then he tossed it away.

Sera flicked her wrist, and a tendril of her magic snatched the pebble from the air. She held it aloft. Meeting Lord Rowan's gaze, she grinned.

"What have you done?" he gasped as his body slumped. Only the grip of the soldiers kept him upright.

"Exactly what you did to me. Except you just... threw away the spark of your magic." She held the pebble between her thumb and forefinger. An almost imperceptible trace of magic rippled over its tiny surface. Once it nestled among thousands of other stones in a riverbed, it would be indistinguishable and virtually impossible to find.

Lord Rowan's eyes widened in sudden, awful

understanding. His mouth opened and closed for a moment before he yelled, "Stop her!"

Before anyone could understand what was happening, Sera threw the small stone into the sky.

In an instant, Erin shifted into a crow and flew after the object. In mid-air, she snatched it up in her beak and in a few flaps of her wings, had disappeared amongst the amassed clouds. Sera had asked the Crow if her plan was successful, to catch the stone and drop it into the Thames.

"Give it back! Make her give it back!" he yelled, looking to Lord Ormsby for assistance.

The Speaker cast a narrowed gaze at Sera. "What have you done?"

She shrugged. "No more than he did to me. Lord Rowan has just thrown away the spark of his magic. He has no power anymore."

The other mages stared at Lord Rowan with a mixture of disbelief and horror on their faces.

"Take him away," King George said.

Instead of a fierce mage king, the soldiers dragged away a defeated old man with less magic than a seventh-generation aftermage maid, whose only gift was a tiny flame with which to light the kitchen fire.

The air hung heavy with a blend of smoke and relief as Sera and her companions surveyed the smouldering battlefield. The once-pristine cobbles of Charing Cross were now scarred with scorch marks and debris, evidence of the struggle that had taken place.

"Someone tell me where...that...came from." King George pointed to the shadow behind Sera.

Somehow, she had forgotten that Ebonfyre still guarded her back.

"This is Ebonfyre, Your Majesty. They are guardian of the Fae realm. Queen Deryn sent them to assist your cause." The dragon lowered its gleaming black head. Sera reached out and stroked their obsidian muzzle.

A range of emotions flowed across King George's face before he could stop them. "Queen Deryn?"

"Yes," Sera replied. "She did not wish any harm to come to Your Majesty, or to your son."

The king started to say something, then changed his mind and coughed instead.

Sera ran her hand along Ebonfyre's black scales as she addressed them. "Thank you. Your debt is paid, and you are free to return to your realm."

The dragon huffed a warm breath over her hand, then leapt into the sky. In a few beats of massive wings, they disappeared into the clouds.

"We expect to see you at court tomorrow, Lady Winyard," King George said as he turned his horse and left Charing Cross, his guards closing around him.

When the sound of the cavalcade faded, Lord Ormsby approached Sera. "I don't like you."

"I believe we established that some time ago," Sera replied.

"It's not because you're a girl. I always thought Dewlap's taint would make you like him. I never thought Rowan would prove to be the traitor among us." He put his hands on his hips, which made him resemble an angry teapot. "It is forbidden to strip another mage of their magic unless directed by the Speaker of the Council and the king. But in this case, such permission is retroactively granted. You did the right thing, for once."

Sera ran his comment back through her mind before she decided there was a rather well-hidden compliment in there. "Why don't the others know about the Nereus?"

He huffed. "That is confidential information, known only to the Speaker and his second, if the man is trusted."

"Which, fortunately, I am. I understood the horror Lord Rowan thought to unleash upon us." Lord Pendlebury joined them. Lord Dench had climbed into a hackney and huddled in a corner with Lord Gresham propped up beside him.

"This is why we don't allow female mages. So there cannot be a Nereus." The speaker glared at Sera as if the entire affair were her fault.

Anger surged up her throat. "*That* is your justification for snuffing out lives? Women can be trusted to make our own decisions if we are informed of the consequences."

Lord Ormsby crossed his arms. "And did that stop Lord Rowan from trying to make Lord Tomlin..." His voice trailed off, and he grimaced as though his breakfast might fight its way back up his throat.

Sera curled her hands into fists. "Women are blamed because men cannot control themselves. Perhaps all men should be extinguished, instead? That would equally solve the problem."

Lord Pendlebury coughed, and Hugh squeezed her hand. At least Kitty looked as indignant as Sera felt.

The deep frown lines on Lord Ormsby's face evened out a little. "Perhaps it is time for this council to consider adopting a policy similar to that of our counterparts in Europe. Women mages could live a scholarly life in quiet seclusion. You would, of course, be expected to set the example."

Sera stared at Lord Ormsby, her hands curling into fists and sparks dancing over her knuckles. "No one will ever cage me again."

The Speaker shifted and cleared his throat. "Well, yes, I think you have established your worth here today, Lady Winyard."

Sera snorted and wondered if it was too late to call Ebonfyre back.

As if reading her thoughts, Kitty muttered, "You should have kept the dragon. We could have had a matriarchal society established by suppertime."

"I'm starved. What say we leave someone else to clean up this place and go for a pint and a pie?" Elliot suggested.

Sera laughed and wrapped her arms around Hugh. "I think we've all earned the best meal Imp can provide."

Twenty-Four

IT SEEMED ONLY FITTING that they return to the Apothecary's Poison to celebrate. Sera, as Nyx, was cheered and toasted by the patrons. After a meal that made her stomach swell and a sufficient quantity of ale, they adjourned to Kitty's Mayfair mansion. Sera wanted to luxuriate in a large bath and a soft bed. Hugh tiptoed down the corridor to join her after everyone went to bed, as the staff had placed him in his own room some distance from the two young women. A situation they had to remedy.

The next morning, after Hugh had crept back to his room, the Napier staff prepared Sera to attend court. She was bathed again, primped and preened, and dressed in a cream silk sack-back gown, covered in embroidered leaves and tiny black velvet pansies.

Kitty and Hugh accompanied her. Elliot was still abed when they left, as Kitty kindly thought the footman deserved a day off.

When they walked the wide halls of the palace to the throne room, the very atmosphere of the palace had changed. Now it was charged with hope. The gloomy pall that hung over everyone when the king was secluded had lifted. The group stopped at the grand doors. Sera took Kitty's and Hugh's hands.

"We did this together, and I would not be standing here without both of you." Then she kissed each of them, Kitty on the cheek, Hugh a quick kiss on the lips.

Then she let them go, folded her hands before her stomacher, and nodded to the guards. They flung the doors open on a packed crowd. Everyone had crammed into the audience chamber to see King George restored to them. People peeled away in front of her like waves parting, leaving a clear path for Sera and her companions to walk towards the red velvet–draped canopy.

The immense room stretched out before her, its walls adorned with life-sized portraits of previous monarchs. The high ceiling glittered with intricate golden patterns. Beneath her shoes, the floor had been polished until it gleamed and reflected the light of mage-crafted chandeliers. The soft fragrance of hothouse flowers perfumed the air, wafting from enormous arrangements on the sideboards.

When she reached the raised dais with its golden thrones, Sera curtsied gracefully, keeping her eyes downcast until her presence was acknowledged.

"Lady Winyard," Queen Charlotte said warmly, her voice resonating throughout the room. As she stepped down from her throne, the rustle of her elaborate gown preceded her.

When Sera rose and met the queen's gaze, she found the royal eyes full of gratitude. "Your Majesty," Sera murmured.

The queen took her hand and embraced her. A wave of emotion crashed over Sera. She had doggedly navigated her own course since she turned eighteen and had done what she believed to be right. In the process, she had saved not only a king but a man deeply loved by his wife.

Letting her go, Queen Charlotte patted her cheek. "You have done all that was asked of you. Thank you."

"Yes, thank you, Lady Winyard. You freed me from the grip of a curse that not one of my physicians or mages had detected." Here, the king glared at Lord Ormsby and the old doctors clustered to one side.

The king rose from his throne and held out his hand. As Sera took the outstretched hand and kissed the jewelled signet ring, her senses tingled with unease. A trace of darkness lingered within him. A faint shadow left from years of the entropy stone's poisonous effect, like a soot stain left in a disused chimney. Would it have any effect on the king's mind in the future?

She didn't know, so chose to keep silent. For now.

"It is my honour to serve, Your Majesty, and use the gift in my veins to benefit yourself and this country," Sera replied, keeping her concerns for the future to herself.

"The Fates did something right when they

bestowed such a gift upon one who has used it in our defence, even when it endangered herself." Now Queen Charlotte glared at Lord Ormsby, who shuffled from foot to foot.

Sera basked in the warm regard and gratitude of the royal couple. But fresh worries sprouted in her mind. The darkness within King George may have been subdued for now, but it had not vanished entirely. One day, they might need to face the consequences of the entropy stone's lingering influence.

On the more personal side, would the Speaker demand that she be sequestered in a nunnery to stop any other mage from trying to create a Nereus? Did her actions mean any female mages born in the future would live, or would the council redouble their efforts to snuff out every gifted woman?

A hush fell over the vast audience chamber as the royal couple returned to their thrones. King George kept hold of his queen's hand. The love the two shared was obvious to all in their court. Sera waited, unsure what would happen next.

"Lady Winyard," the king began, his voice firm yet laden with gratitude. "In recognition of your extraordinary talents and unwavering dedication to our kingdom, we have decided to create a new position within the royal court." He paused for a moment, allowing his proclamation to echo through the hall. "You shall henceforth be known as the People's Mage, tasked with using your magic to serve the needs of our subjects."

Sera froze for a moment. The king had just endorsed Lord Ormsby's practice of giving her the dirtiest jobs requested of the mages. Well, it could have been worse. They could have officially changed her title to the Duchess of Drains.

"You will, of course, be given the authority to call on other such magical assistance as you require to serve those citizens of this kingdom who can least afford to engage a mage," Queen Charlotte added with a wink.

Ha! Which meant she could direct Lord Tomlin to clean the fat blockages in the East End if she wished. Which she would. She had not forgotten his support of Lord Rowan's plan.

"You honour me, Sire." Sera curtsied again. Nyx would support the common people, just as they had supported her in Charing Cross. No army could stand before them.

"As you navigate your own path, Lady Winyard, we know you will continue to uphold the values of justice and compassion that we prize, and which seem to be sadly lacking in the Mage Council," Queen Charlotte said.

Sera bit back a smile as Lord Ormsby continued to squirm on the royal hook. She had always liked the queen, with her direct manner and the way she protected the rights of women. The queen's words confirmed that Sera was free to live her life as she wanted. No one would ever cage her.

"Speaking of justice, there is another matter that must be addressed." King George waved a hand, and from a side door, guards escorted Lord Rowan into the room.

A gasp went around the crowd, and a sharp, feminine cry drew Sera's attention. She knew that voice. Somewhere behind the press of courtiers lurked Lady Abigail Crawley.

The old mage, who had once resembled a wise scholar, was gone, replaced by a feeble and sad figure. His once-proud demeanour was now slumped and shuffling. Red-rimmed eyes were wild as he cast about him. His long white beard appeared to have tangled with spiderwebs and dust, and he had lost the soft hat that usually covered his bald head.

"*Mr* Ernest Rowan." King George stressed the new form of address. "You committed a heinous act of treason against the crown. You unleashed a foul curse upon your king, then plotted to steal our kingdom. For these acts, you are stripped of your magic and your title, and all your property is forfeit." The king's words rang with an air of finality.

A conflict arose within Sera. Satisfaction at seeing the old mage pay for his crimes warred with sympathy. Without his magic, he was a weak old man who seemed unable even to lift a book. What sort of life would he lead now? Perhaps he might find employment as a gardener. Sera recollected something Kitty once said— most old people liked to potter in gardens.

"Bring forth Lady Abigail Crawley," commanded Queen Charlotte. Her voice echoed through the hall with an air of authority that sent a shiver down the most stoic of spines. The queen's displeasure was a terrible thing to behold.

The crowd parted. People pulled back from the noblewoman as though standing too close to her might see them punished alongside her. Lady Abigail cast about her, looking for a friendly face. Finding none, she drew herself up and walked with a proud step towards the monarchs. She curtsied, but it was a small thing, and she rose immediately, without permission, as though she considered herself an equal.

"You have been complicit in your grandfather's crimes," Queen Charlotte began.

"I—I beg your mercy if you believe I had any part in his treachery," Abigail protested.

The queen narrowed her gaze and continued in a cold tone. "We are well aware of the part you played. You poisoned our mage."

Sera wondered which one the queen referred to—Abigail had handed over the poison that had taken Lord Branvale's life and then poisoned Sera's tea to help steal her magic.

Abigail glanced at Sera, and for a moment, pure hatred burned in her eyes. Then it was gone as she adopted a demure and helpless expression. "I was under his control, Your Majesty, and did not understand the gravity of his actions."

Sera's snort cut like a knife through the silence. She couldn't help but scoff at the pathetic display. Abigail had been a willing participant in her grandfather's schemes, not an ignorant ingénue. She thought to rule over the court as queen once her grandfather had England under his thumb.

Queen Charlotte rose and stared down at her former lady-in-waiting. "You expect us to believe you were nothing more than a pawn in his twisted game?"

"Please, Your Majesty, I swear it! I would never knowingly betray my country." A tear trickled down Abigail's cheek.

Sera thought it a fetching performance. But she had seen behind the mask. Abigail's concern was only for herself and her status. She was a woman who had proven herself willing to aid and abet murder in order to become a duchess—and then a queen.

Queen Charlotte knew the nature of her ladies. She fixed her gaze on Abigail. "Lady Abigail Crawley, for your involvement in Mr Rowan's treachery, you are hereby banished from court. You are dead to us from this day forth."

Abigail's eyes widened, but already Sera could see the calculation in them. Her parents were still wealthy. She would shortly be married to the heir of a duke, and she would be a duchess when his father died. She would create her own court.

But the queen wasn't done yet. "Furthermore, any who support or associate with you shall also face ostracism from both our court and all good society."

Even Sera winced at that pronouncement. What was a grand duchess if no one attended her soirees, balls, and garden parties?

The future Abigail imagined away from the court

dissolved in front of her eyes. "Please, Your Majesty," Lady Abigail whimpered, her voice barely audible. "I meant no harm...Sera, my friend, you know how I like a good jest."

Her former friend turned towards her, expecting a reprieve or intervention on her behalf. But she would find none. She had made her choices. Now she had to live with the consequences.

There was no more discussion. The king turned to converse with one of his courtiers, and Abigail was simply...forgotten. As though she had been made invisible. She retreated, casting about wildly for anyone who might support her. Then she spotted her betrothed standing at the back with a cluster of young bucks. Abigail threw herself at him, seeking solace and protection. But instead of embracing her, the young man pushed her away with a look of disdain.

"Control yourself, madam. I do not know you," he declared coldly, his words like shards of ice shattering any remaining hope for Abigail.

"You cannot abandon me. We are to be married in a few weeks." She stretched out her hands towards him in a futile plea.

"*I* am to be a duke, madam. I will marry a woman worthy of being my duchess, who will be a pillar of our society and respected about court. Not one who despoiled herself with a footman and who betrayed our king and country." Having said that, he turned his back on the woman he had once declared he loved, and he laughed with his friends.

Sera's heart clenched as Abigail ran from the throne room. Her sobs were lost amid the rising conversation.

Queen Charlotte moved to her side and turned her back upon the court, her gaze fixed instead on the face of her beloved George. "In life, Lady Winyard, we must make the right decisions, even if they are difficult ones that cause us pain."

With those haunting words lingering in the air, Sera curtsied to the royal couple and found Hugh and Kitty off to one side. "I have seen enough," she murmured to Kitty.

Kitty linked arms with her. "It is done. Let us think of more pleasant topics, oh mighty People's Mage."

From court, they journeyed to Sera's little house in Soho. Apparently, Elliot had pulled himself out of bed before noon, as it was he who opened the front door.

"They didn't throw you in prison for being troublesome, then?" He almost sounded disappointed.

"Nor was I rewarded with wealth beyond our wildest dreams, so we will both have to keep working." As she stepped over the threshold and inhaled the aroma of baking biscuits coming up the stairs from the kitchen, she breathed out a sigh.

She was home.

"Oh! Milady, you're returned to us. We've been ever so worried, even though Miss Napier said everything would work out fine," cried Vicky, the young maid.

Sera hugged her. "If Kitty says everything will work out fine, she means it."

Rosie bustled up the stairs. "We are ever so pleased to have you back, milady." The cook wiped her hands on her apron as she hurried into the foyer. "I've been cooking all morning to create a celebratory feast, if you are hungry?"

Before Sera could answer, Hugh's stomach rumbled. She burst into laughter and took the hands of her dearest friends. "Come on. Rosie bakes the most divine cakes, and Elliot can make himself useful and pour tea." She tugged them towards the stairs.

One week later

Early that morning, Sera had sent a message to Kitty asking her to accompany her to the wharves.

"Why are we here, exactly?" Kitty asked as they stepped down from the carriage.

"I want to show you something." They linked arms, while Hugh trailed behind.

As they walked along the raised stone pavement of the dock, a sight below made Sera stop in her tracks. An old man waded in the muck left where the tide had begun to ebb. He muttered to himself as he picked rocks from the mud and placed them in a satchel at his side.

"His daughter cares for him, but he spends his days searching for the pebble he threw away," Hugh murmured as they watched the slow movements of Mr Rowan.

"That should keep him occupied and out of politics," Kitty said in a sharp tone.

Sera peeled her gaze away from the sad sight and focused on the vessel moored further along.

The gangplank was extended, and men bustled up and down, carrying supplies and crates. They nodded to Sera and called out good morning.

"What is this? Apart from the obvious—a vessel." Kitty gestured to the impressive ship bobbing with the gentle motion of the tide.

"It's what you wanted." Sera tugged Kitty closer until the prow of the ship loomed high above them.

Kitty let out a sigh and cast an exasperated glance at Sera. "I told you I wanted a *vote*, not a *boat*."

Sera laughed. "This isn't about a say in politics, sadly. Some things are beyond even my magic. I recollect you asking for an adventure involving pirates. To encounter pirates, we need to be out there, on the ocean." Sera gestured in the general direction of where the River Thames met the North Sea miles away.

Kitty's eyes widened, her mouth made an O shape, and for once, she was silent.

"King George has allowed me a three-month absence from England. I have instructed the captain to sail wherever we wish to go. Your father knows, and your maids have packed your luggage, which is already stowed on board." Sera stared up at the imposing ship. She was quite beautiful.

In her mind, the sails unfurled, caught a breeze, and they journeyed towards the horizon and whatever awaited them beyond it. Her life was her own. No one would ever seek to control her again. Sera had only to grasp the helm and steer her own course.

"I believe Arwyn is also going to join us, as he'd like to see more of the world," Sera added.

"Well, what are we waiting for? To adventure!" Kitty lifted her skirts and practically ran up the gangplank.

Hugh held out his hand to Sera, and she laced her fingers with his.

"Wherever you go, milady, I will follow." Hugh kissed her knuckles.

"How do you feel about growing a roguish beard?" Sera asked as they followed Kitty up onto the deck and a gust of fresh wind brought with it the scent of freedom and adventure.

THE END

History. Magic. Found family.

I DO HOPE you have enjoyed Seraphina's last adventure. If you would like to know what stories I will be penning next, you can sign up for news at:

https://www.tillywallace.com/newsletter

About the Author

Tilly drinks entirely too much coffee and is obsessed with hats. In her spare time, she writes whimsical historical fantasy novels, set in a bygone time where magic is real. If you love found family and comfort reads, come and escape reality in her tales.

Email: tilly@tillywallace.com
Web: https://www.tillywallace.com
STORE: https://www.tillywallacebooks.com

If you would like to support Tilly for as little as a coffee a month, her *Caffeination Crew* read early chapters of her current work, vote on story ideas, and read exclusive short stories and novellas. You can find more information at: https://www.patreon.com/TillyWallace

patreon.com/TillyWallace

facebook.com/tillywallaceauthor

instagram.com/tillywallaceauthor

bookbub.com/authors/tilly-wallace

goodreads.com/tillywallace